P9-CBG-750

THE CUTTING ROOM

LAURENCE KLAVAN

the
CUTTING ROOM

BALLANTINE BOOKS / NEW YORK

A Ballantine Book
Published by The Random House Publishing Group

www.ballantinebooks.com

Library of Congress Cataloging-in-Publication Data is available from the publisher upon request.

ISBN 0-345-46274-2

Manufactured in the United States of America

First Edition: February 2004

10 9 8 7 6 5 4 3 2 1

Book design by Casey Hampton

FOR SUSAN KIM

PROLOGUE

"DON'T EVEN BREATHE, BABY."

I had heard Ben Williams say those words many times, but never in person. And never with a gun pointed at my head. How had I gotten into this position? I had never even been to Los Angeles before, and yet here I was, hardly off the plane, with one of the biggest movie stars in America about to kill me.

Ben Williams, of course, was the star of one of the most profitable action-movie franchises in Hollywood history, the Cause Pain series: the original *Cause Pain*, then *Cause Pain: In Your Face*, and, finally, *Cause Pain: In Da Houze*. His wisecracking, slightly balding, everyman hero always extricated himself and others from international crises with self-effacing aplomb, all the while wearing a weary smile and a torn T-shirt. When he sneaked up on the villains—usually Libyan or Iraqi terrorists—he would always place a gun to their turbans and whisper:

"Don't even breathe, baby."

But now he was using this line—okay, this cliché—in real life. And that made me think that he was nervous, nervous enough not to trust himself, nervous enough to fall back on his screenwriters' inventions. And *that* made me think that he feared me. Me—Roy Milano!

How *had* I gotten here? How had I, an amateur *film* detective, become an actual film *detective?*

As I heard Ben pull back the trigger on his—I could only assume real—gun, my life passed before my eyes, the way writers had always promised me that it would. It didn't take long: I felt that I had only really been alive for a few days, since this whole thing began.

I guess it's time for a flashback, isn't it?

PART 1
NEW YORK

FLASHBACKS WERE INVENTED IN THE SILENT-MOVIE ERA, PROBABLY BY D. W. Griffith. But the pre-credit sequence was first popularized in Lewis Milestone's 1939 version of *Of Mice and Men*, with the main characters, George and Lennie, fleeing a posse before the credits began. *Of Mice and Men* was remade twice, first starring . . .

But I better cut to the chase.

This kind of movie information—arcana, you might call it, or trivia, I'm not ashamed of the term—is what I specialize in. It's what makes up most of my newsletter, *Trivial Man*, which I produce out of my cramped studio apartment in the West Forties in New York City. I write and publish it myself, and you can find it in bookstores and video outlets around town. If you want to order it, write me at: Roy Milano, Trivial Man, 649 W. 43rd Street, Apt. 5C, New York, NY 10036.

As you can imagine, it's not a living. To make my meager version of that, I typeset for companies and do other kinds of graphics stuff. But the newsletter is my love—my only one, at the moment, I will admit—

and it takes up most of my waking hours, planning for and thinking about it.

I'm not alone—I mean, not in my affection for this kind of movie lore, at least. Since the explosion of DVDs, the Internet, desktop publishing, public-access TV and the like, there's now a whole secret community of people just like me. Most are also male (big surprise) and unmarried (of course). There are a few women in the group and, as you can imagine, they are as prized and pursued as I've heard that women are in small mining towns in Alaska. More about them later.

This community of "Trivial People," as I call them, mostly to myself, is connected through the Web, film fan festivals, midnight movie showings, long, information-filled phone calls, and sometimes even face-to-face contact. We know more about movies than the people who've made them. But our need is largely to fit one fact to another, find lost films—or even lost scenes from films—to, in essence, make sense of mysteries and piece together the past. In that way, we are like detectives, and if anecdotal evidence is to be trusted, we are just as dogged.

I like to think that I differ from some of my "trivial" colleagues. I am younger, thirty-five, presentable enough looking, sort of a cross between Gregory Peck and Chico Marx, and I have actually been married. That is to say, for a brief time, I had steady sexual congress with someone besides myself.

It had, of course, to end. When she left me, Jody—who was a film major but not a trivial person and who later became a psychologist— told me, "You just go on and on, Roy, long after anybody else is interested in your information. Can't you see everybody's eyes are glazing over? Can't you hear their merely polite grunting? They're all waiting for you to finish talking! They don't care what the last silent film Buster Keaton made was! They don't care that Red Skelton remade one of them! And you know what? Neither do I!"

I think Jody had hoped my charming enthusiasm about this subject, of which she said I had a lot, would just naturally be applied to other subjects. But the night she heard me muttering in my sleep all the Best

Supporting Actress Oscar winners, the way others count sheep, I think she knew she had made a big mistake with her life.

Still, there are nights when, watching the same old movie on cable, Jody will call me from wherever she is and ask me—with no introductory small talk, not even a hello—who the man playing the waiter is. And when I know, as I always do, she just thanks me and hangs up, and I can hear in her voice relief that there is some security in the world, something stable. And I know that she will call again, and that gives me hope.

Anyway, enough of my "back story."

The call that changed my life did not come from Jody. It came from Alan Gilbert, perhaps the most petty of all the "trivial" men I knew.

Alan was a few years older than me. For money, he wrote the capsule descriptions of movies in the TV section of one of the New York City tabloids. ("*Gone with the Wind,* 1939, Vivien Leigh, Clark Gable. Gal survives the Civil War." You know what I mean.) But his real love was his own public-access TV show—the half hour paid for with most of the salary from his day job—called *My Movies.*

On the show, Alan sat in his tiny East Village apartment and showed forgotten clips from old films, censored scenes, short subjects not seen for forty years, early pornography, and the like. Occasionally, Alan went on location to interview forgotten actors or cult directors. Mostly, though, it was just Alan, his cameraman—fellow trivial fellow Gus Ziegler—a shabby chair, a projector, a screen, a TV, and that was it. The show ran about twenty times during the week—on channel 297 or something—and chances are, if you've ever flicked around at four in the morning, you've seen him.

But while Alan and I had a common interest—okay, obsession—he was never generous about his movie finds; he was competitive, secretive, and unpleasant. His one other personality trait was that he talked a mile a minute, as if, if he slowed down for a second, he would realize who he was. Trust me, that wasn't a good idea for Alan.

So on this day, when I answered the phone, I was surprised by his tone.

"Roy, buddy boy, how're you doing?"

"Hello?" I said, confused. "Who is this?"

"Alan Gilbert, you stupid son of a bitch, who else would be calling you, you're so pathetic?"

That one moment of camaraderie had obviously been as much as Alan could handle.

"Alan? My God. To what do I owe this sudden burst of pleasantness?"

"I'm not being pleasant. I'm gloating."

"Gloating? I shouldn't be surprised. But how come? Did one of the networks finally buy your show?"

I knew this would gall him. It stuck in Alan's craw that some other public-access shows—for instance, one that featured a seventeen-year-old boy shouting obscenely at the camera for an hour—had been picked up by such cable networks as MTV. This seemed unlikely for *My Movies*, given Alan's unkempt appearance, his thinning hair always plastered on his sweating head, and his untucked shirt always billowing out over his emaciated frame. Also, despite his own rattling speech, the pace of *My Movies* made a simple half hour seem like a grueling week.

"Not yet, but one day soon that's going to happen. One day very soon."

"Well, it happened to *SquirmTV*, why not to *My Movies*?" *SquirmTV* was the name of the screaming-teenager show, a bête noire of Alan's, and I just threw it in to annoy him.

"Don't even mention that little scumbag to me—he'll be off MTV in a month, you mark my words!"

"Okay, Alan, we've had enough fun. Why are you calling?"

"I got something big."

I slowly pulled back from the receiver. Alan had never offered to share anything with me before, being distrustful and squirrel-like with information.

"What?

"You heard me."

"What is it?" I asked suspiciously.

"You'll see, and then you'll thank me."

"You know that I'd die before I'd do that."

"Okay, you'll respect me and then you'll worship me."

I couldn't help but pause again, impressed. If what Alan had was so good he was actually going to *show* it to me, then it had to be pretty damn good.

"Why don't you send it over?" I said cagily. "I'm home all night, finishing my newsletter."

"No way is this leaving my sight. I'm taping my show tonight. So come over and watch it and be the first on your block to know how great I am."

I considered this. "Who else is going to be there?"

"No one. Because, besides me, you're the best."

I smiled. This was an odd but touching piece of praise. Awful personality aside, Alan really was the best. But I was happy to be second if it meant not being him. In the "trivial" world, you clung to whatever small life raft of normal humanity you had.

"Okay," I said.

"Taping starts at eight. Be there on time."

The time was a silly affectation, of course. Alan taped *My Movies* and delivered it to the station whenever he wanted. If he paid them on schedule, he never even had to deliver it. One time, for three weeks in a row, he reran the same episode—obscene imitations of Disney cartoons—because he'd had a bad reaction to drugs and had to be hospitalized. (I forgot to mention that Alan had one other interest besides movies: any drug that would, for however long, kill the pain of being him.) So the idea that I was hurrying to his apartment was absurd.

But I had to admit, I was excited. It wasn't every day that something new—that is to say, something old and rediscovered—landed in my lap, even if it was really in the lap of my enemy. In our strange, underground world of arcane movie facts and figures, the idea, of course, was not to have or even to see but to *know*.

I was nearly sprinting when I got to Alan's place.

The front door of his tacky little brownstone on East Third was open, having offered no resistance to the junkies who now smoked crack in its vestibule. I stepped around them, groans in my ears, acrid smell in my nose, and headed to the stairs.

Typically, Alan lived on the top floor, the sixth, the most annoying place. Having taken the flights at an eager pace, I was winded when I pushed open his door.

I didn't have to knock; it was open, too. This seemed hospitable of Alan, but I assumed he was as excited to reveal his discovery as I was to witness it.

The first thing I noticed was not the disarray of the place. My own apartment was stuffed with papers, magazines, books, and videotapes, too. What was unusual was that Gus Ziegler wasn't manning the video-tape camera, as he usually did. The camera stood, as if patiently waiting, on its perch of a tripod, staring as blankly as a bird at the "set," which was, of course, Alan's only room.

There was the TV on which his film clips were shown. It was not turned on. There was his old 16-millimeter projector. It had no film reels upon it. Opposite, his rickety old screen had fallen over and was ly-ing on the floor.

Alan, the host, sat where he usually did, in his fraying, graying, and overstuffed chair. His hair was even more unruly than usual. His mouth was open. And a steak knife had been pushed deep into the heart that, to be honest, I never even knew he had.

"HOW WELL DID YOU KNOW MR. GILMAN?"

"It's Gilbert. So a lot better than you, I guess."

I had called the police. I know they never do that in movies. People are always fleeing crime scenes, incriminating themselves, even when they're innocent. But this was the first dead body I'd ever seen. And, honest citizen that I am, I figured, I'd never had any problem with the police, a crime had been committed, Alan Gilbert had actually been *murdered*, so why not? It wasn't long before I realized the foolhardiness of my idea.

"Well, you know what they say about people who report crimes," the cop said. "It's like that expression, 'He who smelt it dealt it.'"

The other cop chuckled. There were two of them—both chunky, both about thirty, each pretty much indistinguishable from the other. It seemed a new concept in interrogation: bad cop, worse cop. Not that they were brutal. They just cared more about their own questions than any answers I could give them.

"Well, thanks for encouraging good citizenship," I said.

I was surprised by my moxie. I had remembered Bogart in *The Big Sleep*: Playing Raymond Chandler's private eye, Philip Marlowe, he is always being hauled in by police and always ready with the wisecrack. *The Big Sleep* really exists in two different versions. The first one was made in 1944 and was shown only to troops overseas. The other was altered to accommodate Lauren Bacall's sudden stardom and include more scenes with her; this version was the one released generally in 1946.

It should be apparent by now that, recalling trivia—like counting sheep with Oscar winners—was my way of alleviating anxiety. That was why I was staying remarkably cool, with no lawyer, in the third precinct on East Second Street, where they'd taken me.

And this was especially difficult, because I had something to hide.

"The question remains," one cop said, unamused. "How well did you know Mr. Gilbert?"

I thought I better be accommodating now. "We were acquaintances. I run a movie newsletter. Alan runs a public-access TV show. So we knew each other—professionally." I said the last word with irony, since *profession* usually implies the making of money. But they didn't notice.

"Public access?" one asked the other. "What's that?"

"You know," the other answered. "Like those strippers on late at night. They pay for it themselves."

"Ohhh, right. And like that old lady who dances around half nude, with her boobs hanging out."

"Yeah."

"It's kind of sad, but I like watching it."

"Me too," the other said.

"So," the first one asked me now, "that's what the camera was for, and everything?"

"Yeah," I said.

"And what did he do, turn it on and drop his pants or something?"

"No. He usually showed old film clips."

"Oh, wait, I know this guy," the first cop said to the second. "He shows, like, the Stooges."

"That's right," I said. "Sometimes Alan showed the Three Stooges."

They just spoke to each other: "Like Moe cracking up and everything."

"Yes," I said, "rare old Stooges outtakes."

Just to each other: "Right. Whenever I see it, I think, I wouldn't want this to be *my* life, but I like to watch it, anyway."

"Me too."

"I'm sure Alan would have found that a touching tribute," I said.

They ignored me. I remembered what happened at Ernst Lubitsch's funeral. William Wyler had turned to Billy Wilder and said, sadly, "No more Lubitsch." And Wilder had replied, "No more Lubitsch *movies*."

"At Ernst Lubitsch's funeral—" I started.

But as before, the cops were uninterested in any wisdom but their own. "So what were you doing there?"

"Alan had called me. I came over."

"You do that a lot?"

"A fair amount."

"Did you know that his wallet was lying on the floor, empty?"

"No." I hadn't, actually. "I guess I was too rattled to notice anything."

"Did you know that an empty bottle of amphetamines was lying in the sink in the john? And so was an almost-empty bag of grass?"

"No," I said, honest again. "But Alan liked to get high."

"I wonder why," one said, and both of them chuckled.

"*You* like to get high?" the other asked me.

"No," I said. That was true, too.

The cops looked at each other, and each shrugged a bit. They seemed to have nothing but contempt for Alan, and they hadn't even known him. I remembered Red Skelton's famous remark at the hated mogul Harry Cohn's funeral. He looked at the huge crowd and said, "You know what they say: 'Give people what they want, and they'll turn out.' "

I began, "Well, you know what Red Skelton said—"

But they were talking to each other again. They had even more contempt for me, who did not even medicate himself against his own insignificance. Okay, I thought, let them think I'm a bug, a nerd with no life. First off, it was sort of true, though I liked to think of myself as a hard-boiled nerd. Second, it was as good a cloak to hide behind as any other.

"Loser really didn't have a lot to steal," one said.

"More than some other loser did, apparently," the other responded.

On the word *loser*, they turned to me again.

"Okay," the first said. "Just make sure you leave your address and phone number."

"And don't leave town?" I asked.

Again, they were not interested in my amusing remark, a reference to film clichés.

"Do whatever you want," was all one cop said.

On my way out of the precinct, I passed a closed room in which someone else was being interrogated. Through the small window in the door, I recognized one of the junkies who had been smoking crack in Alan's vestibule. I could faintly hear her responding to badgering questions in a forlorn and confused whisper.

I could have stopped and told them that I didn't think she did it, killed Alan. But I kept walking, and didn't look back. They wouldn't have cared what I had to say, anyway.

See, I didn't think Alan was killed for his drugs or for his cash, such as they were. I was sure he had been killed because of what he had told me he had.

He was killed because of Orson Welles.

ORSON WELLES, OF COURSE, MADE WHAT MANY CONSIDER THE GREATEST American film, *Citizen Kane,* in 1941. Though Welles went back and forth about what would be his next project, he finally decided on an adaptation of Booth Tarkington's novel about a disintegrating American family, *The Magnificent Ambersons.*

The story was close to the director's heart, given his own privileged upbringing. Welles had been born in . . .

But I do go on.

To cut to the chase, Welles made *Ambersons* with some of his usual cast from his old radio Mercury Theatre players: Joseph Cotten, Agnes Moorehead, and others. When the film was finished—a dark and heart-rending masterpiece, over two hours—and about to be previewed, World War II was breaking out. Welles agreed to go to Brazil to make a film encouraging Latin American participation with the Allied cause.

While he was down there, his version of *Ambersons* was previewed in California, disastrously. Instead of coming back to help re-edit it, he stayed in Brazil—some say to party, some say to avoid confrontations about his movie and to essentially abandon it, and still others say to fulfill his patriotic duty.

Either way, the film—with the help of his loyal but powerless editor, Robert Wise (who later directed *The Sound of Music*)—was drastically recut by the studio and, in some places, reshot. The new version, running only eighty-eight minutes, was released, basically dumped, on the bottom half of a double bill.

It made little money but received glowing reviews, some critics' awards, and Oscar nominations. Still, the original version, the lost footage, has obsessed film fans, has become in a sense the Holy Grail of the trivial community. While other seemingly lost movies have been found and resurrected, *The Magnificent Ambersons* remains the one that got away, the one that plays on in the imagination of any film detective. It would, many believe, surpass *Citizen Kane* as the greatest American movie ever made.

I left out a crucial part of what Alan had told me on the phone.

"Taping starts at eight. Be there on time," he had said. "You're going to faint."

"Why?" I'd asked.

"Because I've got it."

I'd waited, then pushed on, a faint chill coming over me. "Got what?"

"I've got *The Magnificent Ambersons*."

Would Alan have bragged about it if it weren't true? Maybe, but I suspected that, for once, secretive Alan just couldn't keep his mouth shut. He really believed that this would be his break, propel his show into the big time—or at least into the mainstream—and the thought was too juicy to keep to himself.

Still, I had my doubts—until I got to his apartment. When I saw the reels missing from his old projector, when I saw his little screen toppled over, when I saw him dead, I knew he had been telling the truth. To any trivial person worth his salt, the full version of *The Magnificent Amber-sons* was indeed worth killing for.

I didn't tell the police, because I knew they wouldn't understand. Or maybe I feared they *would* understand, at least feel compelled to include this as another motive in Alan's murder. In other words, they might start nosing around for the film, just to look like they were doing their jobs.

I couldn't have that. I had to find the film myself—not to avenge Alan's death or even to solve his murder, though these were perhaps auxiliary motives. I had to find *The Magnificent Ambersons* in order to see the *The Magnificent Ambersons*, in order to *know* at long last what had been missing all those years.

How many more people had Alan told? Even though he'd said I was the only one, I couldn't be sure. If I had been the only one with Alan's confidence, it would mean that he was even lonelier than I thought. But it would also mean that I had the best chance of finding the film.

Of course, as I left the police station, I realized something else: Even if Alan hadn't told another soul, at least one other person knew. The one who killed him.

That made me know that this piece of detection would be danger-ous. And that made me start to run.

I RAN TO MIDTOWN. THERE, I PACED MYSELF, SLOWED DOWN, SO AS NOT to seem crazed. In fact, I wanted to be appear casual as I began my own private investigation.

"Gus!" I yelled, nonetheless.

I was glad that Gus Ziegler was at one of his many day jobs, the ones he did to finance his—unpaid—position as Alan's cameraman. Gus was an aspiring trivial man, someone who just hung around our fringes, never seemed to have the energy or initiative to do anything on his own. He seemed content to run a camera, to copy pages, to take advantage of others' hospitality, to lurk.

Rare for a man in the trivial community, Gus actually stayed in shape, compulsively, training at a gym for hours every day. Given his stature and Marine buzz cut, this gave him a squat and overbuilt look, bullheaded and thick-necked. His bulky veins and straining skin made him look much older than his—I didn't know, probably thirty-eight—years.

Today, Gus was hiding his stocky frame under doctor's whites. He was working at one of his more peculiar jobs: for a clinic, checking people's blood pressures on the street. As I approached, he was sitting at a little table, squeezing a wrap around the arm of a businessman, as the regular world of commuters, yuppies, cops, and vendors swirled about him.

Did he know about Alan and *The Magnificent Ambersons*? That was what I was here to find out. And it was why I hadn't mentioned his name to the police.

"Gus," I said again, a bit quieter, as the businessman was unwrapped and went away.

"Hey, Roy," Gus said, his voice oddly deep, from what I could only assume were steroids. "Fancy seeing you."

"Have you heard about Alan?" I said.

I thought Gus flinched for a second, but I couldn't be sure. He only said, in a conspiratorial whisper, "What do you mean? Wait, here, put this on."

Sitting on the chair at his table on the busy sidewalk, I let Gus place the wrap around my arm. As we spoke, he pumped his little attachment, inflating my wrap.

"Now, what's this about?" he said.

"He's dead," I blurted out. "Alan."

Gus pumped the wrap so tight that it unpleasantly squeezed my arm. Then, with an apologetic grunt, he let it deflate.

"Jesus Christ. When was this?"

"Last night. You didn't know?"

"No, I . . . how did it happen? Was it a heart attack? I begged him to come work out with me! Anger can be as bad as fat."

"No, somebody murdered him. Stabbed him through the heart with a steak knife."

"Jesus Christ. I told him to stay away from meat!"

Now Gus's grip grew slack. The attachment slid from his hand. Absently, he detached the Velcro of the wrap from my arm. Then he just sat there, his big head bowed, as if in mourning. To any observer, it must have seemed bad news about my blood pressure. Then, after a respectable period, he looked up again.

"How do you know?" he said.

"I was there. I found him."

"That is so weird," he said.

"I know. Who'd want to kill Alan? I mean, for real, you know what I mean."

"No, because—you know, he called me last night. He told me not to come over, that the taping was off. Otherwise I'd have been there. I'd be dead, too."

Gus's self-interest seemed genuine, so I was persuaded to believe him.

"Yeah," I said. "I thought it was strange you weren't around. He seemed ready to go, and nobody was working the camera."

"So the taping *wasn't* off?" Now Gus seemed grave, as if there were teamsters who should have been alerted about Alan's amateur show.

"Apparently not. He didn't tell you what the topic was, or anything?"

There was a pause. Gus looked at me very directly. I couldn't tell if his face showed guilt or anger or complete confusion. His unique combination of sloth and compulsion always made Gus seem totally stupid, but I could never be sure.

"I think it was Abbott and Costello bloopers," he said. "Why?"

"Nothing," I said. "It's just—any information might help."

"But you don't think that that had anything to do with—"

"Oh, no," I backtracked quickly. "The cops are pretty sure it was the junkies in his lobby. He'd been robbed. And his, you know, his drugs were stolen."

Gus shook his head, sadly, the world making sorry sense again. With his steroid-slowed voice, he said, "I kept trying to get him into Health."

"I'm sure."

Suddenly, Gus looked behind me. When I turned, I saw a heavyset woman, impatiently waiting her turn at the table.

"Well," I said. "I better let you get back to work."

"Okay," he said despondently.

Gus spoke as if his job was pointless now; with Alan's show over, what was he working for? Nothing.

"I just thought I'd let you know."

"Thanks." Gus nodded. "Your blood pressure's fine, by the way."

Gus extended his meaty hand, which I shook. I could not tell if the crushing grip in which he held me—for what seemed a terribly long time—was accidental or intentional, sad or somehow angry, or merely typical.

But I couldn't help but feel it was a warning.

I DECIDED TO MAKE A RETURN TRIP TO ALAN'S APARTMENT HOUSE. SOME crime scene tape lay on the ground outside, as if hastily and indifferently discarded. That was the only evidence now that anything untoward had happened inside.

A drawn woman of about fifty, her head covered by a colorful but sagging hat, sat on the stoop. Her legs crossed, her right foot kicking, she read a magazine in the setting sun of the cool September day.

I stood there until she noticed me. Then I gave her a friendly—and vaguely sympathetic—smile. To my surprise, rolling up her magazine, she spoke first, and as if we were old friends.

"So. You hear about what happened?"

"Yeah," I said. "It's a shame. He was a sort of friend of mine."

"I thought I'd seen you around."

"Damn crackheads," I said, and tried to sound indignant.

"Oh, please," she said, her voice rising slightly. "I mean, maybe. But there was so much coming and going last night, it could have been anyone."

I felt my heart lurch a little. I tried to appear calm.

"Is that right?" I said.

"Yes, it's right."

"You tell the police?"

She gave me a look that meant, *Are you kidding?* And since she was black and this was New York, I gave *her* a look that meant, *Say no more.*

"But I'm telling *you.*" She was obviously eager to spill her guts—or merely gossip—about this with *someone.* "This was not a man who entertained many visitors, let me tell you. But I don't have to, right, you knew him."

"Yeah. Alan was a, well, a difficult guy."

"Unpleasant, very unpleasant. And fragrant. Not a bathing sort of man, if you know what I mean."

"I do."

"But still—kill him? I don't know."

There was a long pause. The woman—Mrs. Heater, I later found out, was her name—took out one of those long brown cigarettes. I didn't think anybody smoked them anymore. But if she was going to smoke it, I was going to light it for her.

"Thanks."

"Sure."

I waited patiently, not wanting to push. "Were these people you'd seen before?"

"It's hard to say. My cataracts make it hard."

I couldn't help but grunt a bit, in frustration. But she didn't seem to hear.

"I know one was that muscleman. But her, I'd never seen before."

I just nodded, feigning calmness. But heat was starting to fill my shirt. Gus had been there that night! Even though he said he had not!

"When you say *muscle*, you mean—"

"The short one, who sometimes carried the camera back and forth."

"Right, right. And . . ."

A woman? Alan Gilbert anywhere near a woman? Suddenly, reality was taking a shape I didn't recognize.

"The woman was on the run, I know that. Two steps at a time."

I nodded, with a little "uh-huh." Like her, I was just another neighborhood gossip, more interested in *knowing* than in doing anything.

"She came out first," Mrs. Heater went on. "Then muscleman showed up. And then *he* left. I thought there was a party going on, attended by only one person at a time."

Mrs. Heater laughed at this, a brown ash jiggling off her smoke. Then, sighing a little, she seemed to lose interest in the whole affair. She unrolled and took up her magazine again, as if I wasn't even there.

So I started to leave. But before I did, I turned around, because I had to know one other thing.

"Tell me—"

Mrs. Heater looked up, as if I were a person she was meeting for the first time.

"Yes?"

"Were either of them carrying anything?"

"Who?"

It took her a second to remember. But when she did, she gave a snort of recognition and didn't hesitate.

"Oh! The man had something in a bag. He was clutching it to him, like he was afraid he would drop it. And hanging out of the top of the bag was, like, a tail, or something."

"A tail?"

"Not like a dog's tail. Shinier than that."

"Like a piece of film?"

"That's right. Filmy."

She stared at me a second. Then, recognition again slowly vanished. Mrs. Heater went back to reading, her hat dipping down over her flawed but still observant—to me, very beautiful—eyes.

GUS ZIEGLER LIVED IN A HOLE OF AN APARTMENT HOUSE UPTOWN ON THE West Side, where Columbia University begins to mingle with Harlem. His flat was on the first floor, and his buzzer just said, GUS, as if that was all we needed to know.

I needed to know a lot more.

Standing on the sidewalk, I could see that his one lousy room, which faced the street, was dark. When I pushed his bell—insistently, several times—no one answered. So I thought I'd kill time next door in a magazine store, reading the movie reviews in every newsweekly, glancing out the window every few seconds, until I saw him come home.

I only had to wait a few minutes before I saw the big man lumber by.

To be honest, in his own fashion, Gus was moving quickly, as if he was being pursued by someone. His expression—panicked and fearful—confirmed this, when, as he opened his apartment house door, I tapped him on the shoulder. I said just, "Gus."

He let out his own low, rumbling version of a scream. Then, turning immediately away, he frantically pushed his key into the lock until the front door fell open before him.

I would not go away. I had never been in a fight before—as opposed to being on the losing end of assaults, as I had been through most of my schooling—but being close enough to *The Magnificent Ambersons* that I could taste it made me bizarrely brave.

I attached both of my hands to Gus's broad back and got a secure hold of his shoulders. As I pulled down his shirt, I saw a tattoo on his neck that said HERMAN.

I thought of Hitchcock's *Torn Curtain*, the scene where Paul Newman has to kill an enemy agent. The director insisted that it be long and arduous—the victim kicking and screaming, his head in an oven, his fingers clawing, never giving up the fight—to show how hard it is to kill someone. But when *Torn Curtain* plays on TV, the scene is often cut to be less violent and, ironically, less cautionary for any kids watching.

Tonight, as I traveled with Gus inside, like a fly on an elephant's neck, I hoped our struggle might be edited for TV.

That was not going to happen. The door closed ominously behind us in the shabby first-floor hall. Gus turned, quickly, and his hands reached behind to grab my hands as if he were flinging away a cloak. The gesture lifted me from the ground and sent me into the wall, legs first.

"Gus!" I screamed.

I ricocheted off the wall and landed in a far corner of the floor. I was now at some distance from Gus, who was moving like a small car to his apartment, steps away. My legs feeling a new kind of pain, I managed to half-rise and half-roll after him. I was right behind as, having opened it, he now tried to shut his door. It was as if we were both squeezing into a fleeing subway train.

"Gus . . ."

Try as he might to lock me out *and* get inside himself, it was impossible. Both Gus and I went shooting in, the old door snapping shut behind us.

Here Gus had a definite advantage. The sun had set, the place was dark, and Gus lived there, I didn't. In other words, as I just groped around, idiotically, he was already scrambling efficiently for whatever he needed to defeat, maim, or kill me.

"Gus?"

I heard him reaching and hauling, zipping and lugging. I knew he was not accumulating any homemade weapons. He was instead grabbing whatever it was he wanted to either hide from me or, dragging past me, carry out. And, of course, I thought I knew just what that might be.

"Gus, let's talk about this," I said as my eyes adjusted slightly to the dark. All I could make out were piles of clothing, strewn on every surface, and I did not think I would be more enlightened if the lights were on. "Gus, it's not yours to take."

"I don't know what you're talking about," he said, panting, as he scooped up something and stuffed it down into something else.

"You know exactly." My problem in communicating was: I did not want to just blurt out the words, for what if I was wrong, what if he didn't know? I could just imagine Gus stopping what he was doing, standing there and staring, saying, "You mean, Alan had *The Magnificent Ambersons*?" and then what would I do? So I had to be suggestive if not downright vague.

"You know exactly what, my friend. You know just what."

Suddenly, there was silence. Though I could make out even more of Gus's run-down studio swollen with clothes and remains of meals, I could not make him out any more. In Welles's film *Touch of Evil*, there is a fight in the dark at the end of which, in a shocking closeup, Akim Tamiroff's character is shown garrotted, his eyes bugged out. That film was also recut and reshot, in Welles's absence.

I was hit in the stomach by what felt like a swiftly moving shovel. (I later learned it had been the one-volume edition of *The New York Times Encyclopedia of Film Reviews*, 1926–1970. My one copy was hard enough to pick up, let alone swing around.) The force of the blow bent me completely over. I grasped before me and clawed a terry cloth bathrobe off a chair before going down. Then I lay on the floor, near what looked like a small pile of egg and mushroom omelette that I'm sure Gus had meant to wipe up.

Carrying whatever he had been packing, Gus now started to step over me with his muscle-clogged legs. As he did, I managed to choke out, "Are you going to do to me what you did to Alan?"

I got him with that. Gus stopped, straddling me, his single piece of luggage held in one hand and swinging above my eyes.

"I didn't do that!" he yelled.

That was all he said. He started to go again, the bag pulled away from my reaching hand now, like bait from a fish, as his sneaker grazed my left cheek with its dirty sole.

Switching my target from his bag to his foot, I succeeded in closing my right hand around his thick left ankle, though just barely. My right hand joining forces with my left, I got a firmer hold. I found I could not trip him up but only pull him around, absurdly, like a small child trying to land a giant kite. Gus tried to kick me off, his bloated leg jerking up again and again.

"Please let go," he said reasonably.

Gus managed to kick me off. But his kicking motion had upset his balance. As if he were propelled from a banana peel, both of his feet went flying up before him, and he came crashing down next to me, his bag leaping away and smashing against the front door.

There was a pause. I thought this might instill a sense of comic camaraderie in Gus, but Abbott and Costello bloopers this was not to be.

"You little bastard," he whispered, inches away.

Then he slapped my face like an angry lover.

My whole head rang with the blow from Gus's beefy paw; my face turned, my chin nearly touched my shoulder. When I turned back, a million cries of pain coming from my neck, jaw, and chest, I saw only the wide back of Gus, escaping out the front door. He dragged the bag behind him, like one more piece of dirty laundry.

Gus, of course, could not get a cab.

It was rush hour, New York City's great equalizer: even men pursued by others are left standing on sidewalks, waving their hands. Gus had been at it long enough to let me drag my aching body out the door and down the front hall, after him.

He turned to look behind him—as I'm sure he had done every second—and saw me. Running as fast as his biceps and deltoids would allow, Gus then flew from the sidewalk into the street, across the center island on Broadway, and reached the other side.

From there, he disappeared down into the subway, the top of his fuzzy head visible for a second before he was gone.

Dodging cars—including one available cab, poor Gus—I shot after him, into, across, and down, my sore legs screaming with every stamp on the stairs going toward the Number Nine.

I hadn't had to hurry. Gus stood, swiping and swiping his Metro-Card at the electronic eye at the turnstile, muttering, "Work, damn you, work!"

Mine went through once, clean. Gus now looked up and saw me at the turnstile to his right, bloodied but unbowed enough to smile cutely at him.

The screech of a train coming in got our attention. As Gus's panic caused his MetroCard to finally work, he pulled his bag up from my hand, which was nearly grasping its nylon handle. Then we both pushed through the turnstiles and got onto the train, together.

My heart pounding, strangely exhilarated, I dared to sit right next to him. As we rode, Gus clutched his bag close to his heaving chest, shaking his head at my proximity and his bad luck.

Over the hiss and bang of the train, I bellowed in his ear, "Gus! It's okay that you lied to me! But you'll never get away with it!"

"I don't know what you're talking about!" he shouted back.

"If Alan hadn't been killed, I would understand your stealing it! Maybe I would have done the same thing! But now it's murder! Someone has to stop you!"

"I didn't do that! I didn't kill Alan!"

Of course, the train had stopped at this point, and Gus was screaming his innocence into a silent, crowded car. This being New York, no one even noticed.

Instead, people noticed me. I remembered that the fight had left me smudged with blood, black and blue, with my clothing torn. To all eyes, I seemed the least beloved of all New York residents: the crazy homeless man.

Gus realized this at the same moment I did. Standing up, indignantly, he hugged his bag tighter and said, like an offended old dowager, "Get away from me! Go bother someone else!"

People edged away, some frightened, others disgusted. Then the bell sounded for the closing doors. Through the scrambling mob, the station stop was visible. The doors tried to close, were forced open, tried to close, were forced open again.

Gus saw his chance. While the doors did their dance—opening, nearly closing, opening again, bell going off—he hustled toward escape. Fearing he might make it, I reached for him and grabbed. Unable to stop his strong body, I merely opened one side of his jacket, flung it flat against him, and sent an envelope out of its inside pocket onto the floor.

The bell now insistent, the doors finally closed. As the train spasmed onward, I scooped up the envelope through the feet of nervous, fleeing passengers. Frantically, I opened it as Gus reached down and tried to snatch it from my hand.

I saw airplane tickets to Los Angeles. Then Gus stopped me—and everyone else—with a cry of "Police!"

The tickets were snapped away by him. I looked up and saw, to my shock, coming forcibly through the rush hour crowd, a uniformed cop.

Everyone was staring at me, directing glances of hatred or fear. I started to push through them, saying politely, "Excuse me, excuse me." With the cop doing the same thing, though less politely, I made it to the door between cars.

I thought, if the train kept moving, I might be able to keep avoiding the cop until the next stop, where I could exit and be lost. But first I had to push my way through the next packed car.

"Excuse me, excuse me."

Glancing frantically behind me, I saw the cop finally come through the door, too. The station stop flickered outside; it was only a matter of time.

But I was stuck, crushed in a crowd either hostile or just unable to budge. The cop, however, was making headway. I could see the features of his face now.

At last, the train came to a halt. A river of sweat crashed from my face down the length of my body. All I had to do now was claw my way to the doors and maybe, just maybe, I could get out.

But the doors didn't open. The train just sat there.

The cop was now only two people away. I thought of explaining, of saying that Gus was really the one he wanted, that I was innocent. But I had recently been interrogated, and it wouldn't have looked good. Besides, I might have had to mention *The Magnificent Ambersons*.

Then the bell sounded. The doors flew open. And the stampede of people swept me out onto the platform with them. From the corner of my eye, I could see the cop flailing, his hand above the pressing mob, as I got away.

On the platform, there was a clearing in the multitude, right before a staircase. I took it, ran, and rose to the top of the stairs, never looking back. Behind me, I heard the train take off, carrying Gus, and carrying his treasure.

PRINT IT!

Direct from my L.A. rodents . . . guess which Hollywood subparstar is secretly thinking of starring in—wait for it!—Orson Welles's life story! This lame-o who creates suffering is also planning to direct a remake of *Citizen Kane*! He's been quietly buying up rights to all bios and articles about the big boy and noodling around for rights to Orson's movies! Be afraid, be very afraid. Or, should I say, Hold your breath, Mama.

I scrolled down the story with excitement—and relief. It was a week later, and my wounds were only now beginning to heal. What hurt the most was the thought of having Gus right where I wanted him, and then letting him slip—or, to be more exact, hulk—out of my grasp. Without the money to go to L.A.—or any idea of where Gus had gone there—I was stymied, paralyzed, and more frustrated than if this whole thing had never begun.

Alan's murder was covered only cursorily, as a comic curiosity by the tabloids (MOVIE FAN'S FADE-OUT . . . TV ODDBALL KILLED FOR DRUGS), and in two paragraphs in the Metro section of the *Times*, with a picture of the accused female crackhead, who just looked baffled.

All I could do was halfheartedly return to *Trivial Man* and my typesetting gigs, and wait bitterly for someone else to announce the existence of—and to see!—the complete *Ambersons* before me.

The story in PRINT IT! was my first ray of light.

PRINTIT!.com was a grassroots phenomenon of the trivial community, and the envy of all who toiled there. From his parents' house on Long Island, Abner Cooley had started a Web site devoted to gossip about the movie business. The name, of course, was a film reference but also an ironic take on paper trails versus computer communications.

Soon, through secret sources in movie companies in Hollywood—anyone who copied memos, answered phones, coddled egos, and took crap—Abner had developed the best underground network in the country. He obtained top-secret scripts and downloaded them, ran classified preview screening reactions, even divulged medical and financial truths about the stars.

Though barely twenty-eight, remarkably overweight and diabetic, with only a high school education, Abner was feared and—more than respected—loathed by multimillionaires all over L.A. To neutralize him, they offered him high-paying consultant jobs, even development deals. But Abner wanted to stay in his parents' basement, play with his computer, and know what he knew.

Now he knew something of importance to me.

I don't know how to drive. As I rode the train out to Long Island—far out, more than an hour, to a nondescript middle-class suburb—I rehearsed what I would say to Abner.

I could tell that his typically unsubtle blind item was really about Ben Williams: "creates suffering" meant Cause Pain, his action movie series, and "Hold your breath, Mama" was "Don't even breathe, baby," Ben's catchphrase. I was too obsessed by my own quest to even register disgust over Williams's hubris—imagine remaking *Citizen Kane*! I only knew that I needed what Abner never gave out: his contacts. And I couldn't even tell him why: because Gus Ziegler may have gone to L.A. to call on Ben Williams.

Abner and I were nodding acquaintances, and nod was what he did when he saw me. He sat, full as Falstaff, in his little swivel chair in his parents' rec room, a thin, blond beard trying to lend shape to his babyfat face. Orson Welles had played Falstaff in his own film, *Chimes at Midnight,* also sometimes simply called *Falstaff.*

"Well, Roy," he said, "what brings you all the way out here?"

"I was just in the neighborhood."

Abner laughed. He knew that there was no reason to ever come to Saddleview, Long Island. "Yeah, right."

I came as clean as I could. "You hear about Alan Gilbert?"

Abner only shrugged, indifferently. His trivial influence had become so great now that he placed himself above such public-access trash as Alan. When the time came, there would be no mere Metro section mentions for Abner. So I didn't go down that road.

I said, "I want to know more about Ben Williams and Orson Welles."

Abner nodded, his young jowels wagging. "I was that subtle, ay?"

"You know you never are."

"That's true. Well, what do you want to know?"

"I'm interested in doing some kind of subversion. Screw up his computer systems. I'm talking to a hacker right now."

Abner seemed impressed—not by me, by himself. I knew if I could play on his vanity, his own sense of his colossal impact on the film business—on the world in general—I might get somewhere. I was right. If it were possible, he puffed up further, appreciating his power, a little king.

"I see," he nearly whispered. "Is this why we couldn't talk about this on the phone?"

"Right."

"This seems pretty extreme for you." Abner lit up one of the cigarettes he sneaked while his parents were at work. "I didn't take you for the anarchist type."

"You don't have to be an anarchist to not want Ben Williams to re-make *Citizen Kane*. What's the sled going to say, 'Rosie'?"

Rosie Bryant was Ben Williams's movie star wife, a Southern-fried no-talent with implanted breasts, on whom he constantly cheated and with whom he shared three children.

"Right." Abner laughed. "She could play Marion Davies."

Kane, of course, was based on the life of publisher William Randolph Hearst, whose mistress had been the silent film star Marion Davies. She was far more talented than her screen counterpart rather unfairly portrayed her.

"Well, I like the idea," Abner said seriously. "But I'm afraid I can't help you with it. I need to keep my contacts over there."

"But they wouldn't be involved. I'd make sure to keep them out of it. All I would need to know is who they are."

"Sorry. I appreciate your rage. But if I acted out every time I reported some trashing of film culture, I'd do nothing else."

You mean you wouldn't still be in bed with Hollywood, as you essentially are now, I thought. Abner's disobedience had become his way of being connected to the powers-that-be, just as he smoked in his parents' house but never moved away.

"Look," I said, as if desperate. "I'll offer you something else."

"What's that?" Abner was starting to lose interest.

"My *Revenge* poster."

Abner twirled away from the computer to which he had returned. Greed shone in his bloodshot eyes.

"This is for real?"

"Absolutely."

The original name of *Return of the Jedi*, the third in the Star Wars trilogy, had been *Revenge of the Jedi*. Feeling it was too warlike, the producers changed *Revenge* to *Return*. Some posters with the original name had been printed, however, some of which remained in some people's possession. Through my own sources, I was one of those people, and anyone who had ever visited my apartment knew it.

Abner had been there once, years ago.

"That's a different story," he said.

I was glad to see that Abner's connection to the trivial community—or at least to their salable collectibles—was, in the end, greater than his allegiance to executives.

Still, understandably, he was suspicious.

"You feel *that* strongly about this?"

"Yes." I paused for effect. "And I *would* like to know one more thing."

"What's that?"

"You just posted the Ben Williams thing today. Tell me how Gus Ziegler might have known about it a week ago."

To my surprise and dismay, Abner's jolly face seemed to harden. His eyes squinted; even his nostrils flared. Then he just growled at me, "Get the hell out of my parents' house."

A few minutes later, I stood unceremoniously outside the Cooleys' house. I had walked there from the train station and had no way to get back.

What was up with Abner Cooley?

Because of the simple utterance of Gus's name, I had come away empty-handed. The trail, gone cold, was now tantalizingly lit by new secrets.

"Need a lift to the train?"

I turned at the sound of a female voice. Standing behind me was Jeanine Blount.

Jeanine was one of the aforementioned few female members of the trivial world. She was thirty, small, just five feet, with very long black hair, and glasses. There was a Morticia Addams quality about her—crossed with a bit of E.T.—and this was bolstered by her interest in the occult and astrology, which she pursued via Internet chat rooms, conferences, and the like. What she was doing at Abner Cooley's house was another unknown. But I was happy to see her.

"I work here now," she told me. "I lost my job at the Museum of the Moving Image, so Abner took pity on me. I do his bidding."

"I see. And that includes chauffering services?"

"No. If he knew I was doing this, he'd kill me. So—let's go, okay?"

Jeanine drove me in her huge, slow, 1976 Ford, a legacy from an elderly relative. As always, she spoke with the authority of someone old herself, though her frightening driving style seemed a leftover from her high school days.

"I couldn't help but overhear," she said. "And you said the magic words."

"Revenge of the Jedi?"

"No. Gus Ziegler."

I gripped the door handle as Jeanine took a turn that nearly spun us on two wheels. I couldn't tell if I was growing excited awaiting her information or because I feared for my life, or both.

"What's the deal with that?" I asked faintly.

"You don't think I'm going to tell you just like that, do you?" For her, Jeanine was being almost coquettish.

"I don't know why you're telling me anything at all."

"Abner has gotten too big for his pants—in all ways, I might add. Besides, I'm sort of intrigued. I mean, what's a big star like Ben Williams got to do with Alan Gilbert's murder?"

As we came to a sudden halt at a stop sign, I debated whether to tell her. Jeanine was volunteering knowledge, so I was meant to reciprocate. Besides, the proximity of a woman—even one as peculiar as Jeanine Blount—was melting me a little. As I had mentioned, we don't get many around these parts.

I decided to take it slow. "I don't believe Alan was killed by that crackhead. A neighbor told me that Gus Ziegler had left his place that night. And so had a woman."

"A woman?" Jeanine was as flabbergasted as I was, and even more grossed out.

"Yes."

"Wow. Well, what did they want there, do you think?"

She wasn't making this easy. Neither was the smell of her perfume, which was unpleasant and medicinal, but still, one that only a woman would wear.

"Alan had *The Magnificent Ambersons*."

There was a pause as Jeanine cut around a corner. I could see the train station looming in the near distance.

"A new print?" she asked coyly.

"No," I said. "And you know it. The whole thing."

"Jesus Christ."

Jeanine buzzed right past the station. Before I could point this out, she said, "Screw it. I'll drive you back to town."

———

"Well," she said as we hit the expressway, after a few minutes of silence, "I don't know why Abner hates Gus Ziegler."

"Great!" I said, feeling swindled. "So that was just your sneaky way of—"

"But I *do* know that the two of them were, you know, like, involved."

A faint blush came over Jeanine's pale cheeks. I turned to her, amazed.

"Abner and Gus—you mean—"

"Right."

"Jesus. I didn't even know they were gay."

"They don't know what they are, to be honest. But, apparently, one night, at the Rhinebeck Film Fair"—an annual gathering of trivia people at a tacky but amiable hotel upstate—"the two of them . . . well, whatever."

A vision of the two huge men together—one so soft, one so hard—made me smile, fondly.

"They'd make a kind of sweet couple, actually. But you say it ended badly?"

"I don't know what happened. But, one day, Abner said to me, 'Guys like that give freakish misfit losers a bad name.' Then he just said, 'Herman,' and looked disgusted."

I whistled, slightly, through my teeth, remembering Gus's strange tattoo. Was it the name of another lover? With Jeanine driving, we were getting to the city in no time. Yet now there seemed so much more to find out.

"So that would explain how Gus knew about Ben Williams's Welles movie?" I asked quickly. "Before Abner put it in PRINT IT!?"

"Right. Maybe Abner talks in his sleep. Either way, I've done their charts, and I could have told them it would be a big mistake."

Jeanine cut off a truck, while I tried to put it together.

"So if Gus killed Alan for *Ambersons*—and that's just a hypothesis," I said, "he's now in L.A., trying to peddle it to Ben Williams? Through the contacts he got—or simply stole—from Abner?"

"Maybe so. But don't forget the woman." Jeanine shook her head in sympathy for the poor creature.

"Right, the woman."

Her mentioning this made me glance down at Jeanine's legs, heavily covered in black tights, as she stomped on the brakes at the tunnel. It wasn't only desire. Suddenly, I felt that I couldn't do this alone. There was too much that I didn't know.

How to drive, for example.

"Tell me something, Jeanine," I said.

"Something *else?*"

"Yes." I paused, then plunged in. "How would you feel about going to L.A.?"

PART 2
LOS ANGELES

WE WENT AS COURIERS, THE CHEAPEST WAY TO FLY ANYWHERE. I PUT
Trivial Man on hold, and Jeanine quit Abner's employ. She and I
waited until we were called, and then we were hired—separately—to es-
cort goods to the western part of the U.S. Our cargo was unknown.

I arrived the day after Jeanine. It was my first time there, and Los
Angeles was a revelation. I had spent so many years writing and reading
about the place—or at least about the film business there—that to actually see it was like seeing a palace from a dream. I couldn't quite believe
that it existed.

And I wasn't sure I wanted to know. As Jeanine drove me from the
airport in a cheap rental car—and we passed fast-food places, run-down
motels, endless strip malls, one after another—I could feel mystique
and magic drop away with every mile. If I ever wanted to return to writing about Hollywood, I'd have to forget what I now knew. But once you
knew something, how *could* you forget it?

"Just live in denial," Jeanine said, watching me stare, unhappily, at
a triple-X-rated video complex. "Concentrate on the movie, on *The*

Magnificent Ambersons. That's the mystery. That's what we're here to find. The rest is just, you know, real life."

She had said it with indifference bordering on contempt. Her message: Suspending our study of show business to confront the real thing did not mean we had to be disillusioned. Sometimes you had to maneuver through its muck and mire to find what you wanted. Then you could go back into hiding, and erase the reality.

Jeanine had cheered me up, and I smiled at her. She smiled back, crazy cat sunglasses hiding her eyes.

"Now, let's take a look at those names," she said.

———

We stayed in West Hollywood, in the shabby apartment of Jeanine's cousin Larry, a middle-aged man who wrote graphic novels. Currently attending a comics conference in San Francisco, he had left his black-and-white sketches—highly sexual and scatological science fiction—hanging from clotheslines in the bathroom and kitchen, as if to dry.

"I figure Annie Chin is your best bet."

Sitting on her cousin Larry's lumpy bed, Jeanine had opened up her laptop. She had secretly copied into it Abner Cooley's file of movie company contacts, right before she quit, once she had broken his code.

"It had to do with character names from scripts that Preston Sturges wrote but never shot," she said. "It took me all day. Don't ask."

"Who's Annie Chin?" I sat down beside her.

"Ben Williams's personal assistant. Ever since Ben Williams slept with her, and then acted like it never happened, she's been a little peeved. That's how Abner got those bad preview cards for *Cause Pain: In Da Houze.*"

"And you think that's who Gus contacted in L.A.?"

"Possibly. There would have been no point in contacting Ben Williams's"—she scrolled down a page—"masseuse . . . or his drug dealer . . ." She tapped a final key. "Or his mother."

Jeanine logged off, then shut the little machine.

"So what do we do? Not—call her at work?"

"No. Or at home, either. You want to eliminate whatever stalker vibe you might give off."

"Then maybe it should be a woman. Maybe it should be you."

Jeanine just looked at me, her face softening, taking pity on my innocence.

"I'm not going anywhere," she said.

Jeanine spoke as if she had once ventured out into the real world, been burned, and retreated home again. She would stay inside with the computer now, thank you.

"Okay," I said, not wanting to push it. "But you will have to drop me off."

The plan was for me to run into Annie Chin at her favorite breakfast place, a faux-Fifties diner called Swingers, on Beverly Boulevard. Here was where I waited the next morning, eating granola and watching beautiful but hard-looking waitresses, outfitted in little retro space-age outfits. Most of the patrons were young wannabe actors or models, each more striking than the last, each less dressed. As a trivial person, I was ignored by the staff, so I had to stand and wave down a waitress.

Finally, at a nearby booth, I noticed a kindred spirit, an odd person out. She was an Asian woman of thirty, with a mole on her cheek, wearing a black catsuit under a denim jacket, and reading a script.

I thought of the original *Invasion of the Body Snatchers*. Its downbeat vision had been softened by a hopeful prologue and epilogue, which were later removed for its reissue. Then I got the nerve to approach her.

"Are you Annie Chin?" I said, standing by her, carrying my granola.

She looked up, suddenly, surprised. In this arena of more routine beauty, she was used to being ignored—and maybe even preferred it that way.

"Yes?" she said.

"I'm a friend of Abner Cooley's."

I hoped that this might break the ice, grease the skids, and all the expressions that make your way easier. Instead, Annie Chin's lips curled into an unamused smirk.

"Really. Another one."

I had to take this as encouragement—maybe Gus *had* contacted her! So I slipped into the seat opposite her.

"I'm Roy Milano," I said.

"And what do *you* want?" she asked.

"I want to know if you know a guy named Gus Ziegler."

Annie laughed, with no mirth whatsoever. She closed her script, placed her elbow on it, and put her face in her palm. Then she shut her eyes, as if suffering. When she opened them, they were filled with tears.

"Can't you leave me alone? Don't you know that I wish I'd never heard that name?"

I nearly gasped with a feeling of success. Yet Annie's unhappy responses were making me uneasy. So, commiserating with her, I pulled out the neck of my shirt, where Gus's bruise on my neck still hadn't faded.

"Me too," I said. "That's why I'm here."

There was a pause, then Annie relaxed a little. It had worked; in this painless environment, I was another injured individual. She wiped her eyes on her sleeve, and then on a Swingers napkin.

"That guy Gus is the reason I don't have a goddamn job anymore," she said, more quietly.

"Is that right?"

"Yes. He dropped Abner's name, and who knew that I knew Abner? Well, apparently a lot of people!" She looked at me bitterly. Then she shrugged, because it no longer mattered.

"Anyway, he said he had something that would interest Ben, something about this Orson Welles thing—which at that point was still a secret."

"He didn't say what he had?"

"He said he would only talk to Ben about it. Well, trusting Abner, I trusted this guy Gus, even though I sensed he was a little weird, body-builder, or whatever. I set up the meeting, and a few days later I get a fax. Not even from Ben, from his *new* assistant! Telling me not to bother coming in, I'm fired. And later that afternoon, they messengered me over this envelope with"—tears starting again, she fumbled in her pocketbook—"this printout that I guess they got from Gus."

Annie took out some folded pieces of paper and slid them across to me. I recognized them as pages from Abner Cooley's contact lists, the ones that were safely hidden inside Jeanne's laptop.

"So that's how come he canned you? Because you were one of Abner's sources?"

"I guess." She blew her nose. "He's never even . . . I mean, I haven't heard from Ben since. It's been a whole week."

She blushed then, because her tone had betrayed her to be more than just an aggrieved employee. Relieved to be so exposed, she pointed to the script on the table.

"I'm reading this for him, still," she said. "To see if he'd be right for it. Isn't that ridiculous?"

I looked at her, with sympathy. Even though she had ratted on Ben, she still had such profoundly mixed feelings. She was a trusting person, and easily hurt. She had trusted me, but I was no Ben Williams. I reached out and touched her hand, very, very briefly.

"Not more than anything else," I said.

Annie Chin was comforted by my tone. Instinctively, she touched the mole on her cheek. Then, fully linked to me, she asked, "So why do *you* want to kill Gus Ziegler?"

I laughed a little, as she did, sniffling. "It's Gus who might have killed someone. After he stole something. What he gave to Ben."

Annie nodded, with a small grunt of understanding. But she didn't even care what it was. She just tore off a piece of her paper place setting and wrote on it, stabbed it, with her pen.

"Here," she said. "This is the home phone and address of his new assistant. Her name is Beth Brenner. Just look for a really stupid bitch."

Annie slid the paper over to me, laughing at the depth of her emotions. As she did, the sleeves of her denim jacket rode up and revealed small bandages on both of her wrists.

Though I couldn't afford it, I paid for her meal, anyway.

"SO," JEANINE SAID LATER, SITTING NEXT TO A NEW PILE OF MAGAZINES on her cousin Larry's bed. "Has she called you back yet?"

She was referring to Beth Brenner, Ben's new assistant, for whom I had left several messages.

I shook my head no. "Maybe it was a mistake to mention Orson Welles."

"Don't beat yourself up," she said evenly. "You thought it would intrigue her."

"I think it scared her off."

"Well"—she pulled out a jangling set of rental car keys—"since you insisted, let's go."

It was a late Saturday afternoon. I approached the door while Jeanine waited in the car outside Beth's two-story apartment house in West Hollywood. We had decided that confronting her at Ben Williams's office, or, God forbid, his home—addresses Jeanine had cribbed from Abner—would be a mistake. At Beth's home, I could try to speak my piece, make sure she got it, and run, like a man slipping a menu under an apartment door in New York. Did they do that in L.A.?

I saw none in the small vestibule, where I pressed her buzzer.

"Yes?" came a young female's voice.

"Is this Beth?"

There was a pause. Then, "Get lost, creepo," she said.

The buzzer clicked off, without another word. I waited for what seemed a spectacularly long time. There was only silence.

Then, through the window on the vestibule door, I saw a police car pull up outside.

I remembered that, when the original *Scarface* was released, some states showed a different ending, in which Paul Muni was hanged for his crimes. But since Muni was already working on another film, they just used a stand-in, a trapdoor, and a hangman.

Pressing my back to the wall, I peeked out and watched the cop car park behind Jeanine. The door opened, and a blond cop, in much better shape than he would have been in New York, emerged. He walked to Jeanine's window, and they spoke.

My heart began pounding loudly. I could only imagine what Jeanine was doing—feigning ignorance of the city, or imitating flirtatiousness, or reading his palm. Whatever it was, the conversation soon ended. Jeanine turned on her motor. Then, glancing once furtively at the front of the building, she drove away. After a second, the cop got back into his car and did the same.

Left behind, I waited, swallowing very deeply. Then I exited the apartment house and walked out into the sun.

It wasn't a warm day, by my new California standards, but I was still soaked with sweat. As I walked quickly up the little street toward the broad boulevard—Melrose? I wasn't sure—I glanced behind me.

A young woman was leaving Beth Brenner's building. She was in a hurry.

She didn't fit Annie Chin's definition, by any stretch of the imagination. She was red-haired and long-legged and—if she had called the cops to get rid of me—pretty smart, as well. But, either way, Beth Brenner was heading toward her purple Taurus parked across the street.

I started to run up the block toward Melrose. As I got there, Beth was just pulling out behind me and, making twice the time, heading the same way.

At Melrose, I took a quick right and saw Jeanine's car parked at a mini-mall, as we had arranged. Meanwhile, Beth had stopped behind me, at the light at the corner.

"Let's go," I said, getting in. "There she is."

Jeanine waited until the light changed, and Beth had taken a quick right onto the boulevard. Then she peeled out after her, into traffic.

"I can't believe she actually called the cops," I said.

"I told you she might. Good plan, right?" she said.

"Great plan."

"I did our charts last night, and we make a good team."

"I'm happy to know that. Get left."

"Okay." Jeanine did. "Let me ask you something else?"

"What's that?"

"How do you know that's even her?"

"I, uh, don't."

Suddenly, it was a packed boulevard, all cars speeding, heedlessly. In the same lane, Beth's purple car had weaved ahead and was covered by a larger vehicle. Jeanine put on her turn signal and was about to get parallel. But she was suddenly cut off by a tiny white Porsche zooming in ahead.

A tanned yuppie was at the wheel. Moving at top speed, he pulled up alongside Beth. Honking his horn, he gestured for her window to come down. When it did, neither one slowing, Beth looked over, and he yelled, "Could you give me some directions?"

"Where do you want to go?"

"To your place!"

Flipping the finger, Beth zipped the window up and increased her speed. The yuppie kept pace, still honking, in a game of romantic chicken.

The car ahead of us, blocking us from Beth, now pulled out, cut across lanes, and exited. We were right behind Beth and then, as she floored it, right beside the lovesick yuppie.

He turned and, through his expensive shades, saw two trivial misfits waving at him and blowing kisses. Then—

"Jeanine!"

Beth had suddenly taken a U-turn. To escape her paramour, she cut over double lines and flew across the boulevard, going the other way.

Jeanine, of course, followed.

As she did, a pizza delivery truck shrieked to a halt, swiveling into a skid. But Jeanine was too busy veering behind Beth to care.

"He went through a red light, anyway!" she yelled.

I gripped the door handle, my foot hitting the floor over and over, in an impotent *brake* gesture. Then Beth took an immediate right, off the boulevard, onto neighborhood roads.

Jeanine peeled after her.

She slammed on the brakes, spinning the car half around. An elderly matron stood in the road, blithely overseeing her corgi doing his business. Staring at us, screaming, the woman's mouth was as round as a blow-up sex doll's.

Meanwhile, Beth was disappearing, cruising left, in the near-distance. Jeanine took a fast half-circle around the woman and the dog, and kept on Beth's behind.

"Lunatic!" the woman screamed after us.

We soared left, completing the oval that would get us all back onto the boulevard. At the end of the lane, Beth was at a stop sign, waiting to return to the action. Jeanine pulled up behind her, very innocently. When there was a secondary break in traffic, Beth zipped out, Jeanine tailing her like a small child holding her mother's hand.

There was a symphony of swearing as the two of us dodged other drivers and sailed across four lanes of traffic, going both east and west. Avoiding at last a station wagon filled with a family, we followed Beth into a small mall, Jeanine barreling behind her into the parking lot.

Then she slowed and parked, just another patron at one of about ten tacky stores.

I wiped the sweat from my face.

"I don't know why people from New York hate L.A.," Jeanine said.

"Maybe they just don't know how to enjoy it," I replied.

Then we sat and waited as Beth fixed her hair.

BETH TOOK FOREVER.

"What did you tell the cop, by the way?" I used the time to ask.

"That I was lost."

I saw a crumpled-up map, placed on the floor, for effect.

"Well, it's true, isn't it?" Jeanine asked, with sudden and surprising self-knowledge.

Before I could reply, I saw Beth finally leave her Taurus. Gripping her handbag, she entered a small drugstore. Once again, I left Jeanine behind and set after her on foot.

I followed her through electronic doors into the small, garishly lighted store. Beth walked blithely down aisles, picking up products, then putting them back. Keeping a few paces behind her, I did the same.

In *Double Indemnity*, Fred MacMurray secretly met Barbara Stanwyck in a grocery store. That film's original last scene—which took place in the gas chamber—was cut.

Finally, I saw something that made me stop. Beth had slipped a makeup bottle into her bag.

She did not approach any cash register. She just kept walking, casually, and completed what had all along been a circle throughout the store. Then Beth—whom Ben Williams must have been paying well, who made a lot more money than I did, anyway—left as calmly as she had come in.

I left, too.

In the parking lot, she walked just as easily, did not run, certainly did not open her bag or inspect what she had shoplifted. I'm sure she thought that nobody else knew.

The bottle in her bag was my ace in the hole. I took a very deep breath.

"Excuse me?" I said. "Beth?"

She turned on her heel. Close up, I could see that her face was freckled, her eyes green. She really was pretty. She did not even need makeup, and she wasn't wearing any.

When she heard me, Beth must have thought it was the store detective. But when she took one look, she knew that it was impossible. Besides, I had used her name.

"I called you about Orson Welles?"

Beth stared, first frightened, then shocked, then relieved, and then incredulous.

"Oh, my gawd," she said, with a slight Valley girl accent. "Are you kidding me?"

"No, I'm not."

"Well, maybe you didn't get the message when I called the police on you two minutes ago! That *was* you, wasn't it, creepo?"

"Oh, I got the message all right."

"Would you like me to call those guys over there?"

And indeed another cop car was parked in the lot, with two patrolmen drinking coffee in the front seat.

"You can," I said. "But I think they'd be very interested in what you've got in the bag."

"Oh, my gawd."

Beth seemed to live quickly or, at least, not to think very much. She immediately shifted from anger and cockiness to confusion and despair.

"I get nervous sometimes, *okay?*" she said, a choke in her voice. "Like, because I'm starting this new job now? And I just—well, I take things, okay? And you calling me wasn't helping! Like, already people I don't know are asking me for things! I mean, like, how did you even get my number?"

I felt sorry for Beth. But the way she was going, I didn't think I would have time to show it.

"Don't worry about that," I said. "Let's just go to that phone booth over there. Make one call, and this will all be over, okay?"

Immediately, Beth was composed again.

"Let's use my cell phone."

———

Beth sat calmly in the front seat of her car, the door open, her long legs stuck out, a tiny cell phone in her palm. I stood next to her, dictating.

"Ben?" she said, pulling down her sunglasses. "There's a guy here who wants me to give you a message. I had nothing to do with this, okay?"

"Take it easy," I said.

Her hand over the receiver, she mouthed, "Well, I didn't." Then, into the phone, "He said to tell you just, *The Magnificent Andersons.*"

"Ambersons," I hissed at her.

"Andersons," she said again, as if correcting herself. "And he wants you to call him at this number, if you're interested."

With my coaching, it took three times before Beth got the number right. After she did, she responded, only, "Right, sure, okay, bye," then hung up.

Placing the little phone away, she looked up at me, her eyes now hidden by the glasses.

"Happy now?" she said.

"*Happy* is a strong word," I said. "Enjoy your makeup."

Immediately, Beth's lower lip began to quiver. I stuttered out a rattled, "Sorry I said that." Then I walked back to Jeanine's car, dazed by Beth's ditziness, and by my own success.

That night, on the dusty fold-out couch in cousin Larry's living room, I lay with my eyes wide open. Finding *The Magnificent Ambersons* was turning into a test of ingenuity. I felt like a kid away at college, cooking his own meal for the first time. I just hoped I wouldn't, as it were, set fire to the dorm.

As the sound of Jeanine's tortured snores came from the bedroom down the hall, I repeated, to tire my excited mind:

"Nineteen fifty-eight, Burl Ives, *The Big Country* . . . nineteen fifty-nine, Hugh Griffith, *Ben Hur* . . . nineteen sixty—"

"Peter Ustinov, *Spartacus*," someone else said.

I looked up. Jeanine was sitting on the edge of the bed.

"Best Supporting Actors, right?" she asked.

I hadn't even realized I was speaking out loud. I also hadn't noticed that Jeanine's snores had stopped. Her black hair was let down very long and streaked with a surprising amount of gray. Without her glasses, she had a kind of squinty look. She wore only a T-shirt bearing a French poster for *The Seven Year Itch*, and sweatpants. I couldn't help but notice that her breasts were free and bigger than I had ever known.

"Can't you sleep?" she asked.

I shook my head. "I keep waiting for the phone to ring."

"What are you going to tell him if he calls?"

"The truth. I can't believe Ben Williams would want a movie that someone else was murdered for."

"You think Ben Williams is such a nice guy? Do you think Gus just *gave* him Abner's list of contacts? Just like that?"

I thought for a minute. Had Gus been offered something in return? Or hadn't he had a choice? I shivered about that possibility, and then I became aware of my bare chest.

Jeanine had come closer.

"Are you cold?" she asked.

Her attentions seemed maternal, but not entirely. As she was in other areas, in my bed, Jeanine was a strange mixture of the old and the girlishly young.

She came close, her long hair brushing against my chest. Her perfume had been replaced by the pure smell of soap.

"Here," she said. "I'll warm you up."

It was not that I didn't want her. I had been with no other woman since Jody. Discovering Jeanine Blount's avidity and warmth was arousing.

But Jody hadn't been of my trivia circle, indeed in the end had disdained it. There had been a sort of lifeline in that; there had been hope of normalcy. When I considered being involved with Jeanine, I thought of how blind people like to date someone sighted so they're both not wandering in the dark. Wouldn't we just be trapped by each other?

Luckily, I didn't have to decide. Just as Jeanine's hands found my shoulders, the phone rang.

I scrambled to answer it. The voice on the other end said only, "The Farmer's Daughter Motel, on Fairfax. Room 318. Right now."

It was 4:30 in the morning. Chivalrously, I insisted that Jeanine not drive me. Or had I wanted to be alone, free of her? I wasn't sure. All I knew was that the cab I called pulled up outside The Farmer's Daughter Motel twenty minutes later.

"Maybe you should wait," I told the driver, for what if I didn't return? But I didn't have enough cash to make him stay.

It was across from the Farmer's Market, hence its name. And like its name, the place was so tacky, it seemed to be aware of itself, a postmodern dump. It had Fifties-style trimmings and a neon light that—intentionally?—only worked a little.

I walked in under the drifting eye of an elderly desk clerk. The lobby said "fleabag," as if, again, it was a decorating choice.

"Whom shall I say is calling?" he asked me, in a comical British accent, the receiver of the motel phone on his shoulder.

Before I could even answer, he clicked off. If someone was expecting someone at 4:30 in the morning, it didn't much matter who it was.

Tensely, I rode a rickety elevator the three flights. I thought of the Bates Motel in *Psycho*. Whereas Anthony Perkins had always been the first choice to play Norman, Janet Leigh had not been the only one considered to play Marion. Many other blond actresses had been mulled over, including Eva Marie Saint (who had starred in Hitchcock's *North by Northwest*), Martha Hyer, Hope Lange, and even Lana Turner. As for John Gavin, it might have been Stuart Whitman or Brian Keith—and maybe it should have been.

The elevator reached the third floor. I walked down the dim, grimy hallway, the overhead light flickering "atmospherically." Although I heard nothing from inside any room—no screams or moans, as I had imagined I might—the silence was unnerving. It was as if the whole floor were waiting just for me.

I stood at 318 and knocked. All I remembered next was some heavy object, a gun butt, a blackjack, a filing cabinet, coming down on the back of my head. And then I was unconscious for a long time.

WHEN I WOKE UP, I SAW GUS ZIEGLER AGAIN.

Gus was lying next to me on the floor of room 318. Both of our faces were buried in the gray carpet, which stank of cigarettes and Lysol. We were both tied with our hands behind our backs. The only difference was that I was alive, and Gus was dead.

I was getting good at recognizing dead people. There was a stiff quality to Gus's big body, and his eyes, which were open, stared out in glassy shock. The front of his shirt was ripped down, and his HERMAN tattoo was visible. Gus had two encrusted dark red holes in the back of his head, and something nasty—his brains? I didn't know—had congealed while dripping down his scalp.

With great effort, I stifled a rush of my McDonald's dinner, coming up in my throat. I wished that Gus had had more hair, to make his death less hideous to me and less horrible and undignified for himself.

I thought of him sitting on the street in a doctor's outfit, or yelling "Live Girls!" while handing out flyers for a lap-dancing place, or answering phones for an aromatherapist. Even the crappiest things become nostalgic when someone is dead.

Then I realized that Gus and I were not alone in the room.

I could hear the faint, steady breathing of another human being. I could also hear a television, playing a movie that I couldn't place. Whether this was because I had been smashed on the head or the film was too obscure for even me to know, I wasn't sure.

"I guess this is what they call true love," a woman on the TV said huskily.

"I guess so," a man agreed.

Music swelled for what was obviously "The End." Then, whoever shared the room with us sighed, stood up, and pressed the TV off. As my head ached from the effort of thinking, I realized the movie voices had belonged to Rosie Bryant and her husband, Ben Williams.

The movie had been *Spirit of Love*, a romantic comedy not obscure, but simply too lousy for me to have seen. It had not broken Ben out of his—very well-paying—action-movie ghetto, and it had not established Rosie as anything more than a celebrity wife. But whoever my roommate was, muttered approvingly, "A very touching and amusing film."

This person then grabbed me harshly by my wrists, which were crossed and tied, and pulled me to my knees. I could see out the balcony window of the hotel room, and the light on the brick wall told me it was either dusk or dawn, the time when light begins to fall or come up.

"Upsadaisy," he said.

Kneeling in that painful and vulnerable position, I watched as my companion walked around to face me. He was a handsome black man, middle-aged, dressed in an elegant two-piece suit, with the short lapels so many had worn at that year's Oscars.

I thought that, in the play *The Bad Seed*, the child murderess gets away with her crime. In the film version, she is struck by lightning. Then, in a comic coda, the child actress is spanked, as if it had all just been a stage show. In a sense then, she survived.

For a second, I stared at the man in silence. My mind woozy, I had only one crushing need: to buy time.

"May I have a drink of water?" I asked, for my throat was burning.

"Oh, all right," he said, annoyed.

The man left and returned with a plastic hotel cup, which he held to my lips. Some of the water that splashed out of my mouth went down my front, and some ricocheted off and went raining down on Gus.

"Thanks," I said.

"Right."

The man crushed the cup in what I now noticed was a huge hand. I also noticed something else: His face was familiar.

"Hey, aren't you . . . ," I stammered out. "Aren't you from—"

"*Shatter,*" he said, modestly. "Yeah, yeah."

"That's what I thought." It was a blaxploitation movie from the early Seventies. "You were the police chief."

"That's right. But that was a long time ago."

Perhaps because I recognized him, he looked at me a bit more charitably now. Then, suddenly, he tore down the front of my shirt. Pulling me around like an army drill instructor, he inspected my neck and my back. Then, seeming satisfied, he dragged me on my knees toward a chair.

He lifted me up, painfully, by my elbows, and placed me into it. Was this a perk or a punishment? I didn't know, but I did know something else now: his name.

"You're Dick Burke," I said.

"That's right," he said grudgingly.

"You were the best one in it, in *Shatter.*"

These compliments were helping charm my companion. Yet everything I addressed to Dick Burke was also meant guilelessly. I was glad to see that he was still around and that he looked so well. But couldn't Ben Williams cast him in a better role than his bodyguard?

"So what have you been doing? Just this?"

"Look," he said, "you're not making this any easier."

"Making what?" I asked nervously.

"What the hell did you want to get mixed up with him for?"

Dick Burke pointed at the wide, water-stained body of Gus, lying faced away. Then, disgustedly, he grabbed up a magazine from a table and tossed it at the dead man's head.

"Freak," he said.

Slowly, some of what I was hearing began to make sense. Had Gus been killed for something *other* than being—or so Ben Williams obviously thought—Abner Cooley's spy? Was he guilty of something *else* besides killing Alan Gilbert?

"What are you talking about?" I asked. "I really don't know."

"Look, if you're lying . . ." He looked at me, threatening something unmentionable. Then Dick Burke just shrugged, sat on the hotel floor at my feet, took out a cigarette, and lit it. He sucked the smoke in and blew it out, gratefully.

"Jesus," he said. "If I look in your face, I'll believe you."

"That's because I'm telling the truth." I felt oddly safe with Dick Burke now, the supporting actor I knew. "I wasn't with Gus. I was only looking for him."

"Then why did you mention the same movie he did? *Magnificent . . .* whatever."

I was surprised that an actor as accomplished as Dick Burke had never heard of Orson Welles's second film, but I didn't say that.

"Well, to be honest, I wasn't only looking for Gus; I was looking for the movie. I was trying to get Ben Williams's attention."

"Well, you certainly did that." He laughed. "Mission accomplished."

"What's the . . . what did Gus *do*, anyway?"

Dick Burke rubbed his weary face. "It's not so much what he did—which wasn't great, believe me—it was what he wanted to do. But that's all I can say."

"Do you think . . . ," I was comfortable enough to ask now, "you could maybe untie my hands?"

I turned my back toward him and wiggled my captured fingers. Almost casually, leaving the cigarette in his mouth, Dick Burke reached up and removed what felt like rope from my wrists. I rubbed them, relieved.

Dick Burke waited a while before continuing to speak. Had he really grown to like me? Or did he know that I wouldn't be in the world long enough to squeal? Either way, he went on, pointing at the dead body.

"This Gus guy got to Ben through his assistant—his *former* assistant, Annie Chin."

"That part I know."

"Ben wanted me at their meeting at his office, just to watch, as usual. They had a long talk about this movie—"

"*The Magnificent*—"

"Whatever. I don't keep up on the business much, makes me a little bitter. That Samuel Jackson. Lightweight!"

"*The Magnificent Ambersons* is sixty years old."

Dick Burke's pause seemed unhappy and served as a warning.

"I could tell it wasn't *real* new," he said testily, "because this Gus handed over a bag with a couple of *cans* of film in it, not videotapes!"

Dick Burke calmed down, but suddenly I could see why he might be useful as a bodyguard, and unemployed as an actor.

"They talked money for a while, and arrived at a price. Ben paid him in cash. And then this Gus guy said something that struck me as strange. About the movie, he said, 'I'd sure love to watch it with you sometime, with you *and* your wife.' And he was staring at this little framed picture of Rosie and the kids Ben had on his desk. Then he got up, thanked Ben, and left with me.

"I didn't think Ben had noticed anything. But that's my job, you know? I was driving the guy back to the dump he was staying in, downtown, near the modern art museum. I could see him fidgeting next to me, making like little cats' cradles with his fingers.

" 'Ben's got a nice wife,' " I said, to draw him out.

" 'Very nice,' " he said.

"Nobody said anything then. His fingers were going even faster. Then he turned to me and blurted out, real blunt-like, " 'I'll give you the money.' "

" 'What?' " I asked, not looking away from the road.

" 'I'll give you the money he gave me,' " and he took the roll out of his pocket, like he was proving it.

"I stayed calm, because that's my job, too. 'What the hell for?' I said.

" 'If you' "—and he kind of gulped, like he was swallowing down and then burping back up what he had to say—'get me next to Rosie.'

"I kept driving, keeping cool, you know. I even laughed a little bit, to give him a chance to stop, to say it was all a joke. But from the corner of my eye, I could see he still had his hands stretched out, and the money was still in it.

"I was almost at his place, on a deserted street downtown, late at night. So I turned the wheel suddenly to the right, the tires screeching, and drove into an alley, where I stopped and killed the lights. This all happened in the space of a second.

"As fast as that, too, I turned on the little light inside, up on the roof. Then I stuck my gun right underneath this Gus guy's chin."

Dick Burke paused, but only to put his cigarette out in a can of Coke left on the floor.

"With my other hand, I grabbed him by the front of his shirt. He was a big man, you know, but he was shaking. I think the money fell through his fingers and into his lap.

"I told him to empty his wallet, to show me what was inside. He did, and that's where I found that list of names and numbers, one of which was Annie Chin's.

"And by pulling him toward me, I had yanked down his shirt far enough to see something else. A tattoo."

I was about to say, "Herman," but I didn't, and I was glad.

"Herman," Dick Burke said. " 'Herman?!' I screamed at him, pulling him even closer, and tearing his shirt. 'Herman?!' though, of course, I had had my suspicions."

"Who's 'Herman'?" I couldn't help asking.

"It's not a guy. It's a group. They're a bunch of nuts who believe in 'outing' people who are, well, half-guy and half-girl. 'Her-Man,' get it? They think Rosie is the most famous one like that. They even have their own Web site. And their own tattoos."

I felt the breeze on my collar, where Dick Burke had ripped my shirt and inspected me.

"Jesus," I said.

I *had* heard the rumor about Rosie, but had always discounted it, given Mrs. Williams's undeniable female charms. Why would Gus . . . but Dick Burke gave me an early answer.

"Some people think all the 'Her-Mans' are a bunch of mixed-up freaks like that themselves," he said.

I considered this. Gus having dual sex glands might explain his excessive weight lifting—overcompensation—as well as Abner Cooley's repelled reaction to their tryst. Luckily, I thought, I'd never know.

"We've been bothered by them before," Dick Burke said. "But none ever tried to get inside the house, to find out. This Gus guy thought he had a great idea. He had *The Magnificent* whatever, and Ben wanted it. But he was a rank amateur, and I could tell by the way he was whimpering next to me.

" 'I'm sorry,' he was saying, over and over again. 'I'm sorry, I'm sorry. I'm stupid, I'm so sorry.' "

Dick Burke did a blistering imitation of a weak person weeping. It didn't sound like Gus, but it didn't matter, he seemed to know all about people being that way.

"I heard somebody coming down the alley, some drunk or something. So I told him to turn sideways, and I tied his hands. I stuffed a rag in his mouth. Then I drove him to The Farmer's Daughter. He never gave me any trouble, never tried to run or anything. He was like a guy on death row, or something, resigned. I thought of turning him in to the cops, but . . ." He gave me a look that meant, *I'm black, and this is L.A.* I grunted, understanding. "I knew I shouldn't have shot him. But the guy had gotten me pretty mad."

I tried not to look over at Gus now, but it was impossible. All that muscle, I thought, and he could not be protected from his own peculiarities.

Then I looked back at Dick Burke, whose rage had made *him* helpless, too. He had confessed to me because his guilt was stronger than his fear of being exposed. He had come a long way from featured player.

"Well, if it makes you feel any better," I said, "I think Gus killed someone to get the movie."

Dick Burke seemed genuinely surprised, a bit relieved, then skeptical. "You really think?"

His reaction gave me pause. *Could* Gus have killed Alan? His scheme—though creative—had been doomed to such failure from the start that it now seemed pathetic. Still, anyone who would use *The Magnificent Ambersons* in order to expose a celebrity hermaphrodite was capable of anything.

"Don't forget the woman," Jeanine had said.

Suddenly, I remembered Jeanine, back in the motel.

"If you don't mind my asking," I said, "what *about* the movie? Ben Williams should know how he came to have it. I'd like to tell him."

I had gone a few words too far with Dick Burke. Furious, he stood up and, by my collar, pulled me out of the chair. Then he slid open the balcony window and, my feet grazing the floor, dragged me out onto the small granite terrace. There, picking me up by the belt of my pants, he leaned me far enough over the edge that the brick wall opposite seemed just an inch away.

Change fell from my pockets. We were three floors up. It was definitely dawn.

"Shut up!" he yelled. "You're lucky you're alive!"

"Okay, okay!" I yelled back. "I'm sorry I asked!"

Dick Burke dropped me back on my feet, on the balcony floor. Then, disgusted, he left me there, and went quickly inside the room again.

The storm seemed to have passed. Dick Burke was calmly wrapping Gus's body up in a sheet ripped from the bed. As I re-entered the room, he intentionally turned his back so he could not see me.

I left by the front door.

A cab had dropped me back where I'd started from. Waiting at cousin Larry's, Jeanine had been worried, but not a great deal. After all, to my surprise, I had only been gone a few hours.

"God, that's a shame!" she said, when I explained. "But no wonder Abner was a little displeased by Gus."

"Yeah."

"And Dick Burke. I always wondered what became of him."

"Now you know."

"Well, so what do we do?"

This was the first sound of confusion I had heard from the resourceful Jeanine. It made me think there wasn't much left *to* do. A big movie star had *The Magnificent Ambersons*, and would probably remake it, or use it in some way to promote his misconceived biopic.

"First, I'd like to take care of my head."

"Oh, my God, look at that. Please, let me."

With bandages and peroxide she found in Larry's medicine chest,

Jeanine administered to my wounds, which were unsightly but not deep. She did so with her usual motherly care, capped off with a tenderly romantic touch of my face. We were very close, but I only smiled, gratefully.

"I guess we'll never know how Alan got ahold of the movie in the first place," she said sadly.

"I guess not."

"Or whether Gus really killed him. Or who the woman was. Or whether it mattered."

"No."

"And, most importantly . . ."

She didn't have to say it, I was way ahead of her. We'd never see *The Magnificent Ambersons*, at least not before anyone else. That hurt me more than my head, I was surprised to learn. We had come so far, just to turn back. I thought about planning my next issue of *Trivial Man*, and it paled by comparison.

We were simply stuck in L.A., until our next courier assignment. Wearied by my brush with death, I slept most of that day and all of that night. Then, the next afternoon, we went to Santa Monica to see a festival of precensorship films from the Thirties.

Afterward, as the sun was setting, Jeanine and I walked along the pier. We played Foosball, which I lost, and avoided gang members who pushed past and occasionally rammed into tourists. Looking at the water, we talked about *Baby Face*, the 1933 film we had just seen, which starred a very young Barbara Stanwyck.

"She sleeps her way up the corporate ladder," I said. "It's pretty raunchy, even for that period."

"I know," she said, "but they changed the ending."

"I know. She has to become poor, and be punished—"

"I know, with that crude shot of the smokestacks of the bad neighborhood, cut in from—"

"Right, the earlier scene."

There was no point in either of us mentioning that some speeches in *Baby Face* were redubbed to make them more "moral." We both already knew.

The pleasure of being a trivial person is not just in knowing but in *telling*. Not being able to tell Jeanine anything made me feel more distant from her. Oddly, it made her feel more close. Maybe this was the difference between us, or the difference between men and women, I wasn't sure.

Either way, sitting on a bench, she let her head drop down onto my shoulder. And, either way, I kissed her.

She pulled back, a bit flustered by my mild aggression. Before this, she had made every move, and maybe this had been safer. Just as her actions often seemed conflicted—maternal or amorous? kind or erotic?—perhaps her feelings were, too. I let it pass. I was no one to talk about romantic mental health.

"Thanks for coming with me," I just said.

"Of course," she answered. "I wanted to help."

"But I guess there's only so much that people like us can find out."

"I guess so."

We walked back to the car, left in the pier parking lot. Jeanine pushed the key in the lock, but, strangely, it was already open.

"Oh, no," she said.

"You locked it, right?"

"Right."

We both stood there, hesitant to get in.

"Jesus," Jeanine said. "Do you think those kids, the gangs were . . . are the windows all—I hope they didn't break anything, I didn't buy any insurance in the rent-a-car—"

But she was stopped short in her list of worries. A hard, cold object was placed to the side of my head. Then, a voice—light, high, whispery, one I had heard many times before—spoke into my ear.

"Don't even breathe, baby."

IT WASN'T BEN WILLIAMS, NO MATTER WHAT I THOUGHT.

It was a young gang member, his face hidden by the hood of his jacket. He sat in the backseat as Jeanine drove, his gun trained on the backs of our heads.

"Pretty good imitation, huh?" he said, with a slight Latino accent, and chuckled.

"You sure fooled us," I said faintly.

"Hey, you should hear my Rosie."

This remark, among others, suggested that this was no ordinary Crip or Blood. The route he made us take went not into any dicey neighborhood but straight up through the pricey hills of Malibu.

The sun had set, and there was little light on the roads. Even Jeanine's driving was tested by the conditions, and her breathing was labored, as if she was unable to conceal her fear.

" 'I guess this is what they call true love,' " the boy said, with expert mimicry of Ben Williams's wife. "Good, right?"

Spartacus contained a controversial scene that suggested Laurence

Olivier's character is bisexual. Cut from the film in 1960, it was included in its 1991 reissue. Olivier, however, was dead, and Anthony Hopkins had to dub his voice.

"Okay, stop the car here," he said.

Jeanine did. Way up in the hills, there was only darkness around us, and great gaps between houses. In the distance, we heard some sort of barking or baying, perhaps the coyotes that are said to roam L.A.

"All right, lady," he said, then went immediately into another imitation. " 'Hey, lay-dy! Nice lay-dy!' Who's that?"

"Jerry Lewis, of course." Jeanine still managed to be imperious, but with a shaky voice.

Jerry Lewis's lost film is *The Day the Clown Cried,* a drama about a clown who had to lead children into the ovens in German concentration camps. Monetary problems caused it never to be finished. It may run a close second to *The Magnificent Ambersons* for most coveted lost film.

"All right, lady, that's it for you."

"What do you mean?" I asked.

"Well, you don't drive," the boy said evenly. "Right? So she drove, and now we don't need her anymore."

"But what are you going to do?" I said. "You can't—"

"Don't worry. It's not what you think. We're just going on without her."

"But—just leave her here?" I said. "This is nowhere."

"I'll be fine," Jeanine said, her voice more wiggly.

"First of all, this isn't nowhere, it's Malibu. And secondly, we're not leaving *her,* she's leaving *us.*"

The argument had fatigued everyone. The boy undid his seat belt—which surprisingly he had buckled—and opened the back door.

"You and I'll do the rest on foot."

"I'd like to stay," Jeanine said, "if it's all right with you."

"It's not," he said bluntly.

Jeanine looked over at me, and I could make out her worried eyes in the dark. I winked one of my own worried eyes back at her.

"Bye bye, baby," the boy sang, as a less convincing Marilyn Monroe. "Remember you're my baby, when they give you the eye . . ."

He had finished getting out. I started to do the same, feeling Jeanine's fingers trailing down my hand. I gripped hers before going.

Jeanine drove away, slowly, with obvious reluctance. Then I hoofed up the rest of the steep hill with my young friend. All the while, he had his gun placed squarely in the small of my back.

"That's really not necessary," I said. "I'm here, aren't I?"

"Sorry, but I *am* a gunsel, you know, like that guy in *The Maltese Falcon*." He did a mediocre Bogart. " 'You're taking the fall.' "

Panting, I mentioned, "The John Huston movie was the third version. Did you know that?"

"No," he said, genuinely interested. "Is that right?"

"Yes. One of them starred Bette Davis."

"As Sam Spade?"

"No," I said, actually smiling.

"Well, I should hope not." He did a not-bad Bette.

"In the other, Ricardo Cortez was the lead."

"A Latino? No kidding, that's cool." His tone became more confidential. "I'm a big film fan. That's why this is my dream job."

I was touched by the boy's reaction to my information. Perhaps he was a trivial person-in-training. God knows we are an aging crowd, and we sorely lack minority representation.

I faltered on the stony street, and felt his gun stick painfully into my spine. Just as with Dick Burke, there was a limit to our camaraderie.

Then, through the darkness, a house appeared.

It wasn't much bigger than a shack, but a satellite dish on the lawn hinted at wealth within. So did the two rottweilers slowly parading and protecting the grounds.

"Okay," he said, incoherently using trade talk, "hope you get points." Then he went into Arnold. " *'Hasta la vista, baby.'* I already been where you're going."

Slowly, I felt his gun withdraw. I faintly heard a fizzing sound, and realized that the boy was urinating in the street behind me—from nervousness or ignorance, I didn't know. Then he left me there alone.

I looked at the huge dogs, who looked back, slightly perplexed. I remembered watching a TV movie version of *The Call of the Wild*, starring John Beck. In the scenes of dogs fighting, they are clearly playing, their growls dubbed in.

Hesitantly, I approached the two, and they gathered around me, sniffing, not snarling. Like everyone else I had met in Hollywood, they were a strange mixture of friendly and threatening, and I could never tell when they would turn.

Suddenly, from the small house, a blinding light was snapped on. Guarding my eyes, I saw a silhouette of a man at the glass porch door. With a wave, he beckoned me inside.

Leaving the dogs with a pat on their heads—they had been good and had not killed me—I walked up the small back lawn to where the man stood. Before I got there, he turned and went inside. I followed.

It was one level, a cabin, really, modest by the standards of the rich. A glass coffee table was set before a leather couch, and a skinny standing lamp hung over them both. State-of-the-art video and stereo equipment filled the walls. There was a Sixties bachelor pad feel to it, and the music was Brazilian bossa nova from that period.

"Sit down," Ben Williams said.

HE WAS DRESSED VERY CASUALLY, IN JEANS AND A T-SHIRT, SIPPING A beer, albeit a fancy foreign one. I had once ridden a bus beside Tony Randall, and Jim Belushi once shot a film on my block, but Ben was the first superstar I had ever seen so close. I was surprised by how unimpressive he was. Everything about him was smaller in real life: his height, the amount of his hair, the tautness of his gut. His face was blandly handsome, but the flesh of his cheeks had fallen. His eyes were ringed and watery. Perhaps he was preparing for his role as Orson Welles?

I had met those who served and protected him, who reported on and reviewed him, who fell for and killed for him. *This* was where all those roads ended or began? Still, I had never been much of a fan. I knew Ben's filmography, down to his earliest guest shots on *The Love Boat*. He had only been cast in *Cause Pain* after everyone else had turned it down.

The stars of today could not compare with those of yesterday. Espe-

THE CUTTING ROOM 73

cially when they hired older, out-of-work, out-of-control actors like Dick Burke to do their dirty work. And who knew what else?

"This is my little hideaway," Ben said. "Few people have ever been here."

He acted as if this was a great privilege for which I should be grateful. I nodded, and tried to seem impressed. "It's very nice."

"It's a man's place."

"A clubhouse?" I said, but I knew he meant hiding place, trysting spot, party room. I wondered if he had brought Annie Chin here, and I figured that he had.

"Something like that."

"I'm Roy, by the way. Roy Milano."

He shrugged indifferently. He didn't even extend a hand. For a moment, I wished to annoy him by saying "And you are . . . ," but the feeling passed.

"You're the one who wants *The Magnificent Ambersons?*"

"Yes," I said.

"But you're not one of those, you know, creepy guys, 'Her-Man' . . . guys?"

"No."

"Good. Because if you were, you'd be—"

"Dead."

He stared at me, very annoyed. "I was just going to say, the scum of the earth."

I realized that Ben didn't know what had happened to Gus, and didn't want to know. Ben only ever wanted to know things—and people, for that matter—that would help him. He recovered from this irritating intrusion of the truth, and went on.

"Well, you can have it," he said.

I did not respond with jubilance, because, having been in L.A. a few days, I knew that a condition was yet to come.

"But first you have to do something for me."

This seemed obvious only to Ben, because no one in his world ever gave anything away. He also implied that, given my lowly status in life, my task would be more difficult than most, and that was as it should be.

"What is it?" I asked quietly.

"There's a woman I want you to find."

SHE WAS THE MOST BEAUTIFUL WOMAN BEN WILLIAMS HAD EVER SEEN.

And he'd been with some beautiful women, the most beautiful in the world, the ones other men only dream about. This one wasn't even a star, for God's sake, she wasn't much more than an extra.

It was on the set of his current project, *Terra Nova,* a smart action movie that was allowing him to stretch. He played a scientist called in by the president to hunt down an IRA terrorist. No T-shirts this time, strictly suit and tie. And then—blammy!—fireworks at the finale! The fans wouldn't be disappointed, and the critics would give him some respect. But who cared about them? They were capons, eunuchs. Still, an Oscar wouldn't be a bad legacy for his kids. Forget it, he'd get one playing Welles.

Anyway, the woman was playing his lab technician, had maybe one line, delivered a beaker to him, or something. The minute he looked at her, he forgot his next line! And he was always letter perfect, if the words were worth saying.

She was tall and dark, seemed Hispanic—or Latina, whatever they say now. Early twenties. Piercing brown eyes, enough mouth for two women, and her body! Like Sophia Loren's daughter, or something. Two takes, three takes, he kept going up!

"Are you all right?" she asked.

She wasn't being cute, making fun of him, overstepping her boundaries. She seemed genuinely concerned, there was so much warmth coming off her. He did not doubt her motives for a minute, and that meant a lot, coming from him.

"I'm fine," he said. "You're just—distracting me."

"Is there anything I can do?"

She meant it sincerely, and her Spanish accent made it sound even more innocent. But the crew heard her and, of course, whoops and hollers started coming. She looked as if she honestly didn't know what all the fuss was about. Imagine—a starlet who seemed like a schoolgirl, wrapped up in the face and figure of a foreign goddess!

"No," he said gently. "It's my fault."

The crew quieted down; Ben wasn't going to join them—against her? Screw them! He was the one who'd *protect* her from these animals. That was how he was behaving, and she bought it.

"Let's take ten," Ben said to the director, whom Ben had chosen from music videos, and who thought that was a good idea.

In a corner near the craft services table, she said her name was Erendira. He made her say it twice, then spell it. She came from Barcelona, though she wasn't born there. She had only just moved to L.A., and she wasn't sure she'd stay. Acting was just a lark.

"Well, it's a difficult profession," he said compassionately. "Still, they always need exotics. And if you can speak English, that's a plus."

"I'm an educated girl," Erendira told him proudly. "And not exotic. Just normal."

It just kept getting better. She ate pasta from the table, and told him why it wasn't well done, and what they could do to improve it. Erendira was educated, not serious about show business—she'd asked nothing from him, despite the fact that he'd offered, in his own way—and she could cook! Plus, that shape—she curled around like a canyon road at night—she was dark skinned, that was why he made the connection. How could he resist?

Ben knew that he'd promised Rosie—and himself. After the last one, he'd said it was out of his system. He had to be more careful—that Annie Chin had turned out to be such a betrayer, bringing that muscle-bound freak so close to his house. (And those rumors weren't true—Rosie was all-gal! The affairs were *his* fault, not hers!)

Actually, now that he thought about it, it would have been *Annie's* fault; she probably would have done it whether she was sleeping with him or not. And "sleeping with him"—once!

(He had to make a note to himself: His relationship with Annie Chin was like Welles's with Rita Hayworth. Hadn't she been crazy, too? Or did she just end up with Alzheimer's? He would get that new girl, that Beth Brenner, to look it up. Actually, that Beth was cute and *didn't* seem crazy, but it was too risky for that, forget it.)

So he had no intention of cheating again, and so soon. But when Erendira—to prove her point about the pasta—said, "See?" and placed a fork of it into his mouth, waited until he'd swallowed, and then said, "Mine tastes so much better," he knew he had to have her, right then and there.

"I think we're through for the day," he told the director, who thought that was a good idea.

———

He didn't want to rush her. Erendira was a bright girl, a good girl—and that Latina thing, the church and all, who knew how fast she would go? The last thing he wanted, he thought with a laugh, was a family of big brothers coming after him with machetes. It was scary enough dealing with that kid who had brought Roy there, from the gangs or whatnot! It was scary that night he had a bunch of those kids up to his house for a little private fun.

Anyway, he drove her home, to—get this—an Evangeline Home for Girls in South Central. Very protective, for girls from out of town, no boys allowed in the room. This only served to get Ben more charged.

It tickled the two of them to be sitting outside that run-down place, in Ben's black Porsche! They laughed so hard about it that Ben had to cap it with a kiss.

What a kiss it was. Like slipping hot liquor into his mouth! Sitting outside in his car, she used her tongue like an artist—like a pro, Ben actually thought, and this made him even crazier.

Where had she learned it? Not from the nuns, that was for sure!

"Where I come from," she told him, "everything about love is perfectly natural."

Kindness and cooking, innocence and experience. Plus, a foreign accent. Plus, she wasn't ambitious. Erendira made Ben forget every disastrous affair he had had, made him forget he was even married to Rosie. For a minute, anyway.

"I have a little place up in the Malibu hills," he said. "I'd like you to see it sometime."

I'd like you to see it tonight, he thought. I'd like you to see it right now.

"I'd like to see it right now," she said.

Ben had to admit it, he had not been suspicious. Sure, she was going pretty fast, seeming to do—and be—everything he had ever wanted. But who could blame him for going along?

With her that night, right on the couch where Roy was sitting now, he felt like some fabulous peasant to whom, yes, "everything is perfectly natural." This was no neurotic assistant. This was no climbing costar. Or former agent. Or bulimic wife of a friend. This was, well, it sounds corny, but this was a connection to a past in which he had been a simpler, purer man. And maybe a link to the same kind of future.

Ben proudly showed her his autographed picture from Webby Slicone, the singer-turned-conservative congressman to whom he had contributed money. ("Back at you, Ben!—Webby") But Erendira had only been in the country a brief time, and could not place him.

"So, I want to tell you about my secret project," he said. "Well, what secret, right? It's already been leaked by that goddamn geek on PRINTIT!.com!"

"What is that?" she said.

And why should she know? This was no bimbo, peering through the trades every morning. So, patiently, he explained about his Orson Welles idea, about the history of the Internet and what it was used for, about Abner Cooley, that powerful loser whom he hated, and about *The Magnificent Ambersons*, though he left out the part about Annie Chin, Gus, and "Her-Man," because it might reflect badly on him. Finally, he spoke at length about his identification with Orson Welles, a genius who had been no hero in his own land.

Ben did not know for how long he spoke, but Erendira's attention never seemed to lag. This proved what a real and wonderful woman she was.

"See, my first idea," he said finally, "was to remake *Citizen Kane*—and that secret, as I already said, got out. But what nobody knows is that I actually have *The Magnificent Ambersons*, the entire thing—"

"What's that? Another movie?"

Ben smiled. Where she came from, they probably didn't even have TVs that worked! So Ben explained about that, too, as much as he knew, anyway, since he was still having Beth do coverage on Welles.

"So, what I'm going to do is remake *that* one, the whole thing, the parts that nobody's ever seen. Then I can say I went Orson Welles one better. Somewhere, I think that he's smiling down on me."

She thought a minute, then asked, "And what is it like? The whole film?"

"I haven't watched it yet. I've never gotten through the earlier cut version, to be honest. But I will. I'm going to rise to the occasion."

Kissing him, Erendira seemed sure of it. He did not tell her of his plan to destroy the longer Welles version, have it lost once and for all. He wanted the long *Magnificent Ambersons* to be *his* idea, *his* brainstorm. But he was sure she would have understood, had he told her.

"Let's watch it now," she said.

"What?"

"Let's see it now, I'm very curious."

"But—aren't you tired? And aren't there . . . 'other things' . . . we could be doing instead?"

Ben felt sleazy at that moment, not "natural," but he couldn't help himself. He told her that he didn't feel like watching the movie now, he'd see it later, or maybe have that Beth transcribe it for him.

But Erendira was insistent.

"If it means that much to you," she said, "I want to see it."

How could he say no to that? She was saying "Put up or shut up, be the better man, the artist you know you are and that I know you are."

So Ben set up the projector and screen he had stashed there, the ones on which he sometimes ran vintage stag films that were not on video. Then he broke out the incredible new pot that Stu Drayton had delivered to him. Stu was his dealer and the one who hired the kids from the barrio to make deliveries for him, who gave them "opportunities." That boy tonight had been one of Stu's.

He wasn't sure how Erendira would deal with the drugs, but he was relieved by what he heard.

"Where I come from," she said, "there is no sin in this."

Yes, what a woman she was.

They set up the film and were about to turn it on. But the pot was so strong that, within ten minutes, Ben was laughing uncontrollably, and within fifteen minutes, he was asleep.

When he awoke in the morning, the film was gone. And so was Erendira.

Nothing else was taken. Ben went through his drawers, his safe, all his private places. Even the last taste of pot was left. It was only Erendira and *The Magnificent Ambersons*.

Ben was not angry, he was beside himself. He was sure that someone had kidnapped Erendira while he was asleep. He had many enemies, maybe even some on his own staff. Otherwise, Erendira hadn't been sincere with him, and that didn't make sense, did it? The woman of his dreams? That would mean Ben Williams was a schmuck, and he wasn't, he was a major movie star.

Ben wasn't concerned about *Ambersons*, to be frank. He had several other projects lined up; the Welles thing was just in development. That was why he was asking for Roy's help.

Ben wanted to find the woman; Roy, for whatever reason, and Ben never asked, wanted to find the film. Roy didn't work for Ben, so he was above suspicion. And he didn't know Rosie. (Ben also secretly thought that this would give him some time to stay faithful and work on his marriage. You had to be realistic and keep your options open.)

Ben would provide the backing, first-class all the way, within reason. All Roy had to do was keep his mouth shut and, of course, be successful.

Couldn't Roy use the money? And who was he, anyway, to say no?

Well, that was the story. What did Roy think? About going to Barcelona, he meant?

PART 3
BARCELONA

I WAS FINALLY A REAL DETECTIVE.

What I mean is: In old books and movies, a detective always works *for* someone. He gets paid, instead of just nosing around on his own. This shift into gainful employment gave me greater mobility, of course. But it also meant that I was less free, and beholden to someone else. And that someone was Ben Williams.

"Quit complaining," Jeanine said. "What's the alternative? Back to New York, bitter, with no *Magnificent Ambersons*."

"You're right," I said reluctantly. "I guess this is what they call 'moving up.'"

Like Abner Cooley before me, I had entered into the world of those I judged. But was it really possible to enter? Didn't trivial people's skills at unearthing and exposing make us valuable—and dangerous? Wasn't Abner Cooley really hated by executives? And wasn't Ben Williams just using me? Trivia was turning out to be not so trivial, after all.

"Alan Gilbert thought the *Ambersons* would move him into the mainstream," I said. "And look what happened to him."

"You're not Alan Gilbert," Jeanine said. "You're coming back."

She said this as if she would wait, patiently. All the while, she was adjusting my collar with her usual mix of the maternal and the romantic. It was a full hour before my plane went to Barcelona, but Jeanine had only minutes to catch hers. She was accompanying cargo back to New York.

"I wish you were coming with me," I said.

"I did what I could," she said. "I can drive, but I can't speak Spanish."

They were calling Jeanine's plane now. She kissed me, grazing my mouth with a conflicted kiss, half-aunt, half-amorous. I inhaled her perfume deeply and touched, tentatively, the top of her coiled-up hair.

"Be careful," she said.

Then she was gone.

I had been surprised by the speed with which Ben had ordered up everything I needed. And I had been surprised at who had brought it to cousin Larry's apartment in L.A.

Beth Brenner had been shocked to see me, too.

"Oh, my gawd," she said. "It's the crazy guy!"

"Keep your voice down," I said. "My friend's napping in the other room. Besides, before you cast aspersions, may I look in your bag?"

As usual, Beth immediately began to crumble. But then she pulled herself up, with new self-control. I guessed that Beth was growing into her job.

"I just hope Ben knows what he's doing," she said.

The other night at his house, Ben had snapped a quick picture of me with a camera he kept by his bed for private purposes. Now, with the picture inside, Beth threw a passport at me. Next came a roll of money, an itinerary, and a laptop. Finally—and I backed off as it came my way—she laid before me a small handgun and a permit.

"Jesus Christ," I said. "What's that for?"

"To shoot people with," she said. "Duh!"

I was shocked that Ben thought this job would be so dangerous. I had never even touched a gun, and now I kept this one at a distance.

"So, that's it, okay?" she said. "Oh, there's one more thing."

Beth handed me a manila envelope, which I shook out on the bed. It contained a headshot—that is, a picture and résumé of an actress.

Erendira used one name, like Cher or Madonna or Terry-Thomas. She was sultry, with a huge head of black hair and piercing dark eyes. I could understand Ben's infatuation. I didn't see the look of innocence he had gone on about. But maybe you had to be there.

When I flipped it over, I saw an L.A. address and phone number. Ben had scrawled on it: *Disconected.* He used just the one *n*, not me.

"I don't see what's the big deal," Beth said. "I mean, there already is Jennifer Lopez. How many more of them do you need?"

There was a tone of petulant jealousy in Beth's voice. I looked up at her, suddenly surprised she would be privy to so many of Ben's secrets. But then I knew that Beth was privy to many things about Ben now. No matter how much he regretted Annie Chin—or desired Erendira—Ben had once again been randy and reckless. I wondered how long it would be before Beth became an Abner Cooley contact, too.

"Well," she said, "good luck. Annoy people in Europe now."

On her long, bare legs, Beth breezed from the room. Despite her new confidence, she was still insecure; she took my pen with her.

For the first time in my life, I left the country and flew first class. It was a cushy way to experience a storm in the sky, which seemed to want to scuttle the plane. I was provided with free videos for my own little TV set, two out of three of which starred Ben. Had he arranged for that, too?

In Barcelona, Ben made sure I was picked up by a limo driver and taken to the Carabas, a four-star hotel. Though I had a working knowledge of the language, I didn't have to speak a word of Spanish; I didn't have to make a sound. I had full use of a bedroom, a sitting room, and a giant bathroom with its own Jacuzzi.

I laid Erendira's picture on my enormous bed. Then I unplugged the room phone and plugged in my modem before calling up Web sites from across the sea. I wanted both to be informed and to feel less homesick.

PRINT IT!

Since we reported—without naming names, of course—that a famous star planned to remake *Citizen Kane*, I can now confirm that his plans are off. It seems that after the item made headlines worldwide— okay, it was Ben Williams, baby—the red-faced star is planning a yearlong sabbatical to "spend more time with my family." Since that family includes Rosie Bryant, expect him to be before the cameras in about six months.

From there, I called up the *New York Times* online, and its Metro section, in particular.

MURDER SUSPECT UNDER SUICIDE WATCH

When Lorelei Reed was arraigned last month in a downtown court- room on charges that she killed local TV performer Alan Gilbert, she looked dazed and disoriented. Now she is under a suicide watch.

Gilbert was found stabbed to death in his ransacked East Village apartment. There was no sign of forced entry, but police said money was taken. They had no comment on reports that drugs were also stolen from Gilbert, the host of the *My Movies* trivia program on local late-night cable-access television.

Reed, in her thirties and an admitted crack cocaine addict, is be- ing held on one hundred thousand dollars bail. The suicide watch was imposed after she reportedly tried to stab herself with a pin she had ripped from the hair of a female guard.

As I looked around my gigantic, cream-colored suite, I thought I had come a long way from Alan Gilbert. Finding Erendira might lead me to *The Magnificent Ambersons*, but it would probably not clear Lorelei Reed. Or would it? These days, I was never sure what dead end might open up another avenue.

Before I went to sleep, I buzzed my home phone, billing Ben's phone card. I heard Jody, asking who the woman playing the nun on Landers Classic Movies was. And I heard a few angry subscribers wondering where their *Trivial Man* was.

I wondered the same thing.

Over the next days, I showed Erendira's picture to bartenders, newsstand vendors, theater owners. Despite my fancy new haircut and clothes—courtesy, of course, of Ben—I was treated with contempt. Americans were not their favorite foreigners down Barcelona way.

The only reactions I got were leering approval of Erendira's picture, or annoyed incredulity, as in "Get out of here, quit kidding around." They obviously doubted that I could ever know such a woman.

Otherwise, during the day, I wandered the Ramblas, the broad boulevard that catered to—or tried to trap—tourists with street performers, caged birds for sale, and postcards of handsome soccer heroes. Street children pursued me, aggressively asking for money. A man dressed as Ben Franklin targeted me for attention—sensing my Americanness, I supposed—and tried to block my way, with weird belligerence.

At night, I ordered in room service and flickered through the few TV channels. I watched a popular talent show, in which Spanish residents did impressions of celebrities—some as old as Louis Armstrong, others as new as Madonna—and of handsome soccer heroes. The winner this week, as she had been for many weeks, apparently, was a pudgy, middle-aged woman who "did" Ben Williams.

"Don even breath, bebe!"

She reminded me of my duties. Turning down the set, I logged on for my daily progress report:

Dear Ben,
   Trying hard. No sign of her yet.
               Roy Milano

An hour or so later, I received this reply:

Dear Mr. Milano,
   Ben is not paying you to fool around. Get on the stick.
               Cordially,
               Elizabeth Brenner

I figured that I had now been "given" to Beth, as a symbol of her new power within the Williams camp. I wondered if Ben was losing interest in my assignment.

But the checks that kept coming were for larger and larger amounts. Ben was more desperate than ever to find Erendira, trapped in his usual pattern of family duty and affairs with the unstable. The simple and sensual goddess must be dancing in his dreams, I thought, as the names of supporting acting winners danced in mine.

I figured I had to bite the bullet and call on my own contacts. The trivial community may have spanned the globe, but I knew of only one member in Spain: Ron Gaylord.

Ron was a former film professor and current expatriate, who had followed a woman overseas, where they married and had two children. Soon the woman ran off with their kids, and Ron was left, managing a movie revival house and a serious drinking problem.

I had delayed consulting Ron because he was a nightmare figure of the trivial man: down and out, far from home, with just his film cans to keep him warm. I also feared that he would have an attitude about my new employment, which he promptly did.

"Nice duds," he sneered.

"There's a reason for this, Ron," I said defensively.

"Isn't there always? What is it, you decided to 'grow up,' or something?"

I thought that Ron was in no position to judge, sitting pale, unshaven, and slightly shaky in the cramped office above his run-down theater, which had been carved from a medieval building in the Gothic Quarter. Still, co-option by the workaday world was a sore subject among the trivial, and I felt it.

I wished I could tell Ron what I was really seeking. But his bitterness made him a hard man to trust.

"I'm looking for an actress," I said. "So sue me if I'm being bankrolled."

"By whom?"

I paused, under the withering gaze of withered Ron. To him, there could be nobody worse to work for than—

"Ben Williams."

"Jesus Christ."

"You're just jealous," I said, knowing it wasn't true.

"Yeah, tell me another." Ron drank from a cup that might have contained coffee, but I doubted it.

"Look, I didn't come here for a lecture. And it's nice to see you, too, by the way."

"You're as bad as the rest of them," he muttered. "You symbolize everything that sucks."

"Thanks."

"They're closing me down, you know," he said. "They're building a twin theater, or a plex, or whatever the hell they call it."

I nodded, a bit shaken. "I'm sorry to hear that."

"You think this conglomerate crap is only happening in America. But we're not free of it in Europe, either."

Ron sucked deep from his cup of whatever. I felt sorry for him—and even sorrier for world culture—so I hid behind the job I had to do.

I laid the picture of Erendira out before him. He glanced at it for a second, then looked away.

"Nice," he just said.

"She doesn't look familiar."

"Of course she does. A dime a dozen."

I sighed, putting the picture away.

"The best of luck to you," Ron said sourly. Then he turned to tinker with something, obviously to get me to go. Obediently, I packed up.

"Well," I said weakly, "it was good to see you again."

Ron just addressed the air around him.

"When they've got *you*," he said, "they've got everyone."

In its own way, the remark was a compliment. It almost made me blurt out about *Ambersons*. But there are some people whose self-esteem is so dismal, it's dangerous. Ron was one of those people.

"Good luck," I said lamely, and he snorted back, with derision.

―――

That night, both to occupy myself and, in a small way, to support Ron, I attended his theater.

He was running a revival of *Singin' in the Rain*. I was assured by the sign outside that it was V.O., or version originale, that is to say, subtitled. But when I sank into my seat, I was in for a surprise. Gene Kelly, Donald O'Connor, and Debbie Reynolds clowned and sang in Spanish. Only the taps of their dancing feet were V.O.

Still, I stayed, the film so familiar that I would know it in any language. I remembered that Gene and Debbie's "You Were Meant for Me" number was cut from certain prints and, indeed, it had been here. The few minutes of film were as lost as Ron Gaylord was in Spain.

Misreading the listings completely, I had entered in the middle. So I stayed for the start of *Singin' in the Rain* again, loath to return to my hotel suite and the accusations of failure that flowed into it from my laptop, filling it up as if from a tub left running.

Then I sat up in my seat.

Commercials ran before the feature, as they do in many European cities and in (too many, I think) American ones. This one was a crude but sprightly vignette for a cola called Fizz.

A beautiful woman, wearing a helmet, roared by a cop on her motorbike. Flying from her backpack, a cola bottle hit the street and splattered. On his own bike, the cop started after her, in hot pursuit. At last, she pulled over to the side of the road. Taking off her helmet, she revealed a beautiful mane of black hair and a stunning, full-lipped face. But the cop, of course, only wanted to know if she had more Fizz.

The woman, I was sure of it, was Erendira.

———

No wonder men had been amused that I was looking for the Fizz girl. Who wouldn't be? As the sounds of "Fit as a Fiddle" started from Gene and Donald, I stumbled, shocked, into the lobby.

From there, I rushed to the nearest bodega. Speaking in Spanish, I tried to communicate what I wished to drink. The proprietor, who was playing with me, shrugged his shoulders. He just spoke Catalan.

So, "Fizz," I said. "Fizz."

He made several crude gestures toward his lap and shook his head *no*. They had no bathroom.

Finally, I pantomimed chugging from a bottle, then wiping off my mouth, an insane tourist who would not leave without this one beverage. Tired of jerking me around, he directed me to a refrigerated case.

The stuff itself was sweet and slightly sickening. But Fizz was not what I was after. I peeled off the label with a key, careful not to tear the company name and its address: Cheruba, Inc., 76 Pasaje de Gracia.

I had someone to thank for this. Seeing from the street that his light was still on, I started back to Ron's office above the theater. I took his stairs two at a time, propelled by an urgency I did not quite understand.

When I entered, the place seemed empty. All I heard was a faint, creaking sound coming from within.

"Ron?"

I saw the empty chair first, placed in the center of the floor. Above it, Ron swung, attached by his own belt to a steel fan on the ceiling, which was not turned on. Each tiny swivel of his body turned the blades a bit, which was where the squeak had come from.

His feet were still twitching. All of my senses keen, I stood on the rickety chair beside him. It took several endless seconds to rest Ron's left hip and butt on my shoulder, and ease the pull on his neck.

Then I reached up and, just quickly enough, began to gently unloop the belt.

Right then, I figured that *Singin' in the Rain* was just about done.

ON BARCELONA'S RITZY SHOPPING DRAG, CHERUBA, INC., WAS IN A GAUDI-
designed building, which dripped in the architect's trademark Dr.
Seuss–like style.

The head of public relations for Cheruba was a polite, middle-aged
man named Mr. Fuenta. He made an appointment with me right away.
My occupation had piqued his interest.

"What kind of movies do you produce in America?" he asked.

Behind his desk, he was holding one of the fake business cards Ben
had supplied me with. I smiled, with a sly, producer-ish air.

"I'm preparing a project with Ben Williams now, actually," I said.
"It's in the early stages, but Ben is wonderful to work with."

Fuenta was highly impressed. His English was impeccable, better
than his grasp of Hollywood specifics.

"Well, he's a very good actor," he said, "as is Rosie Burnett."

"Yes. Rosie *Bryant*, actually, is interested in our piece as well."

Fuenta nodded, and muttered abashedly, "Bryant." He took out a little pad and started to make notes.

"And what is the story?" he asked.

"Well, it's a"—and here I was totally vamping—"a love story. A very powerful love story. And there are, you know, space elements."

"Space?"

"Outer space, yes."

"I see." He scribbled. "And how do you see Fizz being involved? Would they drink it in space or . . . here on Earth?"

I paused. "Fizz?"

"Yes. I'm assuming this is about product placement."

I hadn't even thought of that, but obviously I should have.

It had been several days since Ron Gaylord's attempted suicide, and I was just getting back to business. Despite the fact that he had seen Erendira's picture moments before, his motive did not seem to be suspicious. Maybe that was the saddest part about it.

I looked at Mr. Fuenta, regaining my concentration. His assumption of a business tie-in was going to be hard to backtrack from, but I had to try.

"Well," I said, "that's something we're looking at. We'd love to be in business with Fizz."

Fuenta was quietly thrilled. "International exposure is exactly what we're looking for. Penetration into the American market is, of course, one of our goals."

Fuenta began to pass me spread sheets detailing the amazing growth of Fizz from a mere mite on the Spanish scene to a giant. Or, at least, that was what they were projecting for the future.

I had to get out before I got in too deep.

"That's down the road, though," I said, his charts piled in my lap. "What's really piqued our interest, and the reason I'm here, is . . . the Fizz girl."

Fuenta paused. A certain steeliness now crept into his mild manner. "The girl?"

"Yes. Your model. We're very interested in seeing her for a part in . . . the film."

"I see. Erendira."

I flushed, happy to hear him speak the name. But Fuenta was staring at me coldly now. He reached out a hand and gestured for his sheets back. I returned them, uneasily.

"Well, that's something you should talk to her about, isn't it?"

"That's . . . well, that's why I'm here. Would you have a contact number for her? Or even—a last name?"

I had meant the last remark as a joke, but Fuenta wasn't laughing. Before tearing off and crumpling up his piece of paper, he gave a small snort of disgust. Either he was repelled by my lack of interest in Fizz, or he thought I was just a pimp for Ben Williams. That was a position I was sure someone else already filled in L.A.

"All right, I'll give you a number," he said.

He flipped through a Rolodex. Then he wrote a number on another piece of paper, tore it off, harshly, and nearly tossed it across to me.

"Tell *him* what you want."

Fuenta's amiability had completely—well, fizzed. He had said it as a threat, and that made me worry.

The voice on the other end of the line was Spanish. It was also deep, male, and very unfriendly. The man received my message—Ben Williams, a movie offer, etc.—grunted in response, took my number, and hung up. But within minutes, he had called back.

I was to go to an even fancier hotel, the Castilla, the next day at three. Someone would meet me in the lobby. When I inquired how I would know this person, I was told, "Just mention Erendira."

I began to e-mail Ben a cryptic but hopeful letter *(Got info—will pursue)*, then realized I was really communicating with Beth, and sent no word at all.

Before I left, feeling nervous and a bit foolish, I slipped the gun into my pocket.

I COULD HARDLY GET WITHIN A MILE OF THE CASTILLA. THERE WAS NO way to reach the front door, let alone the lobby.

A massive throng stood outside the building, making even approach—forget entrance—impossible. The crowd ringed the entire front of the hotel, jutted out into the street, and snaked across it, where I now stood. Almost everyone in it was female and below the age of consent.

"Jorge!" they screamed. "Jorge!"

Flash cameras held above their heads went off. Festive Spanish rock and roll blared from their boom boxes. Police rode by on horseback or passed by on foot, made cursory attempts at control, then confessed defeat, and fled.

"Jorge! Jorge!"

Jorge was obviously the biggest movie heartthrob in Spain. Amazed at my own provincialism, I had no idea who he was. But why did he have to be staying at the Castilla? I checked my watch: five of three.

With a deep breath, I stepped off the curb and waded into the jumping and squealing mob. It was worse than a thousand New York City subway rush hours.

"Excuse me, excuse me."

Elbows were stuck into my ribs and belly. High-heeled shoes stabbed my shins and stomped my feet. Screams like car alarms drilled into my ears.

"Excuse me, excuse me."

"Jorge!"

As if inventing a new dance step, I wiggled free of one crush, then was flung forward, crushed again, and wiggled free. Finally, I saw the great golden letters of CASTILLA loom before me like the gates of heaven.

"Excuse me."

"Jorge!"

At the door, hotel security had somehow kept the horde behind a single red rope. Only one huge bouncer stood there, bulging from his three-piece suit, a walkie-talkie pressed upon his ear. Spain was a simpler place than America, I thought. I flew free of the crowd's last grip.

"Erendira!" I screamed.

"*Qúe?*" the big man asked.

"Erendira! I'm here to see Erendira!"

This was not a name that anyone else was screaming. Recognition flashed in his small, squinty eyes. He unclicked the rope where I stood. Then, practically grabbing me by my shirtfront, he pulled me quickly through before anyone else could follow.

I was passed from this big bouncer to a wiry, weasly one. Holding my arm at the muscle, he traveled with me through a revolving door into the lobby.

There, it was strangely but wonderfully silent.

"Come with me," he said seriously, in English.

We rode up in an empty elevator, tinny rock and roll playing, as if from far away.

"Movie star?" I asked knowingly.

He looked at me with pitying disbelief.

"Soccer," he said.

"Soccer?"

Shocked, I just shrugged. Europe certainly had a different standard for celebrity. At a top floor, he led me down a long vermilion hallway, until we reached the last of only three suites. He knocked once, then twice, then three times.

Something about the code made me start to sweat.

Suddenly, the door was flung open. My companion moved artfully aside, and I was yanked within by a thick fist attached to my belt.

The door was closed behind me, the bouncer standing at my back. I faced a room of five muscular men, all of whom I thought I recognized from the postcards sold on the street. Where was the rest of their team?

They looked at me, then at one another, with small and unkind smiles. One spoke Spanish to his teammate, who replied. Then another spoke to me, in very fast Catalan, and I only shrugged. *"No comprende."*

This made all of them laugh. Then one nodded to the bouncer behind me. Very roughly, I was frisked. Immediately, of course, he found my gun.

The bouncer chucked it to one of the soccer players. I grabbed for it, but it flew past my fingers. Not adept with his own hands, the player bobbled it, and it fell on the dark blue carpet. I bent to retrieve it, and immediately they all stood and swarmed around the weapon.

One kicked it away from my hand. It slid to the foot of a second, who tapped it to a third. This one lifted it with the tip of his shoe. It went flying into the chest of the fourth, who butted it back down to the floor. As the game went on, they laughed and kept crying, *"No comprende! No comprende!"*

With each kick, I had tried to reclaim my possession. At last, I found myself, panting, on all fours, beside it, surrounded by the team. Each eyed me, hungrily, as if I would be the next ball they bounced.

I looked for any avenue of escape. Rising, I turned right—but expertly, player number one blocked my path, crouched, and ran in place.

So I spun around, toward the front door. The bouncer, weaving more imprecisely, was covering it.

I cut left, only to be stymied by another player, who—adhering to the rules—avoided using his arms. He brought his knee up forcefully into my groin. The pain propelled me backward, right into the extended foot of a third player, who, pushing in the back of my knee, sent me crashing to the floor, from whence I had come.

I lay there, reeling from my effort and agonized by my injury. Then an interior door of the suite opened. The players turned. Another man entered the room.

"Jorge," one of them said, in greeting.

HE WAS TALL, DARK, AND VERY HANDSOME. I DEFINITELY RECOGNIZED HIS face from the postcards. He looked down at me with an oddly familiar kind of disdain.

"What kind of movie producer carries a gun?" he said.

He had been handed the weapon by one of his sycophant colleagues. From his cocksure and impatient manner, I figured Jorge must be the Ben Williams of Spain. I slowly found my feet in front of him. At least he spoke Spanish and not just Catalan.

"I guess you haven't been to America very often," I said.

This made him smirk and so allowed his teammates to smirk, as well. Butt last, Jorge placed the gun inside his belt, like a soccer player playing sheriff. I thought about how Ronald Reagan's famous appearance as "the Gipper" in *Knute Rockne, All American* had been missing from the film's prints for years, and had only been restored recently. Some kind of legal problem.

"Erendira's not interested in whatever you're proposing," he said.

"I really would like to speak to her personally."

The team collectively sucked in its breath. Jorge's right eyebrow rose, in surprise. A scene from a 1993 football picture, *The Program*, was also cut because kids had imitated its characters, who lie down on a highway, for fun.

"That won't be possible," he said.

"Are you her manager?" I asked.

There was more shocked inhaling. Jorge sighed. With a wave of his hand, he motioned his teammates from the room. Casting sorrowful looks at me—they would never see me alive again—they dispersed to other areas of the enormous suite.

Jorge sank into a chair and swung his long, famous legs over one side. I took a seat, too, careful of my insulted crotch.

"I'm more than her manager," he said. "In Spain, there are bigger things than show business."

"Like soccer?" I asked.

Another smirk crossed his face.

"Like love," Jorge answered.

I nodded, comprehending at last. I wondered if the country knew that its favorite soccer superstar was the Fizz girl's lover. Jorge soon cleared that up.

"I am keeping our relationship private," he said. "And I will not have it spoiled by her running off to America to pursue a . . . *career*."

He said the last word with contempt. I wondered if Ben had actually been right about how Erendira had disappeared.

"Did *you* . . . steal her back from California?" I asked.

"I have never set foot in your country. She came back because she wanted to."

"She came back because she had *The Magnificent Ambersons*."

Jorge looked at me warily. "Is that an American team?"

I smiled. "It's a movie."

"Oh, is that all." He shrugged dismissively.

I realized that here was a star as big as Ben, and totally unimpressed by him. So, I figured, now it was every man for himself.

"Look, I'm not interested in Erendira," I said. "I'm just here on Ben Williams's dime and time. I'm really looking for the movie."

Jorge glanced at me with amusement, engaged by my disobedience. To him, I was an entertaining little monkey. Then he only shrugged. "Well, good luck."

Gatekeeper of his girlfriend, Jorge would allow no access of any kind. I wondered how much say Erendira had in any of this. She obviously had not told Jorge about *Ambersons*. Or, more likely, he simply had not cared. Did she even have it? I also wondered something else.

"Doesn't either one of you have a last name?"

I had ceased to antagonize; now I no longer even amused. My audience with the great Jorge was over.

"May I use your bathroom?" I asked.

As I approached one of several marble bathrooms, I passed many closed doors behind which, I assumed, the soccer players frolicked, or whatever soccer players do.

Then the door nearest the john opened.

It opened just enough for me to see a pair of eyes. They were dark eyes, a woman's eyes. For the brief moment I saw them, they bore into me with a combination of yearning, volatility, and distrust. Then the door closed again, silently.

In the bathroom, I splashed ice-cold water on my flushed and burning skin. Erendira was here, just a few steps away! Her headshot had not done her justice. In person, just her eyes, for just a few seconds, gave off the glow that had so entranced Ben Williams.

But in such company, what could I do about it? Jorge's self-centeredness was oddly appealing; how dangerous was he without his teammates? Could I risk confronting her without disturbing him? Could I disturb him without damaging myself? For what it was worth, I didn't even have my gun.

Then I heard a swish.

It was almost inaudible, something sliding across marble tile. When

I turned, I saw that a note had been pushed beneath the door and now lay at my feet.

It had been written on Fizz stationery.

Meet me tomorrow at noon.
                    Erendira

The address she gave me was near the waterfront, away from the tourist trade. I folded it carefully and placed it in my pocket.

"All better?" Jorge asked me when I returned.

"Much," I answered.

———

By the time I left, I was an old friend of the team's. Earlier, Jorge had decided I was no one to fear; now he knew I was no one to hate. I was just a pawn of an arrogant movie star from a smug, shallow, and self-obsessed country. I had even shown a little moxie in defying my boss. He summoned his "boys" back in. We all had a beer, proposed a toast, then had another beer, and another toast. Their earlier attempts to kick me to death were forgotten.

"No comprende!" they called me, in tribute.

In Spain, stars were better company than in the U.S.

When I left, I navigated my way through the huge crowd that still remained outside. I was no drinker, but my beer buzz made it a less uncomfortable, slightly psychedelic experience. So many colors, so much music, so close to so many girls!

At the crowd's edge, I turned back. From his window twenty floors up, the tiny figure of Jorge now stood, waving beneficently to his fans. He was like a kindly king, allowing himself to be loved. Upon seeing him, the crowd roared.

How could you not like the guy?

All the way back to my hotel, the beer continued to give me a pleasant lift. It was only shaken by the memory of Jorge's beautiful princess, who was hidden in his tower—and what she might give me once she was freed.

NOON AT THE BAR BAR MIGHT AS WELL HAVE BEEN MIDNIGHT.

It was a dark place near the Barcelona docks, populated by a few older workmen, looking deep into their drinks. I noticed two obvious male transvestites sitting, undisturbed, among them. The name revealed its lack of pretension: it was a bar, just a bar, and if you wanted something else, get out.

It was past noon, way past, one o'clock. I was beginning to suspect that Erendira would not appear, had not been able to escape. How could she, in the middle of the day like this?

The heavyset bartender had turned on a mounted TV. To the indifference of the patrons, a soccer game now served as entertainment. The star player, cascading across the field, tapping the ball past the opposing team, was Jorge.

I realized: He was at work now. Then, a small woman, her face covered by the chic hood of her expensive sweater, sat beside me.

She loosened her backpack. The hood fell to her shoulders. Lustrous dark hair spilled out below her neck. The same striking eyes, now filled with fear as well as need and suspicion, burned into mine.

"So, who are you?" Erendira asked, in English.

"Just a movie fan," I answered.

Bottles of Fizz stood in clear sight among the Scotches and beers behind the counter. But there was no sign of recognition from the Bar Bar. Either no one cared, or no one could believe that such a woman would be slumming there.

"I'm taking a chance in trusting you," she said.

"I know."

"I heard what you said to Jorge. You might have lied. You might just be here to bring me back to Ben Williams."

"That's true."

"Because, you know, I was burned by him before."

I saw traces of the sultriness and innocence that had knocked Ben out. Mostly, though, Erendira just seemed agitated, and her thumbnail picked nervously at the nail of her pointer. All of her nails had been bitten down, and only traces of red polish were left. Maybe this was why no one recognized her: She was not her image, she was her own neurotic self.

"It was my own fault," she said. "I read that that bastard was going to play Orson Welles, so I thought that he would help me. You see someone in a movie, you think he is actually a hero."

The power of Abner Cooley once again was made manifest. Even in Spain, his scoops had made news. But why had Erendira pursued Ben? I did not dare interrupt her to ask; there was instability in her need to talk. At any moment, she might get up and leave, or simply lash out. The bartender approached, and Erendira impatiently waved him away.

"I had taken such a risk in going. Jorge did not know. If it were up to Jorge, I would just sit in the stands all day and cheer." She glanced at the TV, then looked away. "When I saw that, far from being my hero, Ben Williams himself had the movie, that he was my *enemy*"— she shook her head at her own naivete—"I could have killed him. I should have."

Erendira began to eat nervously from my tiny plate of tapas potatoes. I slid them over to her, and with one abashed look of animal
gratitude, she finished them.

"Now, I don't know what to do," she said. "I'm lost, lost. If you can't
help me, I . . ."

She muttered something in Spanish—or was it Catalan? Or Portuguese? Then she buried her face in her hands.

Slowly, I reached out and dared to touch her arm, to comfort her.
She did not pull away. Instead, Erendira gripped my hand, with terrible
need. Then she looked at me, her eyes filled with tears.

"I want to know who killed my mother," she said.

With that, Erendira put her arms around my neck and burst into almost silent sobs. There was no reaction in the place, except from the
bartender, who walked slowly away, to the back of the bar. On the TV,
Jorge was landing a goal, or whatever soccer players do.

This new information sent a shudder through me. At each stop, the
story had unraveled more, like a film spooling off a projector. It wasn't
the first time I felt out of my depth, but, holding Erendira, I had never
felt so inadequate to my task.

She pulled back and laughed, weakly, at herself, wiping her runny nose.

"I'm sorry," she said. "Here I go again, trusting, trusting."

"You can trust me," I blurted out. "I want to help you. But, you know,
I only wanted to find the complete *Ambersons*. Then I was hired to find
you. And now . . ." I hesitated. "When was your mother murdered?"

"A few months ago."

"And what does it have to do with . . ."

Erendira's eyes widened as she realized she had told me so much,
and had explained nothing.

"My mother had the film," she said. "It was stolen from her."

"*She* had *The Magnificent Ambersons?*" I said, shocked.

"Yes."

"But how—"

At that moment, Erendira saw a car pull up outside the bar. When she looked back, her demeanor had changed. Now she was full of new purpose and new dread.

"I have to go," she said. "Jorge has followed me."

"But when will I see you? I need to know what—"

She gripped my hand again, and this time, she pulled me up with her.

"Come with me," she said.

Before I could even answer, I was running alongside her, through the bar, into the back, past a bathroom, to a boarded-up door.

"Just push it," she said.

I did. The two of us plunged from the dim interior into a back alley, which was almost as dark.

We were looking right at the bartender. His right hand was smacking a lead pipe into the palm of his left.

HE HAD A SQUASHED FACE, ALL THE FEATURES CLOSE TOGETHER. WITH the pipe, he waved me away from Erendira. His expression implied: *Give her up, and you won't be hurt.*

Erendira's hand had not left mine since we'd stood up to go. Now I felt it moisten and tighten. She did not move, seemed in fact paralyzed. She only turned to me and whispered, "It's okay. Go ahead."

That was out of the question. Erendira had become *The Magnificent Ambersons* to me, a sixty-year-old treasure in a twenty-something form. As I did with Gus Ziegler, I felt absurdly brave, standing so close to what I sought. Besides, she had that story to finish telling me.

So I shook my head no. Then, holding Erendira's hand, I started to walk past him, as if he might be polite enough to let us leave.

A gentleman he was not. Stepping forward, swiftly, he started to bring the pipe down—not on me, on Erendira. The air was whipped by the weapon, she dodged, and I jumped at him. Actually airborne for an instant, I wrapped my arms around his muscular middle, and the two of us, like awful acrobats, fell into the earth.

The pipe skittered from his hand, clanging against a garbage can. Erendira ran to retrieve it while I literally rolled around with the Bar Bar bartender. One minute he was top, the next I was. We were like two men on fire, trying to put each other out.

The next time he emerged in the dominant position, Erendira nailed him, snapping the baton into his right shoulder blade. Crying out, his arms instinctively opened as if he were swimming the butterfly in the morning sun. I used the opportunity to slip and slide out from under him.

Finding my feet, I grabbed Erendira's hand again. She was already running. She and I headed for the alley opening, followed fast by the barman. Bellowing like a stuck bull in his country's other sport, he had not been waylaid for long.

We made it into a narrow street. There we pushed past other pedestrians, people wheeling shopping carts, parents and their children. Loping like Frankenstein's monster, our pursuer was always close behind, his screaming stopped, his pace slowed by the demands of propriety.

"Get on!" Erendira said.

She pulled me to the side, where I saw what she was seeking. It was a motorcycle, parked at the corner, a helmet left on it, undisturbed.

With what seemed superhuman speed, she got on the hog, and snapped the helmet on her head. I jumped on behind, my arms locked around her, her backpack at my breast.

"Hold on," she said.

We roared off, spraying past people in the crowded street. On foot, with shocking speed, the bartender was soon at our back wheel, his breathing audible even above the din of the motor.

Then he was actually panting alongside, nearly overtaking us, the bull he had been metamorphosed into a horse. This race would be to the death, apparently, but whose I did not know.

The three of us were approaching an intersection now, scores of Spanish cars racing toward and through the lights, heedless of their own speed.

"Here!" Erendira shouted.

With a fast snap and yank, she pulled off her helmet and handed it back to me. Amazed at myself, I had no doubt about what to do with it.

Wrapping the chin strap around my knuckle, I jabbed it once, hard, into the forehead of the running man next to us. His head snapped back, a single time. Faltering just a bit, he kept running, blood now streaming down his face.

The strap wrapped tighter, I swung my arm in a roundhouse right and clocked him right in the head. This time, he went down.

We flew through a momentary gap in the intersection's traffic. I looked back and saw the bartender's tiny body, curled in the road, as if a million miles away. Then he disappeared from sight.

When I turned back, Erendira's right hand was outstretched. I placed the helmet into it, and she put it back on.

No policeman had made an effort to stop us, and I soon learned why: All around, we heard faint cheers of "Fizz! Fizz!" Apparently, to all eyes—miraculously, without a camera—we had been filming a new commercial.

Erendira pulled off into a side street and came to a sudden stop.

"You better go," she said. "I don't want both of us being followed. If Jorge knows people at the Bar Bar, he knows them everywhere."

"I'm at the Carabas Hotel," I said.

Erendira nodded, taking in the information as fast as she could. Then, from her backpack, she pulled out a pile of typewritten pages, hugged by a rubber band. She handed them over to me.

"Here," she said. "I had it translated. It's my grandmother's diary. It should explain most of it."

Holding it, I hopped off the bike. Then, a second later, I watched her whirr away. A small black sedan was right behind her.

Today, I was dancing in the streets.

Who wasn't? It was the first day of carnival. Many, many masked men and women, some on floats, others just on foot, went mad in the streets of Rio. It was my first carnival, now that I am away from Mommy and Daddy's house and married to Bruno. Mommy and Daddy had never allowed me to go, of course. Bruno did not want me to go, either, but who is he? He is my husband, not my keeper! I left him, standing, yelling, in the doorway.

I kept covered up. I was not bold enough to parade around as shamelessly as some of the women did. Perhaps someday. But for now, it was enough to just dance and dance, and feel free in the streets. Being twenty-one is wonderful.

Many foreigners joined us in our crazy celebration. I think they were shocked at the kind of behavior we like in Brazil. One young American in particular kept smiling and nodding at me, his face so red, I thought he would burst. He was handsome, a little pudgy—and going wild!

Each neighborhood has its own carnival, of course, and each carnival has its own samba. Today, we danced in celebration of President Vargas (I will say no more about him—who knows who will read this?) and of Charlie Chaplin, the movie comic.

The young American followed me, and asked me to teach him the Chaplin dance. He was not well coordinated, but he was a very serious pupil. He told me I was "gorgeous." To my shock, he took out one of those movie cameras and filmed me dancing!

"Are you with the secret police?" I asked him, flirting. I knew he wasn't, but why would he be carrying such a thing, anyway? Even though I was confused, I couldn't help but pose for him a little.

"I'm an American movie director!" he screamed, in very bad Portuguese, above the music. "I'm down here to help my country!"

How was he helping his country by filming me dance, and only below the neck, I should add? He screamed some explanation, but I lost it in the noise. I figured he was telling me a big story, but I was still intrigued.

People were spraying perfume bottles at everyone else. I don't think they contained perfume, because it made us all feel so funny! Soon the American and I were dancing very close, the camera hanging limply from his hand.

"What is your name?" he asked me.

"Sonia," I said. "What's yours?"

At first, I thought he said, "Are Son," but it turned out to be "Orson." He said he was very famous, but I didn't care.

"I think I love you!" he screamed, and his face got even redder and fatter.

The young American and I ended up in a doorway off to the side of the carnival. There I let him . . . but dear Diary, I'll leave the rest to your imagination.

He asked where he could reach me. I told him I had no telephone—but I didn't tell him that I was married. That soft American boy would be no match for Bruno.

He gave me *his* address, which was a very fancy hotel. Then he drove me there in his convertible car, with police on motorcycles in front of us, their sirens blaring. I was amazed. He must have *been* famous!

I know I am a wild girl, but I do not care. What a wonderful day!

February 10, 1942

Today, Orson started filming the carnival. Not the real carnival—a fake one! He's built a whole street scene inside a studio and filled it up with people. There, along with many others, I danced the same samba and acted like I was having a great time.

I learned that, if I crawled up on an actor's shoulder, I would stick out more in the shot. Orson told me I'd "make an actress yet!"

What with all the stopping and starting, this carnival felt even longer than the real one. But Orson didn't seem to notice—he kept filming and filming and, after everyone was exhausted, he still wanted to samba!

Then, his face drenched with sweat, he made a speech. He told us, very seriously, that he had been sent to Brazil by the U.S. government and a movie company, to make a film to help relations between our two hemispheres, there was so much trouble in the world. He said he wanted so badly to be our "good neighbor." Nobody listened to him, but everyone liked him, anyway!

Afterward, I went back with Orson to his suite, and we had another wonderful afternoon. He got a cable from America, but he crumpled it up, laughing that "RKO worries too much."

I didn't get home till late, and Bruno cursed at me about my new activities. He told me that actresses were whores, Americans were pigs, and something good about Hitler. He said I should go to church and ask for forgiveness. Then he slapped me. I just hope that the bruise does not show up on film.

March 1, 1942

Orson was very cranky today. He said it was because the U.S. government won't let civilians fly overseas anymore since there's a war and everything.

So his friend from California, Robert Wise, can't come with a copy of his new film for them to work on. He raged and raged, but it was nothing compared with Bruno—it was kind of funny to watch, really.

I told him that I thought he was working too hard, shooting so much film here and going out every night, and still working on that movie in the U.S. He yelled that if he wanted a wife, he would marry Dolores Del Rio! She's the woman whose calls he keeps avoiding.

I calmed him down, in the usual way. Then I made him promise that he will write me into the next part of his film, the true story of the jangadeiros fishermen, who made a brave voyage. Maybe one of the fishermen needs a wife! I said.

He took a pill, and his mood improved, and then he had lots of energy again. He dragged me out dancing, and he stayed long after I left. The way he was samba-ing, I thought he would sweat the features right off his face.

Bruno had already left for work when I got home.

March 11, 1942

Another bad Orson day. We were shooting in the *favelas* (Mommy and Daddy would kill me if they knew), and the crowd turned on us, throwing rocks, bottles, and bricks at Orson's big convertible. We had to put the top up.

I had warned him not to go, that the slums were dangerous, and they might not like Americans around. But Orson insisted. He even went through a voodoo ritual, though he had someone else bite off the chicken's head. I think he has lost a bit of his mind here in Brazil.

Later, a big package came from the U.S. It was the film that Orson's friend Robert Wise (a funny name I said, but he didn't laugh) was not able to bring in person. Orson said, what good is it now, the preview is just six days away, there's nothing he can do with it. And he complained like a little baby.

Then he told me he could not see me tonight, he had more work to do. I asked him if he was seeing other girls, but he told me he would do as he liked. I cried, and he slammed the door on me.

Because I was home early, Bruno tried to force himself on me. But luckily, he was so drunk, it was not to be. Then, lying next to me, he cried himself to sleep. I bet, wherever he was, Orson wasn't shedding any tears tonight!

Note: Tell the big shot that he left his package in the cab when he put me in it.

March 17, 1942

Pomona! That was all Orson was going on about today.

It's all the way back in California, I told him, put it from your mind. But still, he was going on, Pomona this, Pomona that!

So all right, I said, so the preview audience there didn't like your new movie, *Magnificent* something-or-other.

Didn't like?! he screamed. Didn't like?! They laughed and hooted and booed! And he was helpless to do anything about it!

So, go home, I told him. Go home and fix it up.

"Don't you see? I can't!" he said. "I'm here to serve my country! Maybe you can't appreciate a thing like that!"

Then he called me names that I didn't understand, but which I knew were awful.

Before I walked out the door, Orson got a cable from someone named Joseph Cotten (another funny name), and he tore it up, screaming, "Judas! Judas!" Then he started throwing furniture out the window. I told him that Vargas's police were probably watching him, and he should be careful. But he only responded by calling an ashtray "Joseph Cotten" and then hurling it into the street.

Giving up on him, I escaped, and had beers with the crew. Gary, a boy doing sound, told me that they all want to go home, but that Orson, "the patriot," stays in Rio just so he won't be drafted in the U.S. I asked him if he thought Orson was maybe seeing another girl, and all the boys laughed so much at me that I started to cry.

I told them I thought I hated moviemaking now. Gary walked me home and apologized, and I let him kiss me good night. But he was very nice, and didn't try anything else, Diary.

April 8, 1942

Orson has stopped calling completely. That's okay with me!!!

But Bruno brought me flowers tonight. Then he spoke very sweetly. He said he would stop drinking. He said I could keep on being an actress if I wanted. He told me I could do anything I liked.

I told him the truth: I didn't think I wanted to be an actress anymore. Then we went to bed for the first time in a long time.

I think the damage has already been done, but I'll leave that to your imagination, Diary.

May 10, 1942

I was very sick today.

Gary dropped by and told me a terrible story about Orson. (Gary's very sweet, but I have to be a good girl now. Besides, I have broken out and gained so much weight that no one else besides Bruno would want me.) He said the company had just come back from starting the jangadeiros fishermen section. (I did not even know Orson had gone.) He said that, while they were shooting this true story about their perilous boat trip, Orson kept pushing and pushing, until one of the real fishermen drowned! Things here keep getting worse and worse for the big, famous American.

I didn't say it to Gary, but I'll say it to you, Diary. I wish Orson himself had drowned.

I have to go be sick.

June 8, 1942

Gary and the rest of the gang went back to America today. He dropped in to say goodbye, and Bruno was even polite to him. I'll miss him, the little gentleman. Maybe not all Americans are such scum, after all.

Gary said that Orson wasn't going back with them. He was staying to finish the fishermen (hasn't he already done that, ha ha?) in the little town of Fortaleza. Orson wanted to go all by himself, and the crew gave him its crummiest camera. Gary said he looks haunted, very thin (!), bearded, and as dark as any Brazilian. Well, good luck to you, Orson!

Bruno doesn't let me do any of the work around the house anymore. He says I need my rest, if I'm going to be a mother.

July 29, 1942

I heard that Orson finally went home today. I also heard that he was fired—or whatever they call it—by RKO. I guess they decided he had "served his country" long enough. It's foolish to have hoped he would call me before he left. I guess he had lots of other girls to call. I wonder if he's left something behind with them, too.

It's not just the baby. I still have that package, the film he said he was so concerned about. I guess he gave up on it, *The Magnificent Ambersons,* because he never even asked me about it.

Bruno will never know the truth about any of this, and neither will Mommy and Daddy. Only you, dear Diary, will keep my secrets.

I never want to see another movie as long as I live. Carnival seems like a hundred years ago.

"YOU'RE ORSON WELLES'S GRANDDAUGHTER," I SAID.

Erendira only nodded. It was two o'clock in the morning, and she was standing, hugging herself nervously, in my hotel suite. She had not removed her sweater, nor, indeed, its hood from her head. Then, suddenly, as if weakened, she sank into a chair.

Her distant past now paled in importance to her recent one. She slipped off her hood, and I saw that her face was streaked with blood.

"Jesus Christ," I said.

Wearing just my complimentary hotel bathrobe, I broke some ice from my mini-fridge. I wrapped it in a damp towel. Then I placed it against her cheek, washing away dirt and flecks of paint and plaster, and she winced, before thanking me.

Shaking my head, I could think of no worse curse than, "That soccer-playing bastard."

"Don't blame Jorge," she said. "Like a dumb animal, he doesn't know any better."

"Well, he will soon," I said.

Erendira only smiled a little, painfully. "He might be here any minute. And he won't be alone."

"Of course not. Cowards never are."

The thought of confronting Jorge—this time, without the buffer of his charm or fine-fellow feeling—unnerved me. If he knew that I was harboring his disobedient mistress, the goal of tonight's game might be my murder. Still, "I'm not afraid of him," I lied. "Stay here."

Erendira did not need much coaxing. She had only to be led to the bed before she had slipped beneath its covers and into sleep. Before she passed out, she saw the pages of her grandmother's diary stacked on my nighttable. She opened her mouth to comment, but she never made a sound.

"Here," I said. "Eat this."

Not trusting room service to keep a secret, in the morning I went out and bought Erendira breakfast of a bun and coffee. Still wearing last night's dress, her black hair flowing onto her pillow, she smiled, causing creases in her cut face.

"You are a very nice man," she said.

I had slept in the same room, on the other spacious bed, beside her. It had been a night filled with fearful fantasies of fighting angry soccer players. Even the names of the Best Original Screenplay Oscar winners had not made me drowsy enough to sleep.

"So," she said, "you read it?"

"Yes. And now I know . . . almost everything."

"Here's the rest. Last year, my mother found the diary and the film when my grandmother died. Long before, Bruno had moved the family to Spain and died there. The genius Welles might have been amused that his secret daughter had grown up to be a loving but ignorant woman, barely literate, who never even heard of him.

"In what I guess was a tribute to her real father, my mother just changed the name of her pension—the little boardinghouse she ran in Seville, where I grew up—from Casa de la Noche to Los Ambersons Magníficos.

"My mother never told me the story—she was ashamed of it, also. I was more like my grandmother: wild, interested in the arts or maybe just in having people look at me. But I must admit, I'd never heard of the movie, either."

"It was made a long time ago," I said.

"That's no excuse, but thank you. Only when this"—she swallowed, hesitating—"thing happened to my mother, did I read the diary, and find out."

I did not press her for details, though, of course I was hungry for them.

"I had moved to Barcelona to be a crazy girl, to party, to meet people, and to become a model or an actress. That was how I got to be the Fizz girl, and how I met Jorge. I learned English and always kept up on entertainment news, and that's why I read about Ben Williams becoming Orson Welles. That's why, after it happened, I thought he'd be my big daddy."

By now, the bun and the coffee were finished. Erendira had an appetite—which was a good thing—and I placed another ice pack on her face, for which she touched my hand in thanks.

There was something about being near her. It was not just her beauty or her skittishness, though she had both in abundance. It was not even her ability to turn on both innocence and worldliness whenever she wanted to—she was an actress, after all. It was her link to greatness, the part of Orson Welles that was in her blood. Erendira was the closest I might ever get to the past that I had spent my life reporting and reconstructing. I could not help it, I moved a little closer to her on the bed.

I finally got up the guts to ask, "So, what exactly did happen?"

She sighed deeply, her swollen eyes closing, then reopening, with difficulty.

"A few months ago, there was a film festival in Barcelona. When I spoke to my mother on the phone, which I did every day, good girl that

I really am, she told me that she had tenants who had come down the coast for a vacation after it was over. It was off season, and they were her only guests.

"They had been drawn by the name of the place, she said. It was a man and a woman, both big film fans. They kept grilling her about the new name, and kept flattering her about it. She wasn't used to anyone paying attention to her, since my father died. Every night, they drank with her, apparently, and my mother didn't drink well.

"One night, when we talked, she was very tipsy, and she kept going on and on about these guests, how wonderful they were, how excited they seemed about her stories. She said the man had even videotaped her for an American TV show.

"I was getting a little worried about them. What did they want, you know? That's when I decided to go down there myself, to see."

Erendira whipped one side of her heavy hair over onto her shoulder. The next installment seemed to hurt even more than her bruises.

"My mother was in her bed. She'd been smothered with a pillow. When the police came, I found her instructions about, you know, in case of her death. And it described her own mother's diary, and the movie, and . . . that's when I read the diary and when I realized that the movie was gone."

She gave a long groan and fell, as if in slow motion, back onto the bed. Then she wept for what seemed forever. Ice packs and food were now inadequate; there was nothing I could do to help her.

Except find her mother's killers, of course. I had the sneaking suspicion that I knew who at least one of them was.

"I'm sorry to pursue this," I said, once she had subsided. "But did she describe them? The guests at Los Ambersons Magníficos?"

Erendira shrugged. "She said they were young, though young to her was anywhere from twenty to forty. She said they weren't the cleanest people on earth, and for once, in her own hotel, she didn't care. That was about it."

Now her voice grew more excited. "I should never have left home. I should have stayed and helped her run the place, the way she wanted.

What have I gotten? A boyfriend who beats me up. And meeting a movie star . . . who, it turns out, stole the film himself."

I tried to tell her that Ben Williams had not stolen *Ambersons*, only bought it. But she was right: On some level, Ben was an accomplice to her mother's murder. And, as Ben's employee, so was I.

Guilt plus awful memories plus her own physical ordeal made Erendira sleep again, this time to escape. She twitched and moaned a little, from bad dreams.

There was a lot I had to report, and to one person in particular. I did not turn on my laptop. Instead, using Ben's calling card, I dialed long distance to the States.

"Jeanine?" I said. "Gus Ziegler may have killed Alan Gilbert for *The Magnificent Ambersons*. But first, Alan Gilbert killed somebody else for it."

MAYBE I SAID THE WORDS *VULNERABLE* OR *BEAUTIFUL* TOO MANY TIMES. Maybe I stressed how very different Erendira was from her image. Maybe there was an obvious gush in my voice.

Either way, Jeanine thought the whole thing seemed fishy.

"Have you seen it?" she said.

"Seen what?"

"*The Magnificent Ambersons,* for God's sake. Have you seen it?"

"Well, no, not yet," I said, caught. "I mean, the poor woman has had a terrible night, she's barely been conscious, and—"

"Look, that's all you care about, am I right? The movie?"

I paused, for an unfortunately long time. Jeanine came back with, "Roy, Ben Williams can afford to be a schmuck. You can't. And, by the way, Ben wants the girl back. I seem to remember from your stay at The Farmer's Daughter, and our little trip into the Malibu hills, that he's got people who will remind you of that."

I took this tongue-lashing in silence. I knew that she was right, yet I didn't care as much as I might have.

"Besides," Jeanine went on, "Alan Gilbert going to Spain? I never knew him to leave the country. He couldn't afford it."

"But he went to film festivals, to interview people, didn't he? He taped Linda Blair that time, remember? And that old guy who said he was Louise Brooks's lover?"

"Alan later found out that guy had escaped from an asylum. Anybody can say that they knew famous people." Jeanine's tone was especially pointed here. "Besides, one of those interviews was at a horror convention in Trenton. The other one was at the Rhinebeck Film Fair. Both were train rides from New York."

I had to admit all of Jeanine's points were well taken. But when I heard the rustle of Erendira's body behind me, and her slight squeal of reawakening, I hurried to get off the phone.

"I'll see it," I said. "Don't worry. I'll see the movie."

"I hope so. Or else you're helping no one, least of all yourself."

"I've gotten your point."

"And you forgot one other thing. Even if Alan did travel overseas, he wouldn't have done it with a woman. Who would have ever agreed to go with him?"

"There was that woman leaving his apartment that night."

"But—*traveling* with him?"

This remark was the final flick of Jeanine's lash of common sense. Discombobulated, I nodded in silence, instead of speaking, and then I suddenly hung up on her.

From there, I turned to see Erendira sitting up in bed, her feet dangling over its edge. She was smaller than I thought, almost tiny.

I approached her, carefully.

"How are you feeling?" I said.

"Better. It felt surprisingly good to have said all that. And to someone who understands."

I couldn't have explained to Jeanine if I'd tried. But I swore that Erendira looked at me with the same kind of kinship I felt toward her. We were joined by a genius, held together by film history. Now I knelt beside her, like a serf requesting entrance to that kingdom.

"I want to see it," I said.

She smiled a little, naughtily. "You come right out and say it, don't you?"

"The movie, I mean."

"I know you do," she said gently. "And you will. Soon. But first . . ."

Was knowing a hard-boiled nerd a relief after an abusive macho man? Was she only grateful? Should I not undersell myself, had I actually profoundly endeared myself to her? Or, as I imagined, had the forces of time and artistic talent set up this encounter? I only knew that, after many months alone, Erendira was the woman for whom I had been saving myself.

"We've had this date with each other from the beginning," Brando as Kowalski tells Leigh as Dubois in *A Streetcar Named Desire*. The scene had been censored in the Fifties, then restored in 1993.

Erendira slowly pulled her dress up her light brown legs, and, very obediently, I followed it with my lips.

"I DON'T HAVE THE FILM," SHE SAID AFTERWARD.

I just stared at Erendira. That is to say, I pulled back, since she was in my arms and had been for hours, and *then* I stared at her.

"What do you mean?" I said.

"I mean, I have *a* film. But it's not *the* film. Not *The Magnificent Ambersons.*"

I tried to keep my voice from becoming shrill. "Don't you think this is something you should have told me *earlier?*"

Pulling the sheet over herself defensively, she looked me straight in the eyes. "Would it have made a difference?"

I realized what she meant. As calculating—and as insecure—as Erendira was, she had seduced me simply to keep me willing to help her. Had she done the same thing with Ben Williams? Probably.

That morning, I had not known how much I wanted her and how much just *Ambersons.* That morning, the two had seemed the same thing.

Now, at dusk, I surprised myself. I did not care about Erendira's motives. Or, to be honest, about the movie. I just cared about her. Ignoring Jeanine's prescience, I moved back and embraced her.

Encouraged, she explained. "In L.A., Ben passed out, of course, before he showed me the film. I ran it here, on an old projector in the basement of the theater in my mother's town. I watched it with the owner of the place, whom I had known since I was a girl. Imagine my embarrassment when it turned out to be a stag film from, I don't know, nineteen thirty-eight." She smiled a little, bitterly. "Ben probably thought I wouldn't know the difference.

"Actually, what he really thought was: I would get turned on by it. He had bought that innocent but fiery Latina thing I was doing."

She got up, letting the sheet fall. Far from being the happy peasant she had portrayed herself, in private, in bed, Erendira had been unsure physically, and her posture now, when nude, was slightly stooped and self-protective. Like many actors, for her, attention was one thing, intimacy another.

"Sorry I'm not so good at this," she had told me, as we began.

First off, I was no expert. Secondly, I did not care.

Erendira made her way to a closet, where she put on the other complimentary hotel bathrobe.

"You don't think it was an accident?" I said. "That Ben just made a mistake?"

"No. I don't."

"Is it possible that there never was a real movie? That Alan Gilbert, that Gus Ziegler—sorry, you don't know these names—that your *grandmother* never had it? That we've all been following, forgive the cliché, a phantom?"

"No," she said flatly. "It exists. I'm sure."

Erendira said it, irrationally, because she believed her mother. And I nodded, irrationally, because I believed her.

"That means that Ben still has it?"

"Or he gave it to someone else."

She was seated on a chair, her fingers fidgeting, flicking at her nails, her legs crossing and uncrossing. Who knew that Erendira, the Fizz girl, the girl of a movie star's dreams, was really a nervous wreck?

I did.

"Will you help me?" she said.

First, I had slept with the woman Ben had hired me to find. Now I was being asked to work for her—for free, I assumed—in order to corner Ben. Ethically, it was a dilemma.

"Sure," I said.

She smiled, relaxing for the first time since I had known her. She rested back, and placed her feet up on the ottoman the hotel had so generously provided.

Erendira was not at ease for long. Right then, the door—unlocked obediently by a bellboy—flew open. What looked like the entire soccer team appeared.

It all happened so fast. Whispered Spanish slurs were uttered. I heard a scream, curtailed by a hand over Erendira's mouth. A drawer of a hotel desk was pulled open.

"Jorge!" I said. "Remember me?"

Then I saw the Barcelona phone book coming right for my face.

———

When I woke up, I was lying on the floor of the bathroom. To be exact, I lay half in the bathroom and half in the living room, straddling the threshold. Whoever dragged me there had gotten tired before finishing the job.

I was naked, and my broken nose had been bleeding for a long time. I pulled up from the sticky puddle that had stained the white tile and now smeared my nose, mouth, and jaw.

I stood, very shakily. My head throbbed and, with every breath, I heard a crazy trombone blat. I stepped slowly into the suite.

The room showed only mild signs of struggle. Erendira's bathrobe lay on the floor, with both its sleeves outstretched. It looked like a person who had died while crawling to the door.

Foggy and unable to focus, I decided to file a report to my employer. But before I could, the phone rang. I realized it had been ringing the whole time.

The informality of Beth's voice, her use of my first name, had a plaintiveness that, in my haze, merely confused me.

"Roy?" she said. "Come home. The job's over. Ben's dead."

PART 4
LOS ANGELES

IT WAS THE BREAKFAST RUSH AT SWINGERS. ANNIE CHIN SAT IN HER usual booth, finishing granola and reading over a stack of papers. Though Ben's ex-assistant sported a hip new haircut, streaked with a bit of blond, her attractiveness was still more lifelike than the—admittedly amazing—female mannequins who surrounded her.

The mole on her cheek had now been surgically removed. And the scars on her wrists had all but healed.

"So, it wasn't you?" I said.

I slid over a printout of Abner Cooley's latest posting, about the shocking death of one of Hollywood's richest and most mocked movie stars.

PRINT IT!

I guess we all have different definitions for what's "natural," but those close to the source tell me that Ben Williams's death was hardly from the "natural causes" that authorities—and most media outlets—claimed. (What *is* a natural death for a forty-something-year-old, anyway?) My people tell me it was definitely something *un*natural in his system that caused Ben *mortal* pain.

Speaking of unnatural, studio spies allege that Ben's unfinished film, *Terra Nova,* will be completed as planned, with a little script rewrite here and a little digital replacement of Ben's face there. Jeez, if they're going to replace Ben's face, why not do it right and replace Ben completely with . . . oh, I don't know, Orson Welles?

Abner's struggle to control his irreverence was apparent. That he could still be so cheeky proved he had not yet caved in *completely* to the demands of studio bosses.

With a brief smirk, Annie slid it back.

"I haven't contacted Abner in months." She shrugged. "His source must have been someone else."

"Who? Beth Brenner?"

Annie smiled now. "Oh, I think she's been a little too busy for that."

With the last payment that Beth had cabled me in Spain, I had probably been meant to return to New York, and never to be heard from again. But I was in too deep to pull out now. I had flown to L.A. and taken a low-budget room at the funky motel above Swingers itself, determined to stretch out the money for as long as possible.

The first thing I did was phone Jeanine, who did not return my calls. Perhaps she had been burned by my lovesick conversation from Spain, but Jeanine's feelings were always hard to understand, even by herself. Annie Chin, however, wore her feelings on her sleeve, pardon the cruel pun.

My harsh break from Erendira still fresh in my mind—and on my face—I felt strangely allied with Annie now. She had also loved not wisely and, probably, from the brevity of her affair, not too well, either. We were both veterans of unforgettable one-night stands.

Still, Annie was bearing up better than I was, and her lover's fate was more final than mine was. The pages on her table were students' papers, not a screenplay.

"I figured," she said, "that now I'd work with people who have good reason to act like children."

"Congratulations."

"Thanks." She seemed genuinely pleased with herself.

"Well, *I'm* still looking for that thing," I said, acting sheepish about not being able to "let go." "And I was about to go back to Ben about it."

"Bad luck."

"I'll say."

Annie was either glad that Ben was dead or was just hiding deep feelings behind flippancy. I suspected the latter. Or maybe I just hoped it wasn't all she was hiding. I decided to be blunt.

"Do you know anything more than what Abner printed?"

She did not hesitate. "Only what Ben was taking. I guess he didn't have the heart for crack cocaine. Or at least for 'C.C. Ryder,' the new kind of crack that's around. That's all I know, and all I need to know."

As she spoke, Annie cursorily graded a paper, circling some grammar with a red pen. Maybe she really *didn't* give a damn anymore, or the death had added closure for her.

"Crack," I said, genuinely surprised. "Who'd he get it from?"

"Probably his favorite dealer, Stu Drayton."

"Oh, right."

There was silence as Annie moved onto the next paper. She even hummed a little, instinctively touching the place where her mole had been.

"So, what happened to *your* face?" she said, not looking up.

My smile accentuated my bruises. "I had a love affair."

She took this in. "And what's next? Back to New York? What do you do there, anyway?"

We were getting to know each other. "I put out a little newsletter about the movies, *Trivial Man*."

Annie stifled a laugh. "Well, that's a contribution to mankind."

Now I was annoyed. As were many recovering alcoholics, Annie was being a zealot about sobriety or, in her case, abstinence from show business. I had not yet kicked my addictions—to Erendira or to *Ambersons*.

So I used the pitiless wiles of the junkie to lure Annie back to her old habit for my own purposes.

"I was hoping to go to the service today," I said, to tease her. "But I need to know where it is."

She looked up slowly. "You want to go to Ben's memorial service?"

"That's what I said."

"Well, that's an easy one. It's at Rosie Bryant's mother's house in Bel Air. The house that Rosie bought for her. A little bigger than the trailer the old lady was used to."

I smiled. "You seem pretty familiar with the place."

"Sometimes I picked the kids up from there."

"It's too bad I don't drive." I was shameless now.

"Yes," she said, fighting me. "That is too bad."

It was up to me to make it irresistible. "What time is your class?"

Annie was amused by my single—or absent—mindedness. "It's Sunday, for God's sake."

"That's right, I forgot. Well, surely," I said, "you'd want to pay your respects?"

She took it as a test of her new resilience. Annie's eyes stayed dry. Slowly, she began to bunch up her papers. "Why not?"

"Great."

She waited a second. Then she started to signal for the waitress, defiantly. I glanced at the clock: ten of eleven. The newspaper said the service started at noon.

Suddenly feeling worried, I decided to reassure her of her own strength.

"Don't worry," I said. "It won't take long."

Annie's waving hand dropped down, the small scars still suddenly visible.

"It's okay," she said coolly. "Believe me."

Annie stopped off at her place to put on something somber. She loaned me a black jacket that I suspected, from its high quality, had once been worn by Ben. Weirdly enough, it fit me perfectly.

Annie lived in a one-room apartment below Sunset Plaza, near the Viper Room and other hip haunts. There was a tall pile of cassettes stacked near her TV. Though they were turned away, I knew that every one of them starred Ben.

I thought about children taught by a woman so affected by a lousy actor who had seduced her once. Then I thought about a man who would manipulate her to avenge an actress who had once seduced *him*. Was I more ruthless now that I was seeking the *Ambersons* for Erendira? Things had gotten complicated.

Annie had a simpler question.

"How does this look?" she said, emerging from the bathroom.

The elegant black dress showed off her grown-up, real-world beauty. It was so flattering, in fact, that I didn't wonder about her motive for wearing it. She wanted to put her indifference on display for Ben's survivors.

She also wanted me to button up the back of it.

"Your fingers are so cold," she said, with pleasure, as I did.

I felt a flicker of arousal as I blended Annie's buttons with their holes, and she knew it. Annie was trying to prove to me definitively that she had moved on. I decided to let her.

Annie turned around, at the same time that I turned her. Her mouth met mine. And the dress, just fastened, began to come undone.

As we started to make love, maybe we were only playing roles. I was Ben Williams for her; she was Erendira for me. We were stand-ins for stars, and it was one more one-night stand.

But by the end, we had emerged as ourselves again, bit players, perhaps, but in more dignified roles. Annie even called me by my own name.

These were heady times for a trivial man.

"HERE WE ARE," ANNIE SAID.

The big house was hidden behind hedges in a private road in Bel Air. By the entrance was an old guard in a gatehouse, who proudly kept a slew of paparazzi at bay. Apparently, he thought Annie was still in good standing with the Williamses. Happily, he waved her car through.

"Good old Frank," Annie said, smiling, and shook her head.

A phalanx of fancy vehicles overflowed from the driveway into the exclusive street. As we pulled up, a few well-known actors dressed in black were streaming out of a limo, some holding on to others for strength. Annie kept up a narration of their real deficits and desires.

"Oh, look at that hypocrite," she said. "He hated Ben." Or, "I can't believe she showed up, after what she said about him." Or, "That dress really shows off your implants, babe." Or, "Nice hair weave."

Looking in her mirror, Annie checked the dark red lipstick that added the final chic touch to her ensemble.

"Let's just leave it here," she said, and stopped in a no-parking zone.

Without consulting the other, we each put on an attitude of having a right to be there. This meant walking quickly and casually, beside the stars, into the backyard.

There, in the piercing sun, fold-up chairs had been placed in rows before a microphone on a stand. Huge horse race–like flower arrangements stood everywhere. One wreath actually said, HE CAUSED PLEASURE ON EARTH.

"I bet Webby Slicone sent that, to thank Ben for all the campaign donations," Annie whispered, about the congressman. "*And* for introducing him to Stu."

I cocked an eyebrow at this last piece of information. Then, turning to the left, Annie quieted down. There, sitting on chairs near the front, in party dresses and bows, their kicking feet stuck straight out and not reaching the ground, were Ben's adopted daughters, ages three, five, and seven. A Latina nanny kept them company.

The children's touching display of best behavior made Annie turn away immediately. Real suffering took the fun out of crashing the funeral and making catty remarks. Or maybe it just reminded Annie of her own loss, and for a second slowed her recovery. But just for a second.

"Look who's over there," she then said. "I bet this is the biggest audience *she's* seen in decades."

Indeed, it was the largest collection of celebrities I had ever witnessed. I felt digitally placed among them, as Ben would be in his final picture. I thought of Jean Harlow in *Saratoga*, Robert Walker in *My Son John*, and other stars whose deaths during production had caused sleight-of-hand to replace them in the completed film. Bruce Lee. Peter Sellers in the last Pink Panther.

We took seats. Then I saw another familiar face. Dick Burke's.

Dressed as elegantly as ever, the bodyguard was staring right at me, leaning over my chair from the seat behind. His mouth was very close to Annie's and my ears.

"Don't make a fuss," he said, smiling for the benefit of others. "Just get up and come with me. Now."

Annie and I stood, very slowly. With Dick Burke's big hands on our shoulders—and squeezing, none too gently, our necks—he guided us past the other guests. Through the backyard, he directed us around the edges of a pool, toward a poolhouse.

"How have you been?" I said, in a friendly way.

Dick Burke only grunted in response. "I thought I'd seen the last of you."

When I flew back from Barcelona—in coach, cut off from Ben's credit—I had returned to my original status of outsider, nerd, trivial man. Now, getting the boot from Dick Burke had reduced me even further to gatecrasher, nutcase, and scum.

I tried to restore what little credibility I had.

"Look," I said, "I'm still just after the film."

"*The Magnificent*—whatever the hell it was?" Dick Burke asked innocently, though I think he knew.

"Yes."

"I don't give a damn," Dick Burke said wearily. "When this funeral's over, I'm out of here."

I turned to him. "Is that right?"

Dick Burke nodded. "As soon as that sleazy bastard's in the ground." He chuckled. "He don't even breathe, baby."

Annie looked at him, surprised. Dick Burke's total disgust obviously made her suspect something about the man who was pulling us both along.

"You know, Dick," Annie said, "the people outside the gate pay. Abner Cooley doesn't."

A glint of something shone in Dick Burke's eyes, and I feared for both our lives. Then I saw that it was guilt, not rage.

"Hey, I would have been his source, too," Annie said, to further impress him. "In fact, I used to be."

Now Dick Burke looked at Annie with a deep sigh. He saw this for what it was: blackmail. Still holding me, his grip on her relaxed.

"Go on," he sighed. "I won't stop you."

Annie waited a second, to see if I would be allowed to follow. That was not going to happen. So she flashed me a look of regret, and I flashed back one of gratitude. She kissed me, quickly, on the cheek. Then, her surprising survival skills giving me hope for her future, Annie walked back to her car, and all of those papers she had to grade.

"You," Dick Burke told me, "keep moving."

The poolhouse was a modest affair, the female equivalent of Ben Williams's Malibu hideaway. Needlepoint pillows sat on an elegant white couch, which was covered by a quaint country quilt. A rocking chair, still moving, stood in a corner. Paintings of fishing families adorned the wall. It looked like the most expensive room in a Southern bed-and-breakfast.

Rosie Bryant paced before us, smoking a cigarette. She was wearing a short and tight black dress, which accentuated her shapely legs and augmented breasts. Her dark hair was perfectly cropped in a modern pageboy. All-gal, as Ben had said.

Even without speaking, Rosie seemed steely. When she did talk, her faint Arkansas accent made her appear more a canny young matron than a major movie star. Which, as most of America knew, was the case in her movies, too.

"This is the one?" she asked Dick Burke.

"This is him." He nodded.

"Where's the girl?"

"She got away. Sorry."

Rosie looked once, with great disapproval, at her husband's body-guard. But it was his last day on the job, and she knew it.

"All right, whatever." She sighed. Then she turned to me. "Look, I've only recently got wind of the whole thing with He-Man or what-ever it—"

"Her-Man," Dick Burke said.

"I wasn't involved in that," I said.

"So I've heard, and good for you. I'm willing to give you more money than any tabloid could, to say nothing about it, or anything else. How does that sound? Please reply quickly, I've got a funeral to run."

Rosie sounded more the harried hostess than a bereaved widow or concerned mother. But she couldn't have been indifferent. Her gravy train had run aground, derailed by her errant husband, and she was a pro at damage control. Trying desperately to limit the casualties, her first order of business was to eliminate the rats around the wreckage.

But this rat surprised her.

"I don't want money," I said.

"No? Then what do you want?"

"The Magnificent Ambersons."

Rosie paused. Then, impatient fury rising in her face, she looked away from me, to Dick Burke, to translate.

"What the *hell* is this guy talking about?"

"The girl tried to tell you—" Dick Burke started.

But they were interrupted. A high-pitched female laugh came from another room, one at the back of the room we were in. Incensed, Rosie shot Dick Burke a fast, hard glare.

"I thought you took care of her," Rosie said.

As Dick Burke only shrugged, his time on the job ticking down, Rosie strode to a closed door and opened it.

She pulled out a hysterical Beth Brenner. Beth had on her own funeral garb, her long legs demurely covered by black tights. But she was worse for wear, her red hair half undone from its proper perch. She looked like a well-dressed version of the crazy wife in *Jane Eyre*, locked inside the attic. Come to think of it, Orson Welles starred in that movie, too.

Giggling, skidding her heels on the carpet, Beth tried to keep Rosie from pulling her ahead. But the assistant was no match for the wife. Beth ended up on the floor before us.

"My gawd!" She pointed at me. "Look who's here!"

"I thought we told you to keep quiet," Rosie said.

Beth subsided. I could see that her laughter was caused by fatigue and fear, and not amusement or insanity.

"It's what I was trying to tell you," she said. "But you've been too angry to listen!"

"What is?" a steamed Rosie asked. "What is?"

"*The Magnificent Andersons*. That's what all this was about, *okay*?!"

I felt a by now familiar chill of discovery.

ROSIE CLOSED HER EYES AND TRIED TO CONTROL HERSELF. THEN IT WAS her turn to be a schoolteacher, one in a bad school district. "I've had just about enough of this."

She advanced on Beth, and Beth cowered, as if knowing what to expect. Surprisingly, Dick Burke stepped forward, and Rosie stopped in her tracks.

Beth said, quickly, "Stu's delivery boy. The Spanish one. The kid who did imitations. He stole *The Magnificent Andersons.*"

Taking a deep breath, Rosie retreated. It was clear that her incomprehension had been from denial and not stupidity. She decided to quit fooling around and accept the whole awful truth about Ben. There was a funeral to run.

"Apparently, my husband had a few bad habits," she told me, of all people, with a small smile.

"That's right," Beth said, breathlessly, to me. "When Stu found out what the kid did, he came over, to apologize. He and Ben kissed and made up. Then Stu gave Ben a present of crack to smoke." Then she turned to Rosie. "Do you understand *now*? Hello!"

Rosie turned away, with a look of disgust. "Maybe I always understood."

As if forming a new alliance, Beth came over and stood by me, to continue her tale.

"I was with him—all night, *okay?*—but I didn't use any of the stuff, though Ben wanted me to. And when I saw what happened to him, I called an ambulance. Then I got out of there."

"So you never told the cops?"

Beth gave me a look that said, she was a ditzy white woman, and this was L.A. Feeling she was reaching, I only shrugged.

"Well, so what were you doing *here*?" Rosie asked then.

"I came to pay my respects," Beth spat back. "And I thought you might want to know the truth."

Dick Burke gave a little skeptical *pfft*, and Rosie actually laughed.

"You were here to shake me down," Rosie said, "and you know it."

Beth stared at Ben's widow, her eyes narrowing in disbelief. "I can't believe you," she said, like a Valley high school girl.

Now Dick Burke started to chuckle, joining Rosie's growing amusement.

"Well, maybe I *should* go to the police or the papers," Beth said. "It would serve you right. Maybe America would love to know about the big action hero. And his B-movie wife."

Rosie stopped laughing. Though she had achieved high-class status, she was originally white trash. And her rough roots meant she could wrestle in the mud a lot better than Beth.

Reaching into her pocket, Rosie hurled a shining object at Beth's face. The assistant showed enough reflex to turn her head. The projectile—a string of gems—hit the wall behind her, shattered, and sent a dozen sparkling beams into the air, like fireworks.

"First," Rosie said, "you'd have to explain what you were doing with my jewelry."

Now Beth knew she was playing out of her depth. As so often happened, her bottom lip immediately began to tremble.

"Haven't you ever been *nervous*?!" she cried out.

Beth fell silent, her mouth open, in too much incredulous pain to close it. Beth stole things; I recalled trivia; Erendira picked her fingers and kicked her feet. Everybody was nervous. Everybody but Rosie.

"Nice try," she said.

Then Rosie turned and started adjusting her hair in a mirror. Her duties were at an end, and other people were waiting on her.

"Give this gentleman what we discussed," she told Dick Burke, without looking at him. "And get her out of here."

But Beth had more fight in her, more—I'll be honest—than I would ever have expected. As Dick Burke reached out to take her elbow, she yanked it away.

"Well, do you know what this 'gentleman' was doing for your husband?" she said. "Ben was having him track down *another* chick, one he wanted to find so bad that he bankrolled his entire—"

Rosie turned, suddenly. Then she hauled off and slapped Beth once, twice, three times across the face. The force of the blows grew until the third and final one sent Beth flying off her feet, and she collapsed against the nice white couch.

Rosie's strength made me reconsider her, suddenly. Her voice *did* sound a little like Andy Griffith's. And there *was* that tiny line of dark above her lip. Nah, I thought, though still unsure.

It all happened so fast that even Dick Burke could do nothing to prevent it. He stood there, stunned, unsure as to whom he should be protecting now.

A colossus, Rosie loomed over the prone figure of Beth, her fingers clenching and unclenching.

"Go on," she said quietly, her accent truly trailer park now. "Get your ugly ass outta here."

She turned and included Dick Burke and me in her list of leeches, chislers, homewreckers, and lowlifes.

"That goes for you, too."

She had a funeral to run.

"She'll be sorry," Beth said, rubbing her cheek in Dick Burke's car afterward.

"No, she won't," Dick Burke said. "Not about this. Anyway, don't worry about telling the cops about Stu Drayton and everything. They already know."

In the backseat, where Beth and I sat like chauffeured criminals, the two of us looked at each other, surprised. Apparently, on his way out, Dick Burke was giving lots of information to lots of people, profiting from none of it himself. He had the air of someone cleansed.

"Well," Beth said, relaxing, "at least there's that." She looked absently out the window. "Jesus. I never want to see another movie again as long as I live."

Her remark reminded me of what Erendira's grandmother had written at the end of her diary. That reminded me of Erendira. *The Magnificent Ambersons* had become a pawn in a world of murder and drugs. It really needed someone to protect it.

"Speaking of movies," I said, "where is it?"

Dick Burke slammed on the brakes in the middle of the street. Half annoyed, half tickled, he turned around and looked at me from the driver's seat.

"You don't give up, do you?"

As long as Dick Burke was half tickled, I felt safe. Not safe enough to mention that my crusade was less selfish than it had been at the start, however.

"Let's just say I'm not the only one who wants it now," I told him.

Shaking his head, he turned back and started driving again.

"Well, good luck," he said, "and I mean that sincerely."

I thought that any celebrity would be lucky to have Dick Burke as a bodyguard. As long as he didn't tell him too much or make him do disgusting things. But I didn't say that.

"Here you go," Dick Burke said.

We had reached the motel above Swingers. The check from Rosie sat safely in my pocket. Dick Burke gave me one wink in his rearview, and that was enough. I turned to say goodbye to Beth, but she was still looking out the window blankly, as if at the ruins of her young life.

"Well, good luck in your next job," I said.

She did not turn. I noticed that one of her hands was clutched tightly around something. Then her fingers relaxed and revealed several of Rosie's jewels, collected from the floor.

I figured that Beth would do just fine, too.

THAT NIGHT, I WENT BACK TO THE SANTA MONICA PIER, BUT NOT TO PLAY Foosball.

It was the only place I knew to ask after Stu Drayton's lad, the young movie fan who had made off with the most prized movie never made. How had he known to take it?

There was no way I could ask that question of the people I had come to find, the other gang members who hung out on the pier. Here in the arcades after dark, crowded with out-of-towners—as Jeanine and I had been—they hassled and bumped, picked fights and picked pockets or merely annoyed.

Tonight was no exception. While families and kids on dates played video games or classic games like ring toss, the wayward youths snaked in and out, shoving shoulders, pinching bootys, and blowing cigarette smoke. For once, I hoped that being a goofy white guy—I could have trademarked the look—would work to my advantage.

It did not take long. Standing haplessly at a pinball game, losing as badly as I knew how, I soon sensed a presence behind me. Then I felt a shoulder placed upon and pushed against my own. Feigning clueless-ness, as if about to meet a new friend, I turned, with a stupid look that said *Wow, can you believe how much I suck?*

I stopped. I saw the sweatshirt with the face-hiding hood, the hood from the 'hood that was the uniform of those I sought. With a faint Latino accent, the mouth within its shadows made a helpful suggestion.

"Give somebody good a chance."

My companion was as bone-thin as Stu's boy had been. The only difference was that this boy was a girl, or so I was convinced from the shape of the mouth, and the delicacy of the hand that now pulled mine off the knob.

As Ur-dork, I answered just, "Excuse me?"

The girl gently hip-checked me away from the machine. I stood to the side as she finished the use of my fifty cents. With nearly super-human skill, she knocked out a new ball and kept it in play for point af-ter point after point. Her achievement was more impressive since, her hood pulled tight, she could hardly see a thing.

"Hey," I said, "you're really good."

At last, the ball guttered out. Then she raised her gentle hand and gestured out a "gimme" with its long and elegant fingers.

"I need more for another game."

Obediently, I dug into my small jeans pocket; this was how they did things in L.A. But before I handed her the coins, I asked, with inno-cence, "If I make it a dollar, will you do something for me?"

The girl turned with sudden speed. From their cave, hatred now lit and made visible her eyes. With horror, I realized what my question must have implied. I remembered that, when they showed the Elizabeth Taylor movie *Secret Ceremony* on network TV, they redubbed dialogue so that she was a wig model, not a whore.

I pfumpfered, "Uh, I meant—will you *tell* me something?"

The girl relaxed a bit, and, to appease her, I gave her the two quar-ters. But she did not turn back to the game. She placed one hand on her hip and studied me, as if seeing me for the first time.

"They're making cops real skinny these days," she said.

I couldn't help it, I laughed. I should have realized that this is how I would appear; but the idea seemed absurd. Imagine a city patrolled and protected by trivial men! On this adventure, there had been a first for everything.

"Trust me," I said. "I'm not."

"Yeah. Right."

"I'm telling you the truth. I'm only looking for a boy, a kid. He's— he's tall and thin. And he does, well, he does—imitations."

The girl chewed on her cheeks, doubtfully. "Imitations."

"Of, you know, movie stars."

She was about to be even more skeptical. But then she must have realized what—and whom—I meant.

"Ohhhh," she said.

She lifted a finger, the nail of which I noticed was painted with a tiny snake. "Wait here a second. Then come down to the beach."

I hesitated, not knowing to what I was agreeing. As a little joke, as a mild flirtation, she placed the quarters back into my palm, as payment.

Disarmed, I told her, "Sure."

It was a clear evening, beautiful and dry, in the usual L.A. way. Crazed amusement park noise came from the pier; below it, the ocean spat upon the sand, ran away, then spat again. Whites and Latinos mixed, uneasily: young people made out and smoked pot; others tossed a fluorescent Frisbee that did not glow bright enough for catching; still others threw empty cigarette packs into the surf, as far as they would go. Boredom was in the air; so was anger.

Then I saw the girl again.

Her face still covered, she was beckoning me toward the edge of the surf, where she stood with a companion. It was a heavyset young person in sweatshirt and hood, and the roundness of her hips told me that this, too, was a girl.

I got up close but could see her face no better. With their hoods pulled tight, the two looked like twenty-year-old monks in an obscure and female sect.

Imitating them, I removed my shoes and rolled up my cuffs, clamdigger-style.

"So, you're the cop?" the big girl said.

"No." I looked at the thinner one. "I told you that—"

"Just kidding," her friend assured me. "You work for Stu."

"No," I said. "Not that, either."

"Oh. So maybe you're a friend of Ben Williams? And maybe you want some of what Ben Williams liked?"

With her tongue lolling out, she pantomimed male self-abuse. Then the two girls laughed in a way that made me nervous.

"I don't know what you mean," I said. "I mean, I *know* what you mean, of course, but not, you know, how you mean it. I'm just look-ing for—"

"Little Bobby?"

I had a name now; that was something.

"Yes. And I'm looking for a movie."

"Oh. So you want all of us again? For more of that big Ben Williams fun?"

"Look, whatever Ben does—did—with Stu's employees, I don't—"

"Ben. On a first-name basis."

"Look, that doesn't mean—"

As we spoke, I realized that we were walking farther out, into the water. My pants—rolled up to my knees—were being brushed gently by the waves.

I had lost track of my first friend, the skinny girl, behind me. Then I realized her location: at the end of the knife pointed into my back.

"Just don't move, lech."

I had been mistaken for a cop, and then a drug dealer's flunky; now I was a seeker of sex with gang members. This latest investigation wasn't going well.

As the small girl held me in place, the big one came forward and stuck her hand into my pants. She removed my wallet and cracked it open like a clam.

"There's not much," I told her. "I'm sorry."

I had, in fact, left most of Rosie's money hidden in a pillowcase at the hotel.

"Two hundred." The girl shrugged. "Not *too* shabby."

She kept the bills, then dropped the wallet down into the wet. I was about to reach to retrieve it, but the knifepoint pushed in deeper.

"Well, now we can tell you where Little Bobby is," the first girl said.

"Right," her friend agreed, "we can do that."

I smiled, with nervous gratitude. "Great."

"He's right there."

"Yeah. He's right there. Can't you see him?"

With trepidation, I looked where the girls were pointing. It wasn't back to the beach or up to the pier; it was under the water.

In a second, that's where I was, too.

The small girl pushed me; the big girl held my head. Salt and seaweed filled my nose and mouth, and my arms flapped out like a dying bird's.

Inside the ocean, my eyes burned as I forced them open. I saw the fuzzy forms of the big girl's legs, fish floating by, and what looked like a lost pair of plaid shorts. A million pounds sat on my chest, getting heavier.

The beachside love scene in *From Here to Eternity* flashed through my mind: Burt Lancaster and Deborah Kerr in a clinch. Had it been censored or something? I no longer knew.

Faintly, from miles away, I heard the girls curse and laugh as I slapped and kicked at them. Then I heard somebody scream, and the scream grew louder.

It wasn't me, how could it have been? I was swallowing an ocean. The scream slowly removed the girls' hands from my neck and waist, allowed me up, and let me live.

I flew to the surface, water spraying all ways, giving out a massive moan of relief in the air. The girls were already beating their way back to the shore. They were chatting with each other, laughing a little, dragging their fingers in the water. Beyond them, I saw their motivation: police cars, sirens screaming, were approaching the arcade.

The cops weren't coming for them; there were other crimes being committed there tonight. But my friends must have felt it might not look so good if they were drowning me.

I figured they had hurt me because they could, because Stu Drayton and Ben Williams and other people were out of reach. While I wished they hadn't, I understood why they had.

My chest still heaving, I watched them go. Then I pulled over my floating wallet, which bobbed beside me. Unlike the girls from the gang, I would now have to approach the powerful more directly.

When I got home, TV was running footage of the arrest of Ben Williams's drug dealer, Stu Drayton.

"The pleasure of helping find *Ambersons*," I answered. "Forget helping me."

Silent, flickering TV images played in front of me. I sat on the hotel bed, calling New York, this time on my dime.

A few minutes before, Stu Drayton had been paraded in handcuffs before a waiting mob of reporters and cameramen. He had been accused of drug trafficking and indirectly implicated in the death of Ben Williams, at least by the TV anchors. And all on Dick Burke's tip.

Stu was a boyishly handsome man, about forty, with tousled dirty-blond hair. He wore the preppy uniform of a sweater over a short-sleeved shirt, the shirt collar turned up. Studious glasses sat on his face, making him seem even more of an overage student.

Stu's official job description was "art gallery owner" and "cultural speculator." By the end of the day, Stu was out on bail, which had been set at a million dollars. I thought of the junkie Lorelei Reed, still sitting in a cell in New York, for a crime she didn't commit.

Jeanine had made the mistake of answering the phone, and there I had been.

"Look, I hope you're not holding that call from Spain against me," I said.

"I don't know what you're talking about."

"Good." All was forgiven, obviously, even if nothing was understood. "Now, do you still have Abner's contact list?"

"Of course."

"I need some way to find Stu Drayton."

"What for? To congratulate him?"

I smiled. "It's got to do with that little gang guy who drove us up into the hills. He worked for Stu."

"*He's* got *The Magnificent Ambersons*?" Jeanine was aghast.

"Maybe. Maybe he does."

I explained the whole story, as much as I knew of it: the boy's stealing the film; Stu's gift of apology; Ben's untimely demise. Embarrassed, my hair still wet, I left out the part about my trip to the pier.

" . . . and then there's some other stuff that's not important right now . . ."

When I finished, there was a pause.

"I guess it makes as much sense as anything else," Jeanine said at last.

"I'm glad you think so."

"Well, would you like Stu's beeper number?"

"And have the cops think I'm one of his 'clients'? No thanks."

"That might be a problem, mightn't it? How about the private number of one of his galleries in Santa Monica?"

"Thanks."

After I wrote it down, there was more silence before Jeanine said, "When are you coming back to New York?"

"When I have the movie. Or when my money runs out, whichever comes first."

"I could wire you some. I'm working again. Taking tickets at the Film Forum, but there *is* a salary."

"That's okay. Rosie took care of me."

"Be careful. Your chart says there's danger ahead."

"I will."

Neither Jeanine nor I spoke then. There was so much to tell Erendira: that Ben had not intended to show her the wrong film, that I knew who had the right one now. But, at that moment, she seemed a million miles away. Who knew if I would ever see her again? Soccer players had strong wills. There was someone closer, whose very breath was near my ear.

"I promise," I said, "when I get it, you can watch it with me."

There was another break before Jeanine answered, "That's a deal."

There was just voice mail on the number in Santa Monica. I left a message, pretending to be an art patron, looking for information about my "print" of *The Magnificent Ambersons*. I hoped that any cop listening in was not a movie fan.

Several hours later, I received a call back. It was a very pleasant woman's voice.

"Please come to an opening tomorrow night. At the Shutter Gallery in Bergamot Station in Santa Monica. Six to eight. There will be refreshments."

ANYONE WHO THOUGHT STU DRAYTON WOULD LIE LOW WHILE OUT ON BAIL didn't know Stu Drayton. I didn't know Stu Drayton, but I was about to get a crash course.

Bergamot Station looked like a huge parking lot full of art galleries, or maybe a small army base. It played host to the latest in painting and photography, and openings often spilled out the door onto the pavement. That was the scene when I showed up—by cab, of course—the next night.

Trying to look suitably louche, I sauntered into the show, wearing the black jacket I'd borrowed from Annie Chin and never had a chance to return. Luckily, in L.A., what looked funereal one day looked hip the next.

Shutter Gallery specialized, not surprisingly, in photos. Tonight it was the work of Gavin de Klock, a Britisher who took artful exposures in hospital operating rooms. Women in short black dresses and men in faux-Beatnik beards and turtlenecks mingled, heedless of the gaping wounds, severed arms, and bleeding eyeballs that were all around them.

I had signed the book, as instructed. A beautiful young receptionist, her face dazzlingly pierced, read my signature. Then she nodded at a male model/waiter carrying a tray of cheese hors d'oeuvres. He, in turn, nodded at Stu Drayton.

Stu had entered the gallery from the back, from what must have been his private office. He was wearing the same preppy costume he was wearing when arrested. I guessed he always wore this, no matter the tawdriness or trendiness of the occasion.

There was a smattering of applause when he appeared, and the ovation grew as more people became aware of him. Finally, the whole room cheering, Stu made his way to the front of the room.

Anyone who thought Stu Drayton would lie low while out on bail didn't know Stu Drayton.

"You guys," he said softly, like a junior executive at his surprise birthday party. "You guys."

Then, silence falling, Stu spoke to the crowd, standing before a beautiful photo of open-heart surgery.

"I know many of you thought I might not make it here tonight," he said, and there was shocked laughter. "That I might be a little . . . detained." More laughs, more relief. "But I can assure you, wild horses wouldn't have kept me away. Correction—make that L.A. policemen!"

Now the whole room was rocking with hilarity and applause. Stu embraced a tall, bald, slightly rounded fellow beside him, whom I assumed was Gavin de Klock, tonight's featured artist. Glancing at the guests, I saw members of the media, some wielding videocameras. But I wondered who, disguised in hipster wear, were the undercover cops that Stu was so brazenly defying.

Stu paid long, tedious tribute to the work of de Klock—his "vulnerability," his "exquisite tensions," and how the show was "humanity at its most helpless, photography at its most controlled." Then he quieted more applause with raised hands.

"I'd like to close with one thought," he said. "No matter how others distort what I do, I will never stop doing it. In my life and my work, I will stay dedicated to helping the purest and most beautiful of artists. And their work I shall hang on the walls of my mind. Thank you for this, and thank you for coming!"

Deafening cheers then for Stu's L.A. earnestness. It was so loud that passersby gazed in from outside, drawn by the crazy sound.

Stu made his way back through the well-wishers, shaking hands, kissing cheeks, even winking audaciously in a camera. Then, as he approached, I saw him look at me. His smile faded, and the blue eyes behind his glasses grew very cold, as if icing over.

Passing by, shaking another's hand, he whispered in my ear, "Press 'Enter' on the computer in my office."

Then the drug dealer and aesthete, who helped artists get shows and get high, was lost in the love of the crowd.

Stu must have thought there were bugs everywhere.

Maybe he was right. When I closed the door to his office, I had the acute sense of being observed. I felt that my very breathing was being remarked upon downtown, in the D.A.'s office.

In the sparsely decorated room, rife with Asian influences, a bonsai tree stood on a small glass table, and a computer was the only object on a mahogany desk. The screaming figure from Munch's *Geshrei* was its postmodern screen saver. A printer sat, unobtrusively, in a corner. The dim sounds of the gallery party were the only background noise.

I approached the computer, stealthily, as if it, too, were recording my image. Then, with a deep breath, I placed my forefinger onto "Enter" and pressed down.

The screaming figure disappeared. A whirring sound began and slowly built. I spun around, my heartbeat now as loud as my breath.

It was only the printer, commencing its work. One, two, three pages came gently spitting out.

Taking them, I sat on an expensive leather swivel chair, its back designed for peace and comfort. I could hear Stu Drayton's quiet, "contemplative" voice in each word as I read.

TO MY FRIEND.

If you are the man Ben Williams met in Malibu that night, whom Little Bobby—that's how the boy is known—brought to see him, then I assume there is something you want back.

If you are that man, you should know that I want something back, too.

Little Bobby has gotten too big for his Tommy Hilfiger jeans. First, after a night of fun with Ben that I arranged, the movie buff stole a film from Ben. Then, after I gave Little Bobby the lecture he deserved and relieved him of his duties, he absconded both with the film . . . and with a priceless valuable of my own. Perhaps he means to go into business for himself.

Given my recent run-in with injustice, I cannot pursue Little Bobby myself. Nor do I trust anyone else to do so. That is why I am offering you this opportunity.

I have it on good authority that Little Bobby is currently hiding at his girlfriend's house, 35 Cramen St., #4E, in Silverlake. My good authority is his girlfriend, to whom I introduced him, an aspiring painter with a primitive style but a sophisticated sense of self-promotion.

If you are interested, please open the drawer on the desk to your right. The first envelope is for Little Bobby. The second is for you. The third is in case Little Bobby does not accept the first.

Then come see the show again, tomorrow night, after seven.

Please burn these pages with the matches on the same desk, and flush them in the commode in the bathroom to your left.

Close the door behind you when you leave.

Thanks from one art lover to another.

Very slowly, I approached the desk. In the one drawer below the computer, I indeed found three envelopes. As I had expected, the first two contained money. As I had feared, the third contained a gun.

My hands shook a little when I closed the drawer again. It was all very *Mission: Impossible*. After one season, Peter Graves became the star of that show when Steven Hill went off to study Judaism. But TV facts were lesser trivia than movie facts, and so they were less comforting.

I had gone from being a movie star's private eye to a drug dealer's paid assassin. Was *The Magnificent Ambersons* worth it? Was anything?

I kept the door of the inner bathroom closed until I saw the charred pages swirl completely down. Then, nervously, I sat and used the bowl myself. Then I passed through the party—which had grown only larger— one more time.

I stared across the chic revelers, posed against the bloody photos, until I found their guest of honor. The envelopes were in a pocket of my jacket. I caught Stu's eye just long enough to nod.

THE FIRST THING I DID, OF COURSE, WAS PAY A CAB TO WAIT.

I did not wonder why Stu Drayton had trusted me with the money, with the weapon, with anything. Ben Williams's account of me on that night had probably assured him—as the cops had felt back in New York—that I was insignificant and eccentric enough not to betray anyone. And that I was expendable in case I did. They were all right on both counts.

I would have felt a kind of euphoria, an expectation of a long road ending, if I had not seen the other car. The sedan was parked across from my waiting cab, its windows tinted opaquely. It was far too expensive to belong to anyone in the run-down neighborhood. It had an official-looking license plate, which it needed to sit in a NO STANDING spot. I did not get close enough to find out why.

Trying to act nonchalant, I walked toward the door of Little Bobby's girlfriend's building. On the fourth floor, a curtain pulled slowly open, then fell closed again. Sweat starting to heat my head, I pressed the buzzer at 4E. No voice inquired as to who I was. The bell just rang, and I just pushed the door open.

It was a dingy walk-up, and smells of fast food and sounds of rap music filled the staircase. By the time I reached the fourth floor, I was panting, and no match for anyone who got in my way.

Nobody did. And it only took one knock for 4E to open.

The young blond woman standing there—Little Bobby's girlfriend, I assumed—did not say a word. She wore a painter's smock, slightly stained, and smiled once at me, quickly, without pleasure. Then she nodded her head, down the hall, before escaping into another room and closing its door behind her.

I heard faint applause from a TV game show. As I walked slowly down the hall of the large and shabby apartment, I placed my hand upon the pocket where I had stashed the gun. I did not intend to use it—of course, I did not know how—but just feeling it there gave me the illusion of control.

There was no need for such precautions. The door I was seeking was not even shut. I walked a few more steps and saw Little Bobby inside the room, sprawled upon the bed, watching TV. The smell of marijuana was everywhere.

"Hey," he said.

Little Bobby did not even look surprised to see me. Of course, he had the foggy look of someone stoned. But he also had the air of someone waiting for attention, indeed impatient for it. What had taken me—or anyone—so long to come?

"Have a seat."

I had never seen his face before; it had been hidden by his hood. He had a flat nose, a full mouth, and eyes so big, they almost bulged. His skin was covered with acne scars. I picked some clothes off a rickety wooden chair and sat down.

"Do you remember me?" I said.

"Sure." Then he sang, "I've grown accustomed to your face," more like James Mason than Rex Harrison.

"Right. So, uh, Little Bobby—that's your name, right?"

"Yeah. Like a younger De Niro. Or Duvall. Or Redford. Or he's just Bob?"

"Bob, yeah." I paused, hearing the game show shift into a commercial for coffee. "Do you know why I'm here?"

His eyes closed for a minute, then shot back open. "You got something to do with what I took?"

I was surprised by his honesty, though not by his unsurety, given the joint that lay, burned down, in the ashtray beside him.

"The movie is mine," I said.

"It's *yours*?"

He seemed shocked. Of course, it wasn't true. It had belonged to Alan Gilbert, who had stolen it from Erendira's mother, who had been left it by Orson Welles. But I felt I had as much right to it now as anyone. Certainly more than this boy, who was trying to focus on the commercial now before him.

"Yeah," I said, defensively. "Why?"

He shrugged. "Stu had me and my crew go to Ben Williams's place a lot, to drop off stuff and whatnot," he said, still studying the set. "One night, he said he had these old movies, some of them pretty skanky. So Stu called up three of our girls, too. And all of us watched those movies. And then Ben . . . watched us."

"Okay."

"Now I got myself a good girl. She's an artist."

I said nothing in response.

"So, what, then you stole Ben's—"

"Yeah, while he wasn't looking, I took one of those flicks. Of course, I got no way to even show it!"

He laughed at this, uproariously, and ended up coughing. I laughed, too. The thought of a modern urban man struggling with film cans and reels was pretty funny. So was something else.

"You thought you stole old *porn*?" I asked.

"Yeah," he said, looking at me now. "Didn't I?"

"No."

"Huh."

That was the extent of Little Bobby's response, a little burp of bewildered interest. I did not pursue it with him. I only watched what Little Bobby did now.

He reached down, under the bed he was on. Then he pulled out a familiar object by its nylon handle.

It was the bag that Gus Ziegler had stashed the *Ambersons* in, the one I had fought him for on the subway train, the one he had handed over to Ben Williams. The one Little Bobby had stolen from Ben.

I had to restrain myself from reaching immediately for it. Nearness to the film always made me impulsive, sometimes foolishly brave.

I had to save my strength for the rest of the story. Trying to stay calm, I said, "You've stolen something else, too, now, haven't you, Little Bobby?"

Little Bobby seemed to nod off again. Then I realized only one eye had closed; he was winking.

"That I have," he said. "That I have."

He gave one of those *yar-har* laughs, as if imitating an old movie pirate. I thought that, toward the end of his career, Orson Welles had played Long John Silver in an ill-fated foreign-made film of *Treasure Island*.

"And let Stu-pid beg for it."

Little Bobby clicked to another station, one showing a Burt Reynolds car crash movie from the Seventies. He stared at it for a second, blankly.

"I can't do Burt," he said. "Newer ones, they're not so easy."

"Won't you please go on?"

"But I can do the fat guy in *Deliverance*."

Little Bobby started to hop up off his seat, grabbing his behind, crying out, "Ow! Ow! Ow!" Then he collapsed in more drowsy hilarity.

This was also pretty funny, and I laughed with him again. But then he cut it off.

"Stu wanted me to give the movie back, but I wouldn't."

Slowly, I placed one of the moneyed envelopes down on the bed before him. The boy peeked inside, pulled out a few bills, but left the bulk of them.

Then, from Gus's bag, where he had hidden it, Little Bobby threw a little leather-covered object at me. It landed harshly on my chest, then fell into my lap. It was Stu's Filofax, the kind that executives keep. With all their names and addresses in them.

"Let that fool fire me," he said.

"I see."

"Especially now, when he's in such trouble. Meester Beeg." He did Peter Lorre.

"I hear you."

"You should see who's in that goddamn thing."

"I do." Scrolling through, I caught glimpses of familiar names from movies, music, TV. And politics.

"I should be hearing from some of them any minute. That'll be *real* money."

I looked up, not at all sure of what he meant. "You're telling me that—"

"Why not start the bidding now, baby?" Little Bobby did a demented auctioneer. "Do I hear a million? One million! Do I hear two million? I hear—"

"Oh, no. You shouldn't have done that. You shouldn't have called the people in Stu's file."

"No? How come? It's like a, like a scam."

The word—Little Bobby's whole young, misbegotten plan—had come right from the silver screen. So had the idea that losers ever get revenge on the powerful. I knew because, like Little Bobby, I was a loser, too.

My mind went immediately out the window, down to the street. I thought of the car sitting there, too good for its surroundings, the car with the official plates.

I jumped up and, cautiously, pulled the window shade away. The car was still there. My cab wasn't.

Then I heard a woman scream.

It got even Little Bobby's attention. He flinched, suddenly, seeming to be hurt himself, hurt by the assault someone was committing on his beloved new girl, the one who had sold him out to Stu.

Before I could stop him, Little Bobby rose. Then, from beneath the bed, he grabbed another object.

It was not the kind of gun I carried. It was a chunky little machine gun, an automatic weapon.

I covered my face, instinctively. Hoisting the gun unsteadily, he wavered toward the door. At the second he crossed the threshold, before he could even aim, he was collapsed by a foot kicking him, commando-style, in the gut.

The weapon flew from Little Bobby's hands, skittered back into the room, and slid beneath the bed again, as if on purpose. From my cowering position on the chair, I could see Little Bobby sitting on the floor by the door, and a gloved hand at the base of a black sleeve pulling him to his feet.

"Where is it?" the man in the hall yelled.

His bravado gone, smoke blurring his brain, Little Bobby looked up, helplessly. Then he just pointed inside the room.

The man let Little Bobby go, making sure his head slammed hard into the door behind him. Then he stepped over him and entered.

He was small and dressed in a neat, dark pin-striped suit. His face was covered by a ski mask, a jarring touch to his elegant look. Upon seeing me, he stopped. I pulled back from him, reflexively, allowing maximum access to the bag, which lay on the floor.

Just a foot stride away from me, *The Magnificent Ambersons* was stolen again, this time by a masked man.

He hoisted the bag over his shoulder. Then, glancing only once at me, and doing nothing else, he turned to go.

Little Bobby was now standing in the doorway, blinking madly, trying to focus. He clearly intended to be a threat, but he was weaving from one foot to another. Then Little Bobby made the mistake of taking one step forward.

The man pulled out a tiny gun and placed two silent bullets into the young man's heart.

Like a marionette packed away for the night, Little Bobby fell immediately to the floor. Gripping the bag, the man walked past him and disappeared into the hall.

From there, I heard a sudden rustle of feet and a female cry of— "Bastard!"

The man cursed once, then the wall shared by the hall and bedroom shook with the force of a woman slammed against it. I heard something— the body of Little Bobby's girlfriend—sliding down it, softly, onto the floor. She had regretted her decision too late.

I heard the man's footsteps going away. He was humming a tune, an irritating ditty of the late 1960s: "One and one, they still make two. One of me needs one of you . . ."

———

He may have had the bag, he may have even had the *Ambersons*. But he did not have the Filofax. It lay wedged in the belt of my pants, covered by my shirt, pressing cool against my sticky skin. In my fear, I had forgotten to give it back.

SHUTTER GALLERY WAS CLOSED AT SEVEN THE NEXT NIGHT.

Even though it was the time I had been told to arrive, this did not surprise me. I just turned the knob of the unlocked door and walked in. I was getting good at figuring out this kind of thing.

The place was empty. It would have been completely dark, were it not for lights from outside, seeping in through venetian blinds, shooting off the glass that covered Gavin de Klock's hospital photos. It allowed me to see my way to Stu's back office.

Here it was dark, too, but not unoccupied. Stu was waiting in the leather chair by his computer, its light the room's only illumination. A takeout tofu dinner in a Styrofoam dish was on the desk before him.

Seeming genuinely relieved to see me, he waved his chopsticks in greeting. Then, after swallowing a final bite, he beckoned me closer, placing a finger at his lips.

Stu's preppy/mystic cool had begun to crack. He was unshaven, and blond-gray flecks dappled his face. He wore just a short-sleeved shirt, without the sweater. His scent was a mixture of sweat and expensive aftershave.

Still wary of surveillance, he turned and began to type. Standing behind him, I leaned down and read the screen over his shoulder. His message was uncharacteristically brief:

HAVE IT?

I took a deep breath. Then, reaching over Stu, I hit two keys to answer:

NO.

Stu looked up at me, clearly flustered. Behind his wire rims, his blue eyes blinked disconcertedly. Since he did not move to "communicate" more, I took the lead.

LITTLE BOBBY'S DEAD. SO'S HIS GIRLFRIEND. COPS WILL THINK THAT IT WAS GANGS. BUT SOME GOON GOT MY MOVIE. AND WHATEVER IT WAS OF YOURS LITTLE BOBBY STOOL.

My fingers had pressed too hard, causing an embarrassing mistake on the last word: *stole*. Stu didn't even notice. He was too busy standing up and grabbing me.

It was a move not of anger but of desperation. Pulling me by my shirtfront, Stu stared right into my face, with the terrified look of someone who was told he was a terminal case.

Did he wish me to hug him? Stu was that kind of guy. But I only pulled back, to get out of his grasp. I felt sorrier for silly Bobby, his disloyal new girlfriend, even for the king of fools, Ben Williams. There was a long list before I got to Stu.

By now, I had seen murdered people. But I had never seen anyone actually killed. After I called the cops—anonymously, from a pay phone—I had cried in the cab coming there. Did other detectives do that? I didn't care.

I placed on his desk the two envelopes full of money and the third holding the gun. Then I merely shrugged, the universal language for *sorry*.

As I passed through the gallery again, I looked at the photos for a final time. The picture most visible was that of a patient who, despite extreme measures, had not pulled through. He was being covered by a sheet.

"What do you mean, humming?" Jeanine asked me.

"The guy who came in and killed Little Bobby," I answered, "who wanted the Filofax, who took the movie."

"Who lived in the house that Jack built?"

I was too busy packing to respond to Jeanine's little joke.

"He was humming something, and I can't get it out of my head."

There was a long pause as I glanced at the clock. Rosie's money had bought me a last-minute flight, the most expensive kind there is.

"Why does that matter?" Jeanine asked me.

"Because it may lead me to *Ambersons*."

There was more silence. I could tell Jeanine thought it had been a long day for me. Even though it had been, I wasn't raving.

"Look," I said, "I'll tell you when I get there."

"Are you coming into Kennedy or Newark?"

"Neither. I'm coming into Logan. And so are you."

Jeanine's tone now became gentle and slightly cautious, as if she were dealing with the insane.

"But, Roy . . . isn't that in Boston?"

"Yes."

Maybe Stu's paranoia had infected me: I did not say what else I was thinking. I packed the Filofax neatly inside a hotel towel.

Congressman Webby Slicone was in Boston, too.

PART 5
BOSTON

WE BEGAN IN CAMBRIDGE, ACTUALLY. JEANINE AND I MET IN THE HYATT Hotel there, the place where parents of Harvard students stay. It had an open lobby with circular floors, and in the bar, we looked up and down at them and felt we were in the middle of a well-heeled honeycomb.

I did, anyway. Jeanine had other thoughts.

"I keep thinking of falling off," she said. "Hopping up and leaning on the railing, very casually. Then one false move, and—whoops!"

"That'll do," I said. "I thought I would spring for a little luxury— courtesy of Rosie, of course—and now all I can think of is your splattered body a dozen floors down."

"How about your own?" she said. "It could happen to you, just as easily."

It sounded like a threat. Jeanine may have still been steamed at me about Barcelona or just in a morbid mood. She seemed almost vindictively badly dressed—her French *Seven Year-Itch* T-shirt over sweatpants—and her appearance caused stares in a hotel favored by rich Moms and Dads.

This made me feel protective of her, as well as annoyed. I thought I better cut to the chase.

"Look," I said, "wait here."

I stood and approached the aging singer at the bar piano. After he finished his sincere rendition of the song from *Titanic*, I slipped five dollars into his brandy snifter and requested a tune.

When I returned to the table, Jeanine was crankily pressing a maraschino cherry flat with her thumb.

"Visual aids?" she said.

"*Audio*visual."

Before I could finish my word, the piano music began. The singer poured his heart and soul into a bubblegum song of the late Sixties.

One and one
They still make two.
One of me
Needs one of you.
Just one alone
Is oh so sad.
You don't need school
To learn to add.
The new math!
The new math!
The new math!
It's all about love.

Jeanine started to comically sing along, moving her head back and forth, in a parody of "digging it." With a face, I signaled that I understood her "subtle" rib.

"Just bear with me, okay?" I said.

Then the song ended, to my lonely applause.

"It was awful then, and it's awful now," she said.

"But who sang it?"

"The DreamDates, of course."

"And who were the DreamDates?"

There was no point in playing trivia with Jeanine, though pop music ranked below movies and TV in our hierarchy.

Jeanine frowned, as if to ask, what was I getting at. "Webby Slicone and June Faber."

"Well, that's why we're here."

I had kept the Filofax close since leaving L.A. It was still on me, wedged in the inside pocket of the jacket on loan from Annie Chin. Now I opened my coat and flashed the leather-bound object, discreetly.

"Let's just say I've got Webby in my pocket," I said.

"You mean, like big business does?"

"Funny."

Jeanine was referring to the politics of the Republican Congressman from Massachusetts. After the breakup of the DreamDates—and the death of his partner and wife, June, in a drunken car crash—Webby had directed all his energy into business. Impressed by his success, captains of industry backed the diminutive charmer's run for office in his old home state. Only a celebrity—albeit a flea-bitten relic of the Sixties—could have defeated a Democrat in Kennedy country, and that was what Webby had done.

But he had not left all of his old L.A. pals behind. Or all of his L.A. habits.

"Webby's name is in Stu Drayton's Filofax," I said.

The piano player started atrociously tinkling "Born in the U.S.A." Jeanine took a long time to nod. Then she came a bit more to attention.

"I see. So you think—"

"That the guy in the ski mask worked for Webby. He came after Little Bobby for it, after the boy was stupid enough to call him and attempt extortion. Webby's name in that Filofax wouldn't look so good in an election year."

"And you base this idea entirely on a tune that a hitman was humming?"

"Well, not entirely. But sort of."

"So Webby's got *Ambersons*," she said, "and you've got the Filofax."

I nodded. The experience in L.A. had made me angry, and so less shy about suggesting something this outlandish. It was my first pure, detective-like deduction, and I was proud of it. Still, I waited for her response, with trepidation.

Then Jeanine said what she said so often now.

"I guess it makes as much sense as anything else."

I grinned, glad to hear it.

"But I've got just one more question," she said.

"What's that?"

"Why are we in Boston? Doesn't our nation's business get done in D.C.?"

"Well," I said, "it *is* October. Webby's finally coming home, to campaign."

Jeanine nodded. I could see her old feelings for me—whatever they might have been—resurfacing. Spitting gently into a napkin, she wiped off some of the screwdriver that was left on my lips. It had been my attempt at cocktails.

"Why do so many celebrities become right-wing when they go into politics?" she wondered. "Reagan, of course. George Murphy. And that Gopher guy from *Love Boat*—"

"Well, not Miss Hathaway from *The Beverly Hillbillies*—"

"Who lost."

"Right. Sorry, but I don't know the answer."

"Look," she said then, "I've only got two days off from the Film Forum."

"That shouldn't be a problem."

I proceeded to explain. Before I left L.A., I had managed to get myself a little closer to the world of Webby.

A former trivial man, Taylor Weinrod now worked in the sphere of cable television. Taylor was head of acquisitions for Landers Classic Movies, a service devoted to twenty-four-hour golden-age entertainment. Tan and buff, in a suit and tie, with that new combed-forward-balding-guy haircut, he had been appalled to find me sitting in the waiting room of LCM's plush Century City digs.

As if to keep anyone from noticing me, he hustled me into his office pronto.

"Roy!" he said. "Please—please—please come in!"

He cautiously shut the door, very firmly. I had intentionally left my good clothes at the hotel. Looking like an aging loser, I had placed my sneakered foot onto his fancy glass table. He carefully moved aside a framed picture of his wife and son.

"Chic doings," I said, looking around. "It's a long way from Jersey City, right?"

Taylor had once run a movie memorabilia store in that affordable location. Now, smiling unhappily at the memory, he placed his hands nervously beneath his expensive suspenders.

"Well," he said, only half-kidding, "I wouldn't say that too loudly around here."

"Why," I said, "would an alarm go off?"

Taylor did not respond. He just stood, turned, and closed his window blinds, ostensibly to block the sun. But I think he feared *anyone's* view of me, this ghost of trivia past.

He explained, condescendingly, "This *is* a place of business."

I nodded. "I know. That's why I'm here."

Taylor's face twitched a little. "What do you mean?"

"I've been looking to get out of what I'm doing. Climb the ladder a little. You know, you're my role model."

I could see Taylor was complimented. But his need to protect his lifestyle took precedence even over his vanity.

"What did you have in mind, exactly?" he asked, concerned.

"Doing what you're doing. I know a lot about movies, of course. And I'd like to make a lot of money. So, you know," I chuckled, "where do I sign?"

Taylor's eyes widened a bit in disbelief.

"It's not that easy," he said.

"Well, I *know* that. I'm willing to work my way up. But when you start out, they say it's who you know. And I realized—I know you."

Taylor stacked some papers, almost touched, but more unnerved. Then his fingers twiddled on his desk, made of beautiful blond wood.

"There's really nothing that I can—"

"The health insurance is really the attractive part," I said. "I bet you're protected up the wazoo."

I wasn't lying about that; if I had a heart attack tomorrow, there would be no way to pay. But it was my first moment of sincerity.

Sweat was forming on Taylor's upper lip. "As I say, there's really nothing I can . . ."

I was staring at Taylor as innocently as a newborn babe. Maybe I tweaked what remained of his conscience. But I really think he just wanted to get rid of me—and all those trivial memories—quick.

"Look—do you have a résumé?"

"Is that important?"

I was really laying on the fella-on-the-fringe routine. Laughing, Taylor now addressed a savvy, unseen audience.

"Well, it might help!"

"Okay, okay, résumé, that's something I should"—I pulled out a pen and made a note on the back of my hand—" 'Make a résumé,' that's a good thing to . . ."

"Because, without that"—Taylor was staring at that hip crowd only he could see—"there's really nothing *anyone* can—"

"Well, okay, then let's scale it down," I said definitively. "I mean, it doesn't even have to be in the office. It could be something . . . just, well, in the general vicinity."

"The general vicinity."

"Yes."

I saw an idea forming inside Taylor's blue-colored contacts.

Ed Landers was the multimillionaire media mogul who owned Landers Classic Movies, as well as many other stations, sports teams, and high-tech firms. He was heavily involved in Republican politics, and notorious for illegally leaning on his employees to donate both time and money to his favorite candidates. Objections to this occasionally bubbled up, then subsided. Working for Landers was so coveted, and Landers owned so many things.

"Surely," I said, "Ed Landers has such an empire that there must be something that—"

"Well, now that you mention it, there is."

Taylor had said it with relish, as if there were an opening to carry live grenades in your mouth and I was the man for the job.

"Great," I said. "Great."

"Now, it's not working for LCM proper," he said.

"That's okay," I answered eagerly.

"But it's the kind of thing that will give you brownie points with Ed Landers."

"Brownie points with Ed," I said. "Those are good."

"Do you mind"—and here Taylor pretended to take my needs into account—"traveling?"

"Traveling is okay. Except, well—"

"It'll be on the company, don't worry."

"That's what I was wondering."

Taylor started pulling out forms that probably had nothing to do with anything.

"You'll just have to write down where you can be reached. Are you busy this weekend?"

I thought for a second. Then I read the back of my other hand. "Nope. I'm free!"

"Good."

Taylor passed me the forms and showed me where to write. He smiled, as if killing several birds with one stone, placing a feather in his cap, and all those other things that ambitious people thought important.

"This might work out," he said, "after all."

Back in Cambridge, I paused and took a final sip of my OJ and vodka. As the live bar Muzak shifted to Alanis Morissette, Jeanine looked at me, aghast.

"What's the matter?" I said. "You mind wearing a funny hat? I seem to remember seeing you in one now and then."

"No—but what if someone sees us?" she said. "Handing out flyers for Webby Slicone?"

"It's all for a good cause. And not a political one. It's for *Ambersons*."

"You couldn't have just *called* Webby's numbers in the Filofax?"

It was my turn to make a *no kidding* face. "They've all been disconnected. Of course."

Jeanine sighed deeply, trying to find a comfort level.

"Well, I'm not cheering for him," she said.

"Suit yourself."

Jeanine just sat back then. Beneath the table, her foot played lightly and, as before Barcelona, ambiguously, with the hem of my pants.

"Now I see," she said, getting used to it. "Boston. It all adds up."

"Yeah." I nodded happily, pleased with myself. "Like the new math."

NO ONE ON EARTH SUPPORTED WEBBY SLICONE.

Maybe it just felt that way. Certainly none of the indifferent people gathered the next morning at Faneuil Hall were actually *for* him. Everyone was either someone's friend or someone's kid, an aspiring actor or, as in my case, a fobbed-off job seeker. Whoever would be paid to fill the crowd at Boston's waterfront tourist site, that's who our motley crew was, huddled over cool coffee and stale-as-cracker crullers.

"Only the best for us," Jeanine muttered, adjusting her funny hat.

The campaign workers knew that we were fake enthusiasts, but they still spoke to us sincerely of Webby's qualities, as if any cynicism might expose the waste of their efforts and their lives.

But, after all, these were people willing to kill to see this man re-elected.

"There's that handsome devil," one woman worker said, without irony, pointing to a giant photo of Webby that loomed over the square.

A stage had been erected on the cobblestones, beneath the photo and a billowing banner. Like the buttons we were given, it said WEBBY

SLICONE—HE'S PLAYING *OUR* SONG. Since everyone recruited was white, the *our* had an exclusionary feel, and the campaign people did nothing to dispel this idea.

"Stay out of the sun," one of them warned jocularly. "We don't want you any darker than you are."

Along with Jeanine and the others, I had also been given a straw boater to wear, and a little American flag. It was not the most dignified way to conduct—I hoped, to end—my investigation. But it would bring me within a handshake of the congressman, whose future now rested inside my jacket pocket. Unlike an assassin, with a simple exchange, I meant to *save* his life.

There had been a close call when we were patted down, upon arrival. But the security people were on the lookout for guns and not modern, leather-bound address books. Had Webby informed only one favorite henchman of its existence? I didn't know.

Someone else took hold of my arm then, with, as ever, an intention less clear than a bodyguard's.

"See him?" Jeanine asked.

I had been looking closely at the security detail, trying to identify—and avoid—the man in the mask who had shot Little Bobby and let me live. But either pin-striped suits are all the same, or the guy had one ensemble for killing and another for everyday; I couldn't pick him out.

" 'Does this ski mask smell funny to you?' " Jeanine imitated a sneaky technique. " 'Here, try it on, okay?' "

"Good idea," I said sourly.

We were given our final instructions now. Ringing the stage, we were told to applaud, loudly, for our leader, when he arrived to the strains of "May the Best Man Win," another DreamDate stinkeroo.

I thought of Lewis Milestone's film, *The North Star,* a 1940s drama written by Lillian Hellman, extolling the efforts of the Russians in World War II. After the war, it was considered pro-Red, cut, and retitled *Armored Attack.*

"Okay, people," the same earnest woman said. "When he shows up, let Webby know you love him!"

Clearly, this person did, as might anyone drawn to short men with Seventies-style mustaches, comb-over haircuts, and right-wing views.

"Uh-oh," Jeanine said, next to me. "There he is. Be still my heart."

I looked up at the stage. Between two goons, Webby had arrived, all gussied up for his re-election run. His face was remarkably tan, given the cloudy New England fall. His shedding pate was covered by what I assumed were new hairplugs. The mustache was trimmed to a more contemporary length, at least 1984. Even his height, helped by shoe lifts, had increased. Despite all this, he still looked his own age, about sixty.

More and more people now milled in the vicinity, though most were shoppers at the mall stores around us. Piped-in music from loudspeakers began blaring the whole DreamDates canon, building to the song that would be his walk-on cue.

Then, with his one other top-ten hit in the air, Webby waved at the crowd. Since we had only been paid half so far, we cheered back heartily. Our tiny flags waved. Our straw boaters flew, as if it were a barbershop quartet graduation. Around us, tourists, patrons, and brunch eaters pointed with curiosity at a man who had become a celebrity twice, in two different professions.

"I'd yell his opponent's name," Jeanine called to me, "if I knew what it was!"

I did not listen to Webby's speech, which touched on lower taxes, character in government, and late-term abortions—with added show biz jokes and references. I only made sure that, Jeanine in tow, I inched as close to the stage as I could.

"My dream of capital punishment," went Webby's spiel, "is to allow survivors to kill the criminals who killed their loved ones! We shouldn't depend on the government for everything!"

Here we had been told to chant, "Pull the switch! Pull the switch!" his other campaign slogan, which was coupled on a poster with a picture of a voting booth lever.

When Webby had finished—to quieter acclaim, our lunchtime approaching—music recommenced, this time a medley of "The New

Math" and "The Battle Hymn of the Republic." Stepping gingerly on his new heels, the Congressman made his way downstairs into the crowd.

Bodyguard beside him, sardined among us, he began pumping hands, those of his own workers, those of we temporary employees. He tickled a baby's tummy. He got a kiss on his cheek. I admired Webby's ebullience despite his new woes; he clearly loved being famous.

Did he regret buying drugs from Stu Drayton? Did he already have his spin in place if the story blew? Had he ever seen *The Magnificent Ambersons*? I seemed to remember the DreamDates on a Sixties Dean Martin roast with Orson Welles, then in his buffoon phase. I had to check that one out with Jeanine.

"Hey! Thanks for your support!"

Suddenly, Webby was right in front of me.

HIS FACE-LIFT TAUT, HE WAS STILL SMILING BROADLY, AS HE HAD AT THE person before. My heart pounding, I tried to recall the moves I had rehearsed in my head: was it whisper, then open coat? Or was it open coat, then whisper? I would never be a performer like Webby, unflappable in the face of potential disaster.

My hand shaking, I made a move toward my inside pocket, my fingertips touching leather. At the same time, I leaned in close, to catch his ear. But my movements were awkward and incoherent.

Misleading, too. As soon as Webby's bodyguard saw me move toward a concealed area of my clothes, he pulled Webby back, the candidate's smile fading. The goon immediately made Webby cut through the crowd, to greet other people, his only inelegant action of the day. Then he whispered words of his own, into the ear of the congressman. Startled, Webby looked over and stared, for one long minute, into my eyes.

I was already edging out of the crowd. The last thing I needed was to be arrested for threatening a candidate. I would never get out of the clutches of the cops then. While I was stuck in the system, who knew what Webby would do with the bag, which contained what he did not want, just an old movie?

"Roy—"

Jeanine was already out of my sight, her one word wan and distant, her very existence a luxury to consider. I dipped in and out of the group around me, gunning for the daylight just yards away, at the front of the square.

When I broke free of it, my head a blur of flags and faces, I walked as quickly and inconspicuously as possible. Never looking back, I headed for the main road, on which cars were whizzing back and forth.

There was no way to cross, and nowhere else to go. I could have walked back to the square and disappeared into a store. But it was a mini-mall, like New York City's South Street Seaport, and the stores were scaled-down versions of bigger outlets, with only one front door. So instead, impulsively, I ran for a bus that was now passing by and hissing to a halt.

I did not know where it was headed, did not know Boston at all. But I doled out whatever change I had, which eventually caused an approving bell to ring.

Only a mother, a child, and a blind guy had followed me on. My feet nearly squishing with sweat, I took a seat in the back. Through the window I saw two security agents, walkie-talkies at their mouths and ears, search around the edges of the square. Then I watched the red, white, and blue of Webby's rally drift into the distance behind me. I heard "Pull the switch!" and the final notes of a DreamDates song pipe faintly into the past.

I thought of the end of *The Graduate*, with Dustin Hoffman and Katharine Ross escaping on the bus. The part of Mrs. Robinson— played by Anne Bancroft—had originally been offered to Doris Day, as a satiric contrast to her virginal roles. Day, however, had declined.

In the few seconds of peace I now found, I considered one question: When our eyes had met for that one moment, had Webby seemed to know my face? I wasn't sure. And I didn't know what any answer might mean.

The bus seemed to be going into midtown. My brilliant plan was to ride until I recognized a T-stop, take the subway back to Cambridge, and hope that Jeanine would meet me at the hotel.

I pressed for a stop at the base of Beacon Hill.

Emerging at Charles Street, I felt more calm among the browsers and buyers on the elegant, unpretentious block. There was just one thing that caused me new concern.

The blind guy who got on had exited with me.

Ordinarily, this would not have meant a thing. But today, I felt new dread as I snapped my head around to see him.

Walking with a cane, wearing dark glasses, he was speaking into a tiny cell phone.

On any other day, it would have seemed a typical urban accessory and action. Today, I picked up my pace and took a fast right off the main street.

To my horror, he followed.

I looked up what seemed a massive mountain, leading to ritzy Beacon Hill brownstones. Avoiding the skinny sidewalk, I used the center of the street. Picturesquely cobbled, it crunched beneath my feet as my straining legs climbed.

I heard the blind man tapping right behind me.

"Excuse me!" he called faintly. "Excuse me!"

Was he a bodyguard? A Boston undercover cop? Or merely looking for directions? Whatever, he was in better shape than I was; soon he was beside me, panting not at all.

"Excuse me," he said, with a trace of a local accent. "Were you just at the Webby Slicone rally?"

"I, uh . . ." Should I say I was? Or deny everything? Maybe he was just a right-wing blind gay guy seeking a like-minded man. "Yes, I, uh, was."

"Really. Well, maybe you wouldn't mind telling me what you've got in your coat."

The man's own blazer drifted intentionally from his hip. And I saw a gun, lodged securely in its holster.

If I gave up the Filofax now, I would have nothing to barter with, no hope of progress, and no way to get *Ambersons* back from Webby. The road from Alan Gilbert's apartment to Ben Williams's hideaway to Erendira's bed would end here, in shameful failure, on a Boston street.

"What do you mean?" I said. "It's nothing."

There was a very brief silence. Then, with one swift kick, the blind man knocked both of my legs out from under me. My face hit the street stones, and he locked me on the ground, my right arm bent backward, his hand pushed inside and fishing in my jacket. His dark glasses were hanging off, held by a chain around his neck. His eyes looked fine.

"Just don't move," he said, "dumb-ass."

I looked up: A car was heading right at us, coming down the giant hill. I squinted into the daylight reflected off its chrome, and its wheels rumbled deafeningly on the street beneath my cheek.

With one shriek of brakes, it veered around us, wanting no trouble, and went on its way.

Then the man pulled it out, my latest and last ace in the hole. In his haste, the leather covering slid away and landed near my nose. Was it all Webby wanted? Would the man let me go now or quietly, surreptitiously, shoot? There was a chance I would get nothing *and* get killed, a double doom.

He did neither. The man just relaxed his grip on me and pulled away, and let me up.

"Sorry," he said. "But you can never be too careful."

He handed the Filofax back to me, even bending to retrieve its cover as a final courtesy. Then he replaced his phony shades.

"There are a lot of nuts around."

"SO CLOSE, YET SO FAR," I SAID, BANDAGING MY CHIN. "WASN'T THAT A DreamDates song, too?"

"It was 'Close but No Cigar,'" Jeanine corrected me. "It sucked, as well."

I was having trouble dressing my wound in the little mirror on the back of my sun visor. We were in a rental car, heading out of Boston proper, Jeanine swerving in and out of scrapes, as usual.

She had thought it best that we leave: No sense courting more trouble. Also—and I'd forgotten this in my disastrous rush to approach Webby—we had another place to stay. Or, to be more exact now, to hide.

Claude and Alice Kripp were those rarest of trivial characters: a happily married couple. They taught film at Wellesley College, and kept a small and pleasant house in the suburb nearby. Post-hippies, they had met at an alternative Boston paper in the Seventies and been inseparable ever since. Their domestic bliss—which included, shockingly, a child—was looked upon with envy by some trivial folk. Despite this, their example had not been followed; they were still curiosities, not trendsetters.

"They remind me of Barbra Streisand," Jeanine said, our tires shrieking.

"They do?" I said. "How?"

"Well, Barbra was a unique kind of female star in the late Sixties."

"Right. Like Dustin Hoffman."

"Exactly. Both were ethnic, not conventionally good-looking. Yet how many men followed in Dusty's footsteps?"

"Everybody from Pacino to Richard Dreyfuss to De Niro."

"Right. And how many women followed in hers?"

"Debra Winger, maybe. And that was years later."

"That's my point. Claude and Alice, like Barbra, are still two of a kind."

"But the Streisand thing is maybe just the difference between what men and women want. I don't think that Claude and Alice are."

Jeanine looked completely away from the road then, at me.

"Oh, no?" she said.

Suddenly, I saw where this conversation was headed, and I tried to divert its direction as hastily as Jeanine took her next turn.

"Also, you could say that George Segal was even earlier," I said. "Before Hoffman. As a Jewish star."

Jeanine did not reply. So, lamely, I continued the conversation for her.

"Except that Segal had lightened his hair. Like Danny Kaye did in the Forties."

This received no answer, either. I made a last-ditch attempt at diversion, pleading for sympathy.

"The whole side of my head aches," I said. "From where I hit the dirt."

But, not even bothering to signal, Jeanine was taking an exit off the highway. Within seconds, we saw the Kripp house before us, and our treacherous discussion was at an end.

Claude and Alice's home was almost like the others on the unprepossessing block. Yet its overgrown lawn and rickety old station wagon in the driveway implied there were different kinds of people inside. The inhabitants were more impoverished—or maybe just more absentminded—than their neighbors.

But they were warmer, too. As soon as Jeanine cut the motor of our Mazda, Alice Kripp came running from the front door, her arms outstretched, her golden retriever, Gilda, beside her.

Gilda, of course, was named for the movie starring Rita Hayworth in the title role. Several shots in the film—in one, where Rita dares bar patrons to unzip her dress during her "Put the Blame on Mame" number—were clipped for initial runs, then later restored.

Surprised, I realized that anxiety was provoking trivial thoughts. Yet I was not being shot at, pursued on motorcycle, or beaten by a bodyguard. It was a smaller, domestic danger, one represented by the warm hug now being given by Alice, and gratefully reciprocated by Jeanine.

For the first time, I noticed that Jeanine was better dressed than before, her T-shirt and sweatpants exchanged for a fetching little jumper. Perhaps her feelings about me had been resolved, provoked by the Erendira scare. Or else she had never really been conflicted in the first place. Some mysteries existed because people created them intentionally, I thought, and I meant myself.

"Roy!" Alice was saying now. "Get out of the car and come on in!"

I did so, not sure if I were to be in hiding now or exposed to new threats. Arm around Alice, Jeanine went happily up the walkway, the dog wagging up the rear.

I couldn't help it, two issues still nagged. The "blind" peace officer who decked me—obviously working undercover for Webby—had only been looking for a gun. So no one had informed him about a Filofax. *Had* the L.A. gunman really been working for Webby? Or had I been totally mistaken?

The other thing involved the Kripps. As I got inside, patted their dog, pumped the hand of Claude, and received a kiss from Alice, I wondered if they could offer me more than just a place to sleep.

The Kripps were advisers to the American Film Preservation Committee, set up by Congress to restore U.S. movies. Each year or so, they designated more pictures as worthy of being saved, and money was allotted to restore them.

Congressman Webby Slicone was their stumbling block.

It wasn't the project to which he objected, it was some of the films. Anything remotely sexy or violent, anything R-rated—anything, in other words, recent—was rejected by Webby as unworthy, as a sop to his far-right followers.

This surprised some; Webby had, after all, come from "the arts" and should have been sympathetic. But I knew that those days were over and, besides, Webby had always been more interested in money than in the DreamDates' songs. After all, no one could really be proud of "The New Math."

Could Claude and Alice help me get to Webby without my telling them about *The Magnificent Ambersons*? I still didn't trust other trivial people.

But the Kripps were now making it hard to think about any business, nefarious or otherwise. Though only in their mid-forties, they had a funky parental air that immediately put one at ease or on edge, depending on one's relationship with one's parents. (The less said about mine, the better.)

Claude was burly and bearded, with crazy, flyaway hair, and a cherubic face, most of which was cheeks. Alice was his distaff equal, her full face ruddy and cute, with a button nose and cheery, relaxed blue eyes. She, too, was heavy in a hearty and happy way.

I would have felt like crawling into their laps if I had not been planning on using their contacts, while revealing as little information of my own as possible.

"Sit down," Claude said, lighting a cigar. "Our home is yours. Don't hesitate to make yourself comfortable."

Their son was six, and a scruffy, freckled, perfect lad he was. All arms and legs, he was presently placing two action figures in mortal combat against each other on the living room rug. I had not remembered his name or perhaps had just, for my own purposes, blocked it out.

"Orson," his mother said to him, "do you remember Jeanine and Roy?"

He only remembered Jeanine.

The house—as cluttered and informal on the inside as out—smelled of old clothes, coffee, and the broiled chicken dinner that was presently cooking. Books, newspapers, and videos were everywhere, yet the squalor seemed happily domestic and not unhappily desperate. It was amazing what the addition of a spouse—and, of course, a child—could do to the trivial-person atmosphere.

Jeanine was already busy in the kitchen with Alice. They could be heard trading information about recipes that I had no idea Jeanine had. This left me alone in the living room with Claude, the dog, and, beneath our feet, the whirring, hissing form of Orson.

I could tell that Claude was looking at my bruised-up face, but he was too polite to mention it.

"So," he said, "which way did you take to get here?"

The question took me aback. I was about to answer, "Well, through Hollywood, then into Spain, then back to L.A., then here," but I realized that he meant which highway, in the usual manner of suburban men. I could only answer, "Uh, Jeanine would know. I don't, uh, drive."

This did not ruffle Claude, who was, amazingly, a good host in addition to being a trivia man specializing in film noir. He chuckled appreciatively.

"Well, I guess it's a better season in New York than in Boston, ay?"

Now it was even stranger: weather. Well, who couldn't discuss that?

"Yes," I answered lamely, "it's been a beautiful fall."

Claude guffawed, pleasantly, at my misunderstanding.

"I meant that your Yanks are really tearing it up."

My God, I realized to my horror, it was *sports!* That kind of trivia existed in another universe from mine altogether. I did not know anyone from that sphere, although I had heard that baseball statistics closed as many eyes at night as Oscar facts did mine.

Here was a trivia man who had room in his head—and in his home, evidenced by the different kinds of books around—for other interests, small talk, a cigar, and a son! Looking at Claude with a combination of awe and fear, I was unable to answer anything other than, "I don't, uh, follow sports."

My non-response still did not deter Claude, who merely kept smiling good-naturedly. His son, however, began to smell a scary creep; subtlely, Orson moved his battling figures from the floor around my chair to the space near his father's feet, as if for safety.

I remembered the end of *The Heartbreak Kid*, in which Charles Grodin sits with discomfort amidst children at his own wedding, the one he had destroyed his first marriage to have. The original ending had him hitting on the mother of his bride, Cybill Shepherd, to imply his constantly restless nature. After unhappy previews, it was cut.

"Do you smoke?" Claude asked.

I was starting to sweat now. I recalled the original ending of *Where's Poppa?*, in which George Segal—that ethnic pioneer—hits the sack with his own, senile mother, Ruth Gordon, who thinks he is her husband. In the released version, he only drops her off at an old folks' home.

"Close," I said, trying for humor, "but no cigar."

This joke was a lucky one. Claude—who knew music, too, and pop music at that!—came back with, "I think you owe our friend Webby a royalty. And believe me, knowing Webby, he'll collect!"

I laughed, too, and gratefully. This was my chance: an ideal opportunity to swerve the topic away from general interest—and normal life—to my single-minded pursuit.

"So, how often do you two meet with Webby?" I asked.

"You make it sound like we all play bridge, or something," Claude chortled. "There are lots of people on the panel, and we just make our report to him."

"And he generally shoots down whatever films Claude and I suggest," Alice added, re-entering the room. She was carrying a plate full of chicken, and Jeanine followed with salad and bread. Gilda, the dog, stood up and joined them.

"But we *have* arranged to meet with him," Claude said, "to lobby him, I should say, for certain films—while he's here in town."

"You *have?*" I said, my voice breaking.

But that was the end of the subject. It was time for us all to eat.

"Why, what a feast," Claude said, rising to take plates and help.

"Yes," I said, trying to approximate normalcy. "You, uh, really shouldn't have."

"Are you kidding?" Alice said congenially. "How often do we get to see old friends?"

Everyone agreed with this, sincerely. Then we all took our seats at the table, Orson avoiding the chair beside me and choosing the one next to Jeanine. As I opened my mouth to continue my discussion, I saw Alice and Claude join hands.

"Claude, honey," Mrs. Kripp said, "will you say grace?"

The trivial firsts just kept on coming! Shaken, I felt Jeanine take my hand, her head bowed, with real solemnity. My other hand was held by Alice as her husband murmured thanks.

"For good food, health, and fine company."

Everyone chimed in with "Amen," and I came in a moment late, so I said it by myself. This gave the impression of unselfconscious spirituality, and Alice smiled at me beneficently, moved.

"Now, let's dig in," Claude said.

Jeanine helped little Orson—who had brought an action figure with him to the table—cut his meat. She spoke to him in a gentle and whimsical tone I had never heard from her before. Then my attention was diverted to the beverage bottle that sat before him.

To my shock, I saw that it was Fizz.

I reached over to examine it and, as my fingers grazed the bottle, Orson grabbed it back, as if my touch would taint it.

"That's mine!" he said.

Slightly frightened by his hostility, I instead addressed my question to his mother.

"What is that stuff, anyway?" I tried to sound casual.

"Oh, some trial giveaway at school," Alice said. "Apparently it's very popular in Europe. They're trying to bring it to America. Would you like some?"

"Oh, no," I said quickly. "That's really all right. I was . . . just curious."

As Orson turned and sought to shield his drink from me, I saw a tiny figure on the Fizz label. Astride her bike, hair blowing wildly in the wind, a minuscule Erendira appeared only inches away.

A slight shudder went through me as I swallowed the—delicious, by the way—chicken. Would Erendira actually be in the country now? Had Jorge allowed her to leave Spain, or had she broken off with him? The need to retrieve *Ambersons* from Webby suddenly seemed an even more pressing concern.

Yet there seemed no way to re-introduce the subject. Jeanine was either discussing children's eating habits with Alice and Claude—who were very interested—or else bending to "battle" Orson's figure with a chicken leg.

The best I could do was venture into typical trivia territory, hoping to steer the talk back to where it was at least recognizable to me.

"Well, you know what John Huston said about kids, when he was directing *Annie* . . ." I began.

But no one picked up on my segue. There was just as much indifference as there might have been at any other table, as indeed there had been at the police station so long before. I felt my left leg begin to vibrate agitatedly beneath the table, causing Jeanine's plate to rattle a bit beside mine.

She reached over and, with a soothing touch of my arm, said, "Relax. Just for tonight, okay?"

I tried to do as she suggested, just to keep my leg from kicking. For a minute, I banished any thought of trivia, even any idea of *Ambersons*, and tried to concentrate only on the words said around me.

And I found that there was a kind of peace to it. They talked of politics—Webby wasn't mentioned—of home repair, and current academic issues at the college. We ate dessert—a luscious mocha layer cake, by the way—and drank an exotic decaf coffee.

"Care for an after-dinner drink?" Claude asked.

I did.

My mind swirling from the very mild liqueur, I retired to the living room with the others. In the corner, Orson colored by himself. Despite the stacks of videos everywhere, we played Scrabble, and the TV was never turned on.

Alice won, Claude was a close second, and Jeanine a surprisingly strong third. I didn't even break double-digits, and everyone was polite enough not to laugh.

Then it was time for bed.

Claude "airplaned" Orson up the stairs, the boy laughing and squealing, Alice calling "Be careful!" but not really seeming afraid. I ascended the stairs after them, Jeanine walking arm in arm with Alice in my wake.

"I made up two rooms," Alice said, carefully but also kind of coyly. "Is that all right?"

Jeanine gave me a quick glance, and I looked back at her, the drink making me mute. Having relinquished the controls I usually applied in my head, I now had no idea what to do or say. So I left it up to her.

"Two rooms," she said, "yes."

Claude and Alice discreetly went to bed, whispering, "Sweet dreams" to us both. Then Jeanine wavered in my doorway for a while.

"Well," she said then, "that was a lovely evening."

She did not say it casually. She said it wistfully, as if she had witnessed something attainable but ever out of reach. Then she stared at me directly, and I could only look away.

I still restrained myself from introducing any side issues, from asking why Webby had looked at my face as he had, or wondering if the Kripps would help me out, certainly from any utterance about Erendira. And I found that, far from making things harder, it made them easier.

Had everything always been an avoidance? Was even finding *The Magnificent Ambersons* an excuse? By fitting films together, searching for lost pieces, unearthing treasures, was I—were all trivial people—trying to repaint a picture that was missing something crucial? Was it standing in the doorway before me now?

I decided to find out. Taking Jeanine by surprise—indeed turning her back, for she had turned to go—I said, "Why don't you close the door?"

Her brow wrinkled, as if she were about to take offense.

"I mean," I said, "after you, you know, come in."

The jumper had big buttons on the shoulders, like a child's outfit. But it did not make Jeanine seem anything other than adult. Indeed, tonight she didn't seem a mixture of the elderly and the adolescent. She was her own age, which, come to think of it, was not very far from my own.

"My horoscope didn't predict this," she whispered as I undid the buttons and then the straps.

"Jeez," I said, teasing her. "Maybe that stuff isn't true, then."

She hit me a little, comically. Then, deadly serious, she nuzzled at my neck, kissed and bit my lips, and filled my mouth with her tongue.

The jumper fell to her feet, was kicked gently away. I pulled up the turtleneck beneath it, bunching it at her large breasts, and pulled her close. Jeanine did the rest of the work to remove it, and her mismatched underwear—black bra, white panties—made me feel more aroused, and newly close to her. She was so real.

"Forgive me," I whispered, "if I don't last too long."

"Okay," she whispered back, "I'll try to come real fast."

We laughed as much as we moaned. For all the talking we had done, all the movies we had discussed, all the spats we had had, we had never said these kinds of words before.

The first time, I did not, in fact, last long. But only the first time.

Not wanting to disturb anyone else, after many experiments, we found that the bed banged least with Jeanine on top, her back arched, her fingers curled in mine, her breasts shifting ever so slightly as she moved with excruciating slowness.

Afterward, we would have slept forever, had it not been for the sound of screams.

JUMPING INTO MY JEANS, I RUSHED INTO THE HALLWAY. THERE I SAW THREE disturbing sights, my eyes shifting from one to the other, like a crazy moving camera.

Alice stood on the second-floor landing, dressed in a nightgown, her head pitched back, her mouth wide open, shrieking like a banshee beckoning forces of revenge. In pajama bottoms, Claude lay in the center of the stairs, on his stomach, halfway down, his hand outstretched. Running out the front door was the hitman in the pin-striped suit, his face covered by the ski mask. And in his arms was little Orson, who moaned and murmured faintly, his mouth taped, his tied hands waving wildly above his head.

Panning swiftly to the right, I saw through Orson's open door. Its shelves of toys and books were toppled, as if having been hastily searched. Panning back downstairs, I saw the masked man stepping over stuff in the front-door vestibule, which had also been ransacked. Then he was gone.

I glanced back at Jeanine, standing in my doorway, clutching a sheet around herself. Her own eyes, unmoving, were staring straight at me and filled with fear.

Gilda, the dog, barked. But there was only one human being who was conscious, not screaming, and wearing pants.

Taking a deep breath, I raced past the frozen form of Alice and darted down the stairs. Dancing around the prone—I hoped, still breathing—body of her husband, I flew out the door, left open by the masked man in his haste.

I figured it was about three A.M. The neighborhood was dark, except for a single streetlight on the quiet block. The only sound was Alice's outraged-mother cry, which faded, and then ceased.

The man in the mask threw the boy on the backseat of a small black car, which had been parked in the Krippses' driveway. He was about to open the driver's door and get in.

Coming fast for him, my heart booming, I shouted, absurdly, "Hey!"

To my surprise, he turned. I had nothing more to say, of course. I just felt the same foolish, instinctive courage that overcame me whenever *Ambersons* was near. But tonight, was it to save the movie or the boy? I didn't know.

Even more absurdly, I said, "Let's go! Knock it off!"

I sounded like a neighbor scolding children fighting on my lawn. The man dismissed me with a turn back toward the door of the car.

He never made it. Sprinting to reach him, I grabbed at the left lapel of his three-piece suit and pulled.

The next second, I was blinded. The man had yanked one of those long, basement flashlights from the front seat and shone it in my eyes. Lost in a shock of white light, I felt his fist connecting with my gut.

I doubled over and hit the dirt, my second time down that day. When I looked up, the flashlight was off and, in the black, the man's foot—wearing a polished yuppie wingtip—was coming for my face.

Turning at the last second, I felt the impact solely in my bare shoulder. The shoe's sharp tip sunk in like a spike and turned me sharply to the side. But the shoe lingered there long enough for me to grab it, hold it, and—my fingers digging in—remove it.

I brought the shoe up like a tennis racket, a topspin backhand whipped into the masked man's face. He swiveled, once, grunting, as if insulted. Then, my arm still extended, he quickly grabbed my hand, which held the shoe, and pulled me forward.

My arm bent, I went dancing into him. There we stayed, my naked torso locked against his pin-striped chest, my elbow at his belt, like a kinky tango team. His breath blew pot and garlic on my face. With one hand, he pulled my hair back. Then, slowly, his grip of my wrist increased until I felt the bones about to break. At the same time, he pressed upon my bare foot with the shoe he still had on.

Such simple movements can cause such pain: pressing and pulling, bending and turning. He did not have a weapon and he did not need one. I dropped the other shoe, a joke I did not get until later.

"Hey . . . ," I whispered weakly now, "knock it off."

His foot lifting, his hand relaxing, he pushed me away, as if disgusted. I stumbled back, then fell upon the unmowed lawn. I heard a door slam, a boy moan, and an ignition turn.

But it was not just courage that possessed me at these strange times; it was energy. In a second, I was on my feet again and running beside the car as it took off.

A running board would have been nice, but I had something better: the boy. Through the window, Orson's terrified eyes locked onto mine. Then, raising his small, tied-up hands, he unrolled the back window just enough for me to push my fingers in and grab.

The car peeled out, and I held on to the window and so on to the car, my feet skidding on and off the door. Scrambling ingeniously, the boy then jimmied the lock. The door swung open and tipped to the side, with me on it.

The car careened around a corner, and the door tilted again toward closed. As it did, I tried to push my feet inside, onto the backseat floor, and so get in.

But like an angry dad, the masked man slapped at Orson from the front seat. The boy skittered away from him. Then, his own fingers near mine, the masked man pulled the window to shut the back door.

I yanked my feet out, just in time. My fingers came loose from the glass. I went into free-fall, as if pushed from a plane, onto another neighbor's lawn.

I heard the screeching wheels of the car as it disappeared into the night. Then, all I heard were suburb sounds: barking dogs, crickets, and someone else's car alarm.

"Well, it might have been me," I said, "or it might have been you."

"*Me?*"

"That bodyguard at the rally saw you with me, didn't he? And the 'blind' guy had already found *me*."

"I won't take the blame for this."

"Nobody's blaming you—but you could at least say I was right about Webby."

It was our first fight—and on such an unpleasant topic. It wasn't the most auspicious way to end our first night together, huddled as we were in the Krippses' kitchen, Jeanine in a borrowed blanket, me with bandages now practically filling my face. And it wasn't helped by Jeanine's implication that I was responsible, nor by the fact that I essentially—secretly—agreed.

I had not wanted the Kripps to call the cops, of course. But how could I have stopped them? The unconscious Claude needed emergency care, though he had just bumped his head on the stairs while trying to save his son, and had a mild concussion. Alice, on the other hand, was still hysterical, and tranquilized, she now slept, though fitfully, on the living room couch.

When they came, the cops found me noncommittal, but Jeanine wanted to tell them everything. I had to practically beg her not to, and, in the end, she made no mention of *The Magnificent Ambersons*, Webby Slicone, Erendira, Ben Williams, Gus Ziegler, Alan Gilbert, or anybody else. I could see that she hated me for convincing her or, more exactly, herself for agreeing. Maybe she felt that, immediately after sex, she had started knuckling under; what a love affair *this* was going to be!

"Well, at least let me tell the Kripps," she said. "It *is* their child, for God's sake."

"Please," I answered, "it's not a good idea."

"You know, Roy," she nearly spit at me now, "screw Orson Welles, and screw you."

I took her abuse. I couldn't tell Jeanine everything, either. I couldn't tell her that I wanted to handle this, that I felt I was the only one who could. Or that I really wanted to retrieve the boy, and not *Ambersons*. No actor, after all, had ever looked at me like that through a car window.

Maybe I could admit that to myself now, but not to a woman who might get the wrong ideas. That I was actually a decent man, for instance. Who knows what she would do with that kind of information? Like really love me, I mean.

"Look," I said, "just let me handle this."

"Okay, babe. Handle away."

Jeanine pointed to the living room, as if to say, *Start there*. I saw Claude seated on the couch near his sleeping wife, fondly holding the little action figure his son had left behind.

I approached him, very carefully, almost on tiptoes. His father feelings were more foreign to me than Catalan in Spain. I did not want to say the wrong thing.

"Claude?"

Slowly, he looked up. His face was even fuller now from being so swollen. All life had drained from his eyes, which seemed cried out, though I had not even heard him whimper. He managed a raspy, "Yes?"

"What did the cops say, when they left?"

"That they'd be in touch."

I nodded sadly. Then, choosing my words cautiously, not wanting to tip my hand, I told him, "Is there anything I can do to—"

But before I could continue, the phone rang.

I heard Jeanine cry out in the kitchen. I jumped myself. Claude took a deep breath, and his eyes blinked several times, as if awakening. But before he could rise or even speak, I said quickly, "I'll get it."

Before it rang a third time, I walked swiftly to the kitchen, then snapped up the receiver from the wall. As I suspected, a voice on the other end said, "Give me what you have, and I'll give you back the kid."

Then the line went dead.

Though my face was pale, I tried not to betray an emotion as I replaced the phone. To the very expectant Jeanine and to Claude, who had just anxiously entered, I said, "Wrong number."

Claude's face fell, and then he seemed to sink into a chair. He absently fingered another cigar from his pocket, but then just chewed it, unlit.

I took the opportunity to quietly complete my question.

"Is there anything I"—I cut Jeanine off, before she could speak—"*we* can do?"

With stiff upper lip, Claude shook his head.

"Just help me take care of Alice, if you don't mind," he said. "I'll have to carry on, until we know something. There's, you know, work to do."

Jeanine nodded, already making for the living room to sit beside Claude's wife. With her gone, I tentatively placed a consoling hand on the bigger man's arm.

"Don't be such a hero," I said. "You can shift some of the load. That's what friends are for."

Claude managed a touched and gratified smile. Then I dared to suggest what I had wanted to all along, though the reasons for it now had changed completely.

"Why don't you let me keep your meeting with Webby? You're really not up to it, are you?"

Claude looked at me, and tears twinkled in his eyes. Even more moved by my compassion, he slowly nodded yes.

I can love you good
Better than JFK could.
I promise I can sing
Better than Warren Har . . . ding.
I'll tell you the truth.
I'll be yours forever.
So enter the booth,
And pull my lever.
Love's an election.
Make your selection.
And may the best man win.
Hey! Hey! Hey!
May the best man win!

The next day, in his waiting room, I had no choice but to listen to the DreamDates' old songs. Webby had them piped into his Back Bay office, one after another, from all of their albums, and there had been more than I had ever imagined.

Adding to this aural insult were visual ones: framed pictures of Webby with his new (third) wife, a trophy blonde of forty, and Madonna-like paintings of the late June Faber, with her famous frizzy hair hidden beneath a scarf, staring skyward. There were also photos of Webby greeting Reagan, Nixon, Helms, and Goldwater, and stars like Schwarzenegger, Willis, Costner, and, of course, Ben Williams.

There were no photos of Stu Drayton.

I had anticipated a hassle, and I got one. The officious young receptionist—"Pull the switch!" button on heart, straw boater on head—got pugnacious when I told him that, "I'm filling in for the Kripps."

He responded, as if this were objectively false. "No, you're not."

"You don't understand, they've had a family tragedy. Haven't you—" I was about to say "read the papers?" but I remembered that the case, like other kidnappings, was being kept hush-hush.

"I don't care," he said simply.

"Well, that's not very compassionate. I thought that your campaign cared about people."

The young man was about to be equally snide, but then he stopped. Politics did not allow for irony, lest someone think one insensitive.

"We care very much about people," he said deliberately. "But we also care about our candidate's security. I mean—who knows who you are?"

I looked him right in the eye.

"Webby does," I said.

This unnerved him, as I had hoped it might. With a deep sigh, he stood up and raised a slightly shaking finger.

"Hold on just a minute?"

He rushed toward the inner office, where Webby awaited—reluctantly, Claude had assured me—this visit from the Kripps. But the candidate could afford to alienate no constituency, especially since the trivial couple had cornered him on his own home turf. Maybe he'd even work it to his advantage and leak the whole thing to the press. The headline: WEBBY WON'T PRESERVE CINEMA SMUT.

Forget film preservation, I thought. This is about self-preservation. And maybe it always had been.

Like an actor in a farce, the receptionist began to knock just as the door flew open. He faltered and nearly fell, right into the arms of boss, Congressman, and kidnapper Webby Slicone.

"Whoa, whoa, there," the little big man said affably.

"Excuse me, my God, I'm sorry," the young man panted, flustered by having touched and so offended him.

"That's all right. But I thought for a minute we were gonna do the Frug!"

Webby let out a laugh much larger than his receptionist's, who was ten years too young to remember the dance or even the decade from which it sprung.

Still smiling, Webby looked across and right at me. Even from a few feet away, I could see the makeup that covered his eyelids and filled in the wrinkles even his facelift couldn't fix. He gave no indication that he had ever seen me before.

"This, uh, guy was sent by your ten o'clock," the receptionist stammered.

"Well, okay," Webby said agreeably. "What are we waiting for?"

The assistant looked at Webby with a stunned gaze of relief, as if to say, *What a man, oh, what a man you are.*

As I sat opposite him, I realized that I had only ever heard Webby say words from a speech or lyrics from a song. That is to say, I had never witnessed him being himself. But the difference between public persona and private person was minuscule. He still charmed, still sparkled, still smiled. Even when he was being as blunt as to say, "Well, I think you have something I need. Isn't that right?"

I felt a mild shudder at the success of my deductions. My fear was mild, as well. Having been close to powerful people had made me less enamored of them, to put it mildly, and less afraid. Mostly, I just felt disgust.

"And vice versa," I said. "Though I'm interested to know how you knew."

"What do you mean? The Kripps always have some dirty movies to cham-peen. Then we negotiate. That's your bag, too, isn't it?"

I smiled—at Webby's flower-power lingo, not his obfuscation. Though Claude had given me their list of films to preserve—many from the Sixties and still controversial—it sat, folded and forgotten, in my pocket.

"Look, let's not play games," I said. "There are lots of things at stake. Like your career."

Webby made an *I'm impressed* face. Then he shrugged and got down to business, ending his opening act.

"Get up," he said.

I paused. Then, uneasily, I slowly stood, not knowing what to expect. Webby rose at the same time, and approached me.

Without another word, starting at my chest, he patted me down harshly. Then he stopped at the tiny bulge in my front pants pocket.

I had purchased a little tape recorder at an electronics store on the way there. Now Webby removed it, popped out the tape, palmed it, pocketed it, and handed the machine back.

I had been too cute for my own good, and I knew it. But Webby didn't seem angry. Sitting again, he simply proceeded, as if a nasty formality was out of the way.

"I'm just surprised that you've come in person," he said.

"Self-reliance," I said. "Isn't that your credo?"

Webby smiled a bit, but unkindly. "More than you'll ever know."

"So tell me how you were tipped off."

"Maybe I had a report from Mr. Magoo," he said, meaning, I guessed, the "blind" man. "Though I certainly wasn't going to trust a cop enough to tell him the truth."

I nodded, having assumed this.

"And maybe they tailed that little chipmunk lady you were with at the rally." Right again. "And maybe I was surprised when you all landed up at the Krippses'. I never figured the Flintstones for blackmailers."

"They're not," I said. "This only involves you and me. And Stu Drayton and Ben Williams. And a boy named Little Bobby. And Orson Welles."

Webby smiled, and the makeup cracked at the sides of his eyes. He began to sing, " 'Orson Welles, and rain on the roof' . . . *Orson Welles?* What the hell does *he* have to do with this?"

"Never mind. I just want their son back." I paused. "And the bag the guy with the mask took from L.A."

Webby nodded, mildly interested. "*That's* the Welles connection?"

"Maybe."

"Well, I will make no deal 'before its time,' " Webby said, with his usual dated references, in this case to Welles's old wine commercials. "In other words, baby, where's the thing?"

Unlike Stu Drayton, I didn't think Webby's lack of specificity—he meant the Filofax, of course—came from caution. I just thought that "thing" was his all-purpose expression, the way it had been for many people in, say, 1969. Like some celebrities, he was not discreet at all; he thought that everything he did or said was worth celebrating.

"Well, you political guys understand tit for tat," I said, "don't you?"

"The last person who used that expression with me was Raquel Welch," he said, then gave a little Bob Hope–like *grrrr*owl of desire.

I did not smile, and I could have sworn that flop sweat had started on his brow. I was a tough house, and Webby wasn't used to that.

"I want the kid home first," I said.

"First of all, Jack," he said, with a Sinatra-like sneer, "how do I even know you're for real? All I know is that you had a Filofax shaken out of you. What if it's a fake? I mean, I've never even seen you before."

"Oh," I said, starting to sweat a bit myself, "I think you have."

Now I knew the other reason I had wanted to handle this alone. This indeed *was* a personal thing between Webby and me.

Maybe it was the look he had given me at the rally, being hustled away. Maybe it was a feeling I had had, fighting over little Orson at the car. Maybe it was how it felt to face him now.

But something told me that Webby Slicone was the man in the mask.

SITTING THERE, IT HAD STARTED WITH MY REMEMBERING *SECRET CERE-mony*, that Elizabeth Taylor film. It was sold to TV as part of a package that included other—now obscure—late-Sixties Universal pictures. These "adult" movies had new material specially shot for network consumption, creating "acceptable" subplots to replace censored scenes and maintain a proper running time. One of them was *The Night of the Following Day*, a Marlon Brando film about—and here was the connection—kidnapping.

That led me to think about families in general, and circuitously, to *Kings Row*. The old Warner Brothers classic was adapted from a bestseller about small-town life that was shocking for its time. The movie version, as Warner studio memos bear out, had to censor many elements, including the incestuous relationship between a girl and her father. In the film, the relationship just became one of neurotic protectiveness; the father and daughter were played by Betty Field and Claude Rains.

That made me think of Webby's friend, Ronald Reagan, who had his legs removed in the film—"Where's the rest of me?"—and that made me think of Charles Coburn, who played the doctor who cut them off.

Coburn, the portly character actor, won an Oscar for his role in *The More the Merrier*, starring Jean Arthur. But one of his other classic roles was in *The Devil and Miss Jones*, also with Arthur, in which he played a millionaire who secretly went to work in his own department store, to investigate worker conditions.

And that made me think that Webby had done his own dirty work, had indeed pulled the switch.

"And *where* exactly have I seen you?" the politico asked, sweat now obviously caking his face.

"At the end of a gun in L.A.," I answered, "and at the end of a boy in Massachusetts."

I believed it for other, less trivial, reasons. The humming in L.A.— "The New Math"—could have been Webby's need to be found out, a shrink might suggest. Or maybe it was his desire to be recognized, even doing stuff like that, his psycho celebrity thing. Or it might have been mere nervousness, a clutching at the familiar, as I did with facts of trivia.

Or else, by committing his own murders, Webby was that rare thing: a true conservative. No help or handouts for him. You almost had to re-spect the guy for it.

Almost.

"Oh, give me a break," Webby said, rolling his eyes. "You've flipped your wig."

"Not your problem now, with the plugs," I said, pointing to his head.

To be honest, Webby probably did it himself for the same reason Ben Williams surrounded himself with Dick Burkes and Little Bobbys: He trusted nobody. It was a lot easier, I thought, to be trivial than it was to be important.

There was one more, most obvious, possibility: He was simply out of his goddamn mind.

It was, of course, my biggest risk yet. But I was emboldened by the

Sherlock-like skill—if I may say so myself—I had shown of late, with the stakes the highest they had ever been. I was growing into this job, I thought, and not a minute too soon.

"Cheap shot," I said, about the hair. "Sorry."

Webby leaned as far forward as he could without falling headfirst into his desk. His face looked like a desert under a savage sun: blanched, cracked, and split. I feared that his entire surgery might undo itself, his skin falling down, his hair springing off, like some old Warners cartoon.

"Why should I be jerked around," he asked furiously, "by the likes of you?"

I looked him right in his—improbably blue—eyes.

"Because," I answered, "I've got nothing to lose. I mean"—and here I laughed, with a lack of vanity he could never know—"look at me!"

I had him there. Webby just stayed, staring, squinting, growing older by the instant, until he became an ancient.

"Well, after I win the election," he whispered, "you can kiss your bippy goodbye."

He made his fingers into a gun. With a quiet "kapow," he squeezed off a shot and killed me. Then he pressed a button on his desk intercom.

"Send in my eleven o'clock," he said.

No real bullets or blows had been exchanged. There were no bruises or scars to be healed. I had simply been right, and—ironic, wasn't it?—the best man had won.

THAT NIGHT AT THE KRIPPSES', DINNER WAS EATEN IN SILENCE.

It was takeout Chinese this time, no home-cooked meal. Claude, Jeanine, and I ate all we took, if only to pass the time. Awakened from a sedated sleep, Alice just picked. Even Gilda did not beg for scraps, at least not aggressively; in the odd way of animals, she shared the house's unhappiness.

It had been a full twelve hours since my—I thought—successful negotiation with Webby Slicone. Still, there had been no word of Orson.

Jeanine had not approved of my attending the meeting alone, of keeping the Krippses in the dark, of still not telling the cops. She thought I was merely protecting my sole possession of *Ambersons*, and acting inhumanely. I did not disabuse her of this notion, in case I failed, or—fearing a future of intimacy with her—succeeded. The point was moot for the moment, anyway; she had not so much as kissed me since the night before.

"More moo-shu pancakes?" I asked, trying for any kind of response. She shook her head *no*.

I did not tell her about the stamped package now lying beneath the bed we had shared. The Filofax was ready to go to Webby, waiting only for him to make the first move.

"How'd the meeting go?" Claude asked, for the first time since I had returned.

"Fine," I said, with excruciation, as Jeanine glared at me. "But he's adamantly against preserving *Bonnie and Clyde* or *Straw Dogs*. He said, maybe after the election."

"Well, he's always been pragmatic," Claude said. "But imagine someone still fighting over thirty-year-old films. Shows you what power that period of filmmaking still has. Interesting, isn't it?"

Hopefully, he had directed this inquiry to Alice. Trivia ceased to have any interest for her; she returned only an indifferent shrug.

Jeanine lifted her plate loudly and took it into the kitchen. Hearing me lie—and Claude respond to my lies—was just too much for her.

"Well," Claude said, obviously comforted by the conversation's distraction, "thanks for going to bat for us, anyway."

"Sure," I said.

From the kitchen, I heard Jeanine running water much harder than was required to clean her plate.

I thought of the cuts made in Peckinpah's *Straw Dogs*, reducing the sodomy climax of the rape scene—at least in this country—to fast flashes, nearly incoherent. Personally, I thought the Kripps were pushing it by proposing that Webby preserve that one. But I had to admire their audacity, disguised by their homey domesticity.

"Any word from the police?" I asked.

Claude shook his head, as if this truly worsened their unbearable tragedy. Alice bit her lower lip and stared into the distance blankly.

Then the dog raised its head.

Only I noticed Gilda's action or her small, subsequent whinny of unease. Then her moaning grew. She got up and trotted, suspiciously, out of the room.

"Our neighbor usually walks his Jack Russell about now," Claude explained.

I could have taken this as the truth, but I was too jumpy. So, discreetly, carrying my plate, I rose and followed the dog to the front door.

Samuel Fuller's film, *White Dog,* had been held up for distribution in the U.S., on charges of racism. Like the Peckinpah film, it had been released, uncut, overseas. *Dogs* of all kinds seemed to suffer in the United States.

Gilda was suffering, too. Her little yelps of dismay were coming fast and furious, and she now scratched helplessly at the base of the Kripps' front door.

"Gilda!" Claude called faintly. "That's enough now!"

I placed my dirty plate down on a living room chair. Then, trying not to make a sound, I held the bolting dog back with my foot and pulled the door slowly open.

Outside, the moon was covered by clouds, and the single streetlight did little to show me the way. I walked with deliberation, my hand waving out in front of me, as my only guide.

I remembered Webby's final "bippy" remark, his dated decree of my death after his election. I had been a fool to trust him, I knew now. Somewhere, ski mask in place, he waited in the night to break our deal and take his revenge. After all, with me dead, he had no more to fear from the Filofax. How had I been so stupid as not to know that?

Then I heard the sound of a step.

I stopped walking, my hand still outstretched. My mind played a crazy montage of violent images from the Krippses' Seventies films, accompanied by a DreamDates score. I had never known what it meant to feel faint before that moment.

Then I felt a hand grab mine. It took me a second to realize that it was a smaller hand, and that its fingers were holding, not pulling, my own.

"Orson!"

Members of the Kripp family, dog included, all embraced one another in the living room. Claude kept rubbing his boy's hair over and over, as if to make sure that he was real. Alice immediately became her old self, checking Orson for injuries, asking him worried questions, and promising him his favorite meal, which she would cook right away.

"Look who I found," was all I had said.

Jeanine and I watched for a second, then discreetly walked from the room. We did not say anything. She looked at me with a combination of relief, wonder, and exasperation and then just shook her head.

Then she noticed what I was carrying, the thing that little Orson had given me when I'd found him. The bag's nylon handle was wrapped around my wrist.

"Oh, by the way," I said, as an afterthought. "I got *The Magnificent Ambersons*, too."

PART 6
NEW YORK

PRINT IT!

I'm off to upstate New York this weekend, to participate in the yearly madness known as the Rhinebeck Film Fair. It's here that critics, collectors, and just plain kooks gather to catch the latest in old movies: rediscovered gems, found footage, new prints, etc. The event that everyone is looking forward to is a "Mystery Midnight Screening" at which we're promised the "Film Find of the Century"! Even I don't know what it is, and that's saying a lot! It comes courtesy of Roy Milano, editor and publisher of *Trivial Man*, a modest publication that you probably haven't heard of . . . until now.

I didn't know whether to take Abner Cooley's mention as a plug or a jibe, and I didn't much care. I had sent Webby the Filofax after deciding not to simply shaft him. A deal was a deal; and, besides, who knew what a politician who was his own hitman would do if done wrong? Then it became my new determination to share *The Magnificent Ambersons* with the trivial community.

Part of it was guilt, of course. While I felt vindicated in my handling of the Webby matter, I also felt responsible for bringing such horror into the Krippses' home—without ever telling them why. This had made me feel big-hearted and expansive.

Also, after my long ordeal, I had a sense of a homecoming. I had plunged into another world, one populated by powerful people with big money and bad intentions, and had come out with the prize I sought. I felt I should bring *Ambersons* back where it belonged: to the people who did not want to destroy it or ignore it; to the wastrels, nuts, and obsessive fans who cared about it most. In other words, to the people like me.

I did not regret that I wouldn't know the movie first. I was simply sorry that I still didn't know who killed Alan Gilbert.

"Well, this is a new tune," Jeanine said as we pulled up to the Rhinebeck Motor Lodge.

"I thought you'd be pleased," I said.

"I'm not *not* pleased. I just wonder if you're going overboard. We're not all one big happy family, you know."

"I'm aware of that."

"Maybe our world isn't much better than Hollywood or Europe or Washington. There's still jealousy and backbiting and bitterness, only with fast food, that's all."

"I'm not an idiot."

"I never said you were."

After a second of silence, Jeanine leaned over and kissed my neck. Our quarreling had a new tone to it now—and not just because it usually ended in pecks and petting. Since the Kripps, Jeanine felt sheepish for having doubted me; I felt rotten for having started all the trouble. So we danced warily around each other before coming in for more petting and pecks.

"This is the last of Rosie's money," I said. "Did you get one room?"

"Yes." Then she paused, unsure. "Shouldn't I have?"

"No, you should have, that's fine."

"Oh, okay, good. Because we can always, you know—"

"Get another one?"

"Yes, you know, if that's necessary."

"Well, actually, I think the town is pretty booked up."

"Then you can always bunk with someone. Or I can. Actually *you* should, because the ratio of men to women here will be like the U.S. Army, or something, so—"

"It'll be fine. We won't need to."

"Okay, okay, I don't think so, either."

Then there was a long pause. This was, I guessed, how trivial people dated.

I had arranged with the Film Fair organizers for the special showing, but had not divulged the identity of my find. They agreed reluctantly, still burned by a recent "World Premiere" that had turned out to be a waggish trivial man's slides of his vacation. The obscure midnight slot was a precaution in case I pulled such a prank.

Rhinebeck was an affluent Catskills town that featured the country's oldest inn. It was also home to prominent show-business figures who gave it a Hamptons-in-the-mountains type feel. The annual influx of trivial people was a boon for the local economy, and usually generated press coverage. Today there was even a banner hanging over its main street.

WELCOME, FILM FREAKS! it read.

The Rhinebeck Motor Lodge was not the country's oldest inn; it was, in fact, a sterile high-rise on the outskirts of town, and the only place where trivial people could afford to stay.

A shabby yellow schoolbus with an aged driver was donated by the Chamber of Commerce to take us from there to a mall movie Plex, one screen of which was reserved for our Fair. Tonight it would play host to the opening film, which was a new print of a classic. Then it was back to the Lodge's lobby for the reception, held in an old bar renamed especially for us: The Cutting Room.

It was on the bus that night, entering like kids going to camp, that Jeanine and I saw our old colleagues again.

There was Abner Cooley himself, passing around the latest Hollywood trade paper to quote one of his scoops . . . Ron Gaylord, his Spanish theater closed, back in the States looking for work, a high turtleneck covering his suicidal belt mark . . . Taylor Weinrod, dressed to the nines, scoping out films for LCM and seeming as if he were slumming . . . and the Kripps, as ever cuddling, trying unsuccessfully to lead everyone in a round of "Row Your Boat."

All greeted Jeanine warmly, except for Abner, who still smarted from her desertion of him—and he didn't even know that she had stolen his contacts when she'd left. Word of my mystery presentation for the next night had spread, and I was received, as Jeanine had predicted, with a mixture of jealousy, mistrust and, at best, grumpy courtesy.

"Can't you just feel the warmth?" Jeanine whispered.

Let them be small now, I thought, as we took our seats. Once they see what I've unearthed—and have decided to share with them—they'll come around. This would be the beginning of a whole new feeling of community.

"Hey, Milano," Abner said, taking up a whole row. "Tomorrow better be good. I don't want to look stupid in front of America."

"It's too late for that," I answered.

"You're killing me. Look, just be happy I printed the mention at all. And don't bother to thank me for plugging your little newsletter."

I had debated whether to call Abner from Boston with my news. Now I regretted that I had, especially since—if there was new demand for *Trivial Man*—I had not published an issue all season.

"You won't be disappointed," I said. "I promise."

"Well, if it's as good as you say," Abner went on, "next time, lunch is on you."

I laughed—and not just because Abner was famous for sticking others with checks, more often as he became more famous. I did not want *Ambersons* to bring me celebrity, not in the way Alan Gilbert obviously had. I had seen what celebrity—from movies to sports to politics—did to people. Obscurity was looking better all the time.

But try telling that to Abner.

"Yep, I don't know if this town'll be big enough for the both of us," he said smugly, brushing his faint blond beard.

"That's true every day, pudgeball," Ron Gaylord threw in.

Through the bus, there was a ripple of amusement. I perversely admired Ron for not curbing his miserable mouth, even though he was now a supplicant, begging for work. It was a strange, self-destructive form of integrity.

"It's nice to have you back," Abner answered. "I see that the liquor store in town has a 'Welcome Ron Gaylord' sign outside."

"I'll kill you!"

Ron lunged out of his seat and had to be restrained by bulky Claude Kripp.

"That's enough, you two," Claude said in his paternal way.

"I've been on the wagon for weeks!" Ron said angrily. "But *you* can't kick *your* addiction to fudge!"

Nearby, Taylor Weinrod rolled his eyes as if he weren't sure how he had come to be among these lowlifes.

"Will you all just please shut up?" he asked quietly.

Still held in Claude's embrace, Ron leaned forward and snapped Taylor's suspenders once, thwaking his chest loudly.

"Why don't you go back to L.A. and sell out some more!" he shouted.

Audible sighs of dismay now came from Alice Kripp, who put down her knitting to remark, "Well, I think you're all acting like a bunch of children."

"Yes," Jeanine said mischievously. "Let's all just settle down and be happy for Roy."

She glanced at me, as if to say, *Still proud of your plan?* Then she touched my hand, to take the sting away.

This gesture, small as it was, did not go unnoticed by the bus's other passengers. Now, reducing camaraderie even further, there was jealousy of Jeanine and my relationship. The Kripps were one thing—they were parents, chubby, and middle-aged. But Jeanine and I were still hovering on the edges of youthful sexual function, and so must be destroyed.

"Well," Abner said lewdly, "I see *someone's* going to have his own special midnight show tonight."

"Yeah," Ron chimed in, "and there should be more laughing than at *Rocky Horror!*"

A general air of malicious merriment took hold, seeming to rock the bus. Then, "Driver!" Taylor called comically. "Let me out! Right here on the highway, it's fine!"

The nasty buzzing grew quieter, the Kripps having abstained and smiling at us with a parental glow.

Then Taylor came and sat on the seat behind me.

"Well, Roy," he whispered, "don't you think you owe me something for my little favor?"

"What favor?" I honestly didn't remember. "Oh, you mean working for Webby."

"Yes. You know, if your find is something LCM would be interested in, I'm sure Ed Landers would love to know about it. I assume you're still interested in a job? I can't promise anything right now, but . . ."

A real job at LCM was now the farthest thing from my mind. Still, there was the question of what to do with *Ambersons* after it premiered. I didn't even know where Erendira was.

"Let me think about it," I said.

Taylor winked. He assumed I was being cagey, not merely confused. "I see you're learning the ropes of the biz. Good for you."

"No, it's not that, I genuinely don't—"

"Okay, you player, keep it to yourself. But remember my offer. There's voice mail in my room, in case you want to spill the beans and make a deal, before tomorrow."

Unlike the rest of us, Taylor was staying at the country's oldest inn, courtesy of Ed Landers and LCM, and the bus had made a special detour to pick him up. Before I could comment, he had slipped his business card into my front shirt pocket. Then he slithered back to his seat, filled with new, totally mistaken respect for me.

Among the hostile group, Taylor was not the only one nosing around. In Boston, Abner had already grilled me about what I was pre-

senting. But his ego was so great that he couldn't conceive of any discovery "out there" that was unknown to him, so he had shrugged it off.
Still, I knew that his banter about my becoming his equal had been
based on fear, not excited anticipation.

Ron, on the other hand, had less ego and more need. He was in my
ear now, having taken Taylor's spot behind me. His breath smelled of as
many mints as he could consume to disguise a decade of heavy drinking,
so I guessed he was serious about sobriety.

"You don't know what a pleasure it is," he said, "to insult someone
again in English."

I smiled. "It's good to be back home, isn't it?"

"Yeah. Especially since I've got some backing to start a new revival
house. Did I tell you that?"

"No." Ron's backing seemed to have come through as soon as he'd
heard about my screening. "That's lucky."

"Yeah. It's gonna be out of the city, in a small town like this one. I
won't be hiring much more than maybe one other person." Strangely,
Ron seemed to believe that he and I now had a bond, just because I had
cut him down from a ceiling fan. "Any interest?"

Jeanine was seated beside me, all but ignored by these—shy and sort
of sexist—trivial men. Silently, she drew two words on my open palm:
no and *way*.

"Well, let me think about it," I hedged. "Maybe you'll see the thing
and you won't be so excited, anyway."

This sounded as lame to me as it obviously did to Ron. He shook his
head with barely concealed disgust. Then he rubbed his lips agitatedly,
as if a cold one would go down real good right now. Then he dragged
his sorry self back to his seat.

Only the Kripps were left to approach me as we made our way to the
Plex. They, too, I was surprised to see, were soon in the coveted spot
near my ear.

"So, have you shared your little secret with Jeanine?" Alice asked,
purling one on a garment I later learned was a hat for her dog, Gilda.

"She knows," I admitted.

"Does that mean I hear wedding bells?"

"That was just the bus horn," Jeanine answered, and I smiled, relieved.

"Leave them alone, for goodness' sake," Claude said good-humoredly.

Alice's agenda was complex: As our fairy godmother, she wanted to keep Jeanine and me together, and as a trivial person, she wanted to know what the movie was.

"Little Orson sends his greetings," she said, to further build a bridge.

I smiled at this. Though the boy and I had never exchanged a word, he and I were now linked forever. But only I knew how securely.

"Tell him I said hi," I said, not biting.

"Finished now?" Claude asked his wife, with comical impatience.

"I guess," she said. "You know, Roy, you make Webby Slicone look malleable."

"It's funny, you'd think Webby believed in preservation," I said evasively. "Look at his face."

We all chuckled.

"Ten points up in the poll today," Claude added with a sigh.

With the conversation becoming general, Alice gathered up her yarn.

"Well, if you change your mind . . ."

"I'll let you know." I smiled.

The Kripps moved away, arms about each other, as the elderly driver took a shaky turn into the mall.

"Well, why didn't you tell anyone?" Jeanine asked. "I mean, don't you trust them? Isn't that the whole point of this?"

I didn't answer, but I was pricked by the question. Given everyone's competitiveness and self-interest, perhaps I *had* been a Pollyanna.

"I'm just trying to build suspense," I said, and I sounded unsure, even to myself.

Jeanine squeezed my hand tightly. Was she telling me to be careful? She didn't take her hand away until the ride came to an end.

ALL OF THESE FEELINGS BECAME IRREVELANT WHEN WE ENTERED THE sixplex. We walked past theaters showing the latest science-fiction sequels, animated musicals with singing furniture, and Ben Williams's next-to-last action epic, *Make Hurt,* a transparent *Cause Pain* imitation even his fans had avoided. Then we crowded into the smallest theater with the most minuscule screen.

Inside were more trivial people, who had been brought in earlier busloads. I waved to some I knew and liked; I avoided those I knew and hated. I couldn't help but notice that our ranks had grown from the year before. There were even some fans in costume, dressed as Scarlett and Rhett, Elvis, and Dumbo.

Did more technology just mean more access to movies? Or was the accumulation of power in fewer hands in America making more people grow, as it were, smaller? I didn't know; I only knew that I had liked our world the way it was.

Then *Citizen Kane* began.

There had been some derision that this was the opening-night choice. New print or no, it was so obvious. But I for one felt it would position *Ambersons* beautifully for the following evening. And besides, once the picture began, the carping ended.

Everyone sat, transfixed, as soon as the opening shot, the closeup of the "K" in Kane, was revealed. And they stayed silent, mesmerized, as the film—now in scrubbed, almost shining black-and-white—unfolded.

It didn't matter that many people in the audience held more than one job, lived alone, or had deeply disappointed their parents. They saw themselves in the story of a multimillionaire, propelled to power, driven to destroy himself, because of the little sled, the childhood love, he had lost. After all, trivial people were looking for things lost in the past, as well.

When the flames devouring Rosebud faded, when the lights came up, there was a general, uneasy silence. Then the place erupted in applause and cheers, loud enough to be heard in the theater next door, the one whose chase music had been seeping through the walls of our own, during *Citizen Kane*.

"Let's party!"

Someone actually yelled that as we filed into the reception at The Cutting Room. It was a run-down hotel bar that had been repaneled in imitation redwood. Befitting its new, opportunistic name, there were now stills of movie stars on the wall. Most of them had been clipped from recent magazines, so there was no actor older or younger than Tom Cruise or Julia Roberts.

Still, tonight there were balloons and crepe-paper banners and an open bar. And consequently, someone—I never learned who—started yelling, "Let's party!"

Banquet tables had been laid with cold cuts, a dangerous sight for trivial people. Within seconds, a swarm of them descended upon the free food and consumed it, to the obvious dismay of the waitpeople, who couldn't replenish it fast enough. Soon the bar's employees just stood off to the side and watched the attack, in surprise and horror. I noticed Ron Gaylord sneaking in, late, and expressing loud annoyance at the mere scraps of meat that were left.

Most guilty of gluttony was a man able to pay, Abner Cooley. His plate piled high, looking very Henry VIII, he walked off to a table, where he held court. People crowded around him, eager for tips on how to turn trivia into gold, without leaving your parents' house.

Finally, our self-appointed host for the evening, Abner, tapped on a water glass with a knife. It took so long to divert the crowd from chewing and swallowing that his glass cracked and sent water flowing onto his food.

"Hey, hey!" Abner yelled, annoyed. "Let's all listen up now, okay?!"

Abner did not deign to stand, so all of us had to crane our necks to see him still sitting at his place.

"I think it's time to acknowledge how much we've gained since last year," he said philosophically.

Ron whispered, "How much *you've* gained," and there were a few titters.

"Also," Abner went on, oblivious, "it's time to acknowledge what we've lost. I'd like to have a moment of silence for Brian Grayman"—an elderly critic who succumbed to a heart attack—"and Louis Romais"— who wrote questions for a movie trivia CD-ROM and was hit by a bicyclist in Central Park—"and, perhaps most tragically, Alan Gilbert."

Even those who did not know the first two names recognized the last one. At the mention of Alan, there was a murmuring of sympathy or anger or maybe just relief. Then, before the respectful silence could begin, someone called out, "How about Gus Ziegler?"

There was an uneasy pause. Then a few other voices seconded it: "Yes! Gus! Gus, also!"

Even from my bad seat, I could see Abner's face contort irritatedly. He muttered, "Her-Man" beneath his breath. But then he rose to the occasion, if not from his chair.

"How could I forget?" he said, with imitation sorrow. "Gus, as well, left us this year. And now, a moment of *silence*." His tone on the last word prevented any more additions to the necrology.

We bowed our heads and, for this moment, there truly was no sound. I noticed the Kripps coming in late, chatting innocently with each other, then being shushed.

Music ended our mourning. From two large speakers a specially made tape featured a disco version of the theme from *Psycho*. A surprising amount of trivial people, well fed and happily drunk, got up to dance.

There were, of course, more men than women. I saw the Kelman twins, middle-aged women who worked in the Lincoln Center Library, cutting a rug together . . . Hiram Leigh, an ancient Britisher who ran a public-radio film show, *Hat's Off to Hollywood!* shaking by himself, as if electrocuted . . . and the Kripps, boogying unselfconsciously, as if having returned to Woodstock. I also saw Taylor Weinrod, fleeing from the room, discreetly, mortified. A minute later, Abner followed him, seeming to desperately seek a urinal.

I extended my hand to Jeanine.

Never much for dancing, I remembered that Marlon Brando had not been the first choice for the movie of *Guys and Dolls*. Gene Kelly had originally been sought, in order to reunite him with his *On the Town* pal, Frank Sinatra. In the end, Brando had had to fix his singing in the editing room.

"Don't worry," Jeanine said, "you'll be fine. It's an inexact science."

It was our first time together on any floor. Jeanine couldn't really dance, either, but she made fists and shook them above her head, as if flinging loose her chains. As in bed, it was her avidity that made her erotic, not her physical perfection. I couldn't take my eyes off her.

Suddenly, the *Psycho* music stopped, and a romantic arrangement of "Also Sprach Zarathustra" from *2001* began. Jeanine and I ended up in each other's arms, rocking back and forth, only shuffling our feet occasionally.

"On the slow stuff, you really have to know what you're doing," she said, subdued.

"I know what you mean," I replied.

Still, pressed against each other, we felt, to put it mildly, stirred. Jeanine whispered in my ear, "Let's go up to the room."

"Okay."

When we disengaged, I saw what seemed a thousand envious eyes drilling into us from the dance floor. As before, only the Kripps smiled, with encouragement.

"You go first," I said. "I'll follow."

Why be too brazen and engender more hostility? I thought. I would need as much goodwill as possible for the following night.

Reluctant but understanding, Jeanine agreed.

On my way up, I shared the elevator with the Kelman sisters, one twin more tipsy than the other.

"What did the monolith mean?" the first groggily badgered the second.

"Rosebud," the second answered, faintly.

They got off on my floor, and I heard them fumbling, cursing at their lock as I approached my door.

I had expected to find Jeanine already nude or lounging in a night-gown or wearing just her *Seven Year Itch* T-shirt. Instead, she was sitting on the bed, fully dressed, her graying hair down, her face white.

The nylon bag—which had gone from Gus to Ben to Little Bobby to Webby to me—was in the middle of the floor. It was wide open.

Jeanine kept looking at it, and then she looked at me.

"*The Magnificent Ambersons,*" she said, "is gone."

THERE WAS A SECOND BEFORE I COULD RESPOND. THEN, SUDDENLY SOBER after two glasses of wine, I stammered out, "What do you mean?"

"I mean, the bag is empty."

"I can see that. But, well—was the door open?"

Jeanine shook her head. "Maybe one of the cleaning people let somebody—"

"Except who would have enough money here to pay anyone off?"

Jeanine and I looked at each other, and the number of suspects immediately dwindled.

"That's just a supposition," she said. "We shouldn't put too much stock in it."

"You're right."

I was pacing now, as if by walking furiously, I might bump into the answer.

"Jesus Christ! Who the hell would *want* to do this?" I said, at last.

"Who wouldn't? It's like *Murder on the Orient Express*."

I gave a small grunt of concurrence. What a fool I had been to trust the trivial community! A few hours away from unveiling the Everest of film finds, and I was back where I began, all those days ago.

Maybe someone felt I would lord it over them, when I had only meant to bring us all closer. I should have known that group hugs would not go over at the Rhinebeck Film Fair.

"It's too bad." Jeanine sighed. "Agatha Christie films haven't been big since the early Eighties."

"Tell me about it!"

I remembered that in 1980's *The Mirror Crack'd*, Natalie Wood had been replaced by Elizabeth Taylor, garnering the latter her best reviews in years.

"But either way, it's Albert Finney, Peter Ustinov, and now you," she said.

"Don't forget Tony Randall. He played Poirot in *The Alphabet Murders*."

"Actually, I see you more as Margaret Rutherford, Miss Marple."

Jeanine had meant this as a joke, and I smiled, momentarily relieved.

"The weird thing is," I said, stopping my march, "they all disappeared for a few minutes from the party. Or came in late. Abner, Ron, Taylor Weinrod, the Kripps . . ."

I was trying to trust myself again, as I had in trumping Webby. But it took so much effort to recapture the energy, after I had believed that I was through. How had Peter Ustinov done it, case after case?

"So any one of them could have come in and taken it."

"Yes," I said. "And—besides resentment of us—they all had a motive. Taylor would want the movie for his station, to impress Ed Landers. Ron to jump-start his career. And Abner as a coup for his column."

"What about Claude and Alice?"

"I don't have a motive for them," I admitted. "Maybe they found out about me and Webby?"

Jeanine made a face. "That's reaching."

"You're right, but still."

I sat on the bed, beside Jeanine. Exhausted and dispirited, I leaned against her. Then, slowly, I began to nuzzle at her neck, the need for comfort now paramount.

But Jeanine was a practical woman when she wished to be, and a hard-nosed one, too.

"I don't think you want to stay here too long," she said.

"What do you mean?"

"I mean, you've only got until tomorrow night. If you want to keep any credibility as a person."

"You're right." With a deep sigh, I stood up.

She kissed me deeply, and that had to suffice. There was only one advantage this time. At least I didn't have to cross a country or travel to another continent.

"This time, *Ambersons*," I said, "is somewhere in this hotel."

THE PARTY WAS WINDING DOWN.

Only a few stragglers remained, swaying slowly on the dance floor or slumped, unconscious, in their seats. The music was now just a tinny broadcast from a local radio station.

Ron Gaylord was among those left. He stood at the banquet table, rolling the last pieces of meat into a napkin and placing it into his pants. Then, folding up scraps of lettuce that were left, he inserted these into his front shirt pocket and tapped it flat. Then he made for the exit.

Peeking in through The Cutting Room's door, I backed away and hid in a hall as he came out. Ron walked, unsteadily, his pants and shirt stuffed with food. When he pressed for the elevator, I shot around the corner and went up the stairs.

A few minutes earlier, I had asked innocently at the desk for the room numbers of all of my suspects. Now I was grateful that Ron was on four, and not thirty-five.

Panting, I emerged from the stairwell just as the elevator opened. Ron wiggled out, moving at his constipated gait. I waited until he had fumbled out his card key and inserted it into the slot in his door. Then I whispered heatedly, "Ron?"

Gaylord turned, with a look of pure terror. I didn't think he was afraid of having his food confiscated. I was betting that he was hiding something else.

I approached and he responded, with a quivering smile, "Hey, uh, Roy. What are you, uh, doing here?" Then he segued awkwardly into innuendo. "Isn't somebody a little lonely in your, uh, room?"

"Don't worry about that. I just had a thought regarding our conversation on the bus."

"Our conversation? Which, uh, one was that?"

"You know—the one where you talked about starting your own theater. It sounded pretty exciting."

"Ohh, right. Well, it's gonna be. But I'll have a clearer head in the morning. Why don't we, uh, discuss it then?"

The door was hanging open an inch or two. I stood at Ron's shoulder, glancing into the darkness of the room.

"I thought we should talk about it now. I want to know . . . how serious you are."

These words made Ron flinch. Then he looked defiantly into my eyes. "I'm serious."

"I bet you are. My question is . . . how far are you willing to go to do it?"

Ron's defiance hardened into pure rage. "Get lost."

With that, Ron shifted his shoulder into mine, to push me away. But, taking a step past him like an encyclopedia salesman, I pressed down on his door with the toe of my shoe.

The door swung open, with a surprising squeak. Ron was still shoving me to the side, so I slammed into the jamb. But, grappling along the wall for the light switch, I got in, regardless.

The room exploded into light and, walking swiftly around, my eyes took in every inch of it.

"I told you to get lost!" Ron exploded, following fast behind.

I saw a pile of porno magazines on the bed . . . Ron's suitcase, flung open, as if gutted, on the floor . . . and newspapers hanging like a sun hat over the TV. Then I nearly ran toward the other room, the smallest, as they say, in the house.

"What the hell are you trying to pull?!"

"Ask yourself that question," I said, and opened the bathroom door.

Here, it was pristine, as if Ron were meticulous in this one area of his life alone. A Dopp Kit was neatly opened on the top of the toilet, and shaving cream, deodorant, floss, and other goods were stacked like soldiers at the sink.

Then my heart began to race. Another object lay in the bathtub, hidden beneath a towel.

As I reached down to reveal it, Ron pushed me with both hands. Losing my balance, I caromed off the sink and went flailing onto the floor, my head missing the toilet by sheer luck. I pressed on the floor and tried to rise again, my shoulder aching. Ron was pulling the shower curtain closed, like a modest matron.

"You've got no right to come in here!"

"I've got a right, Ron, for God's sake. Let me take it now, and I won't tell anybody."

"*Tell* anybody! You're damn right you won't!"

To prove it, Ron grabbed at the collection of cans upon his sink. Expertly flicking off the cap, he began spraying the deodorant wildly at my eyes. Closing my lids against the toxic mist, I slapped at him blindly until I felt the can at my fingers and made it fly from his hand. I opened my eyes in time to see the can smash into the medicine chest mirror, cracking it starburst-style, like a bullet on a bus shelter.

Ron just stood and stared at the damage, stupefied. Then "You're paying for that!" he shouted.

Once more, I tried to move past him to the tub, but Ron was wielding another weapon. Gripping a can of Colgate Aloe for Sensitive Skin—and pulling me toward him by my shirt's middle buttons—he pressed clouds of shaving cream into my face and hair.

After a second of shock, I sputtered the soapy billows from my mouth, then forced his wrist to the side, as if deflecting a gun, and he sprayed the cream onto the wall. With his right hand so angled, I took the opportunity to push my fist into his stomach three times.

Grunting furiously, Ron pushed me away, sending me slamming into the wall, where I splattered the sloppy cream and slid down it, again to the floor.

There I sat for a second. Ron stood above me, panting, politely recapping the can.

"Finished?" he said. "Finished now?"

Beaten, I made to nod. Then I leaped from the floor and ran right at Ron's midsection. We flipped over the edge of the tub, Ron crying out, cold cuts flying from his pockets, his clawing fingers ripping the curtain from its rods. Then we sank together in a pile of plastic onto the towel.

As we hit bottom, I heard the unmistakable sound of crunching glass.

There was a long pause. Ron and I lay in each other's arms, covered by the curtain, upon the—now apparently broken—object. Then he looked at me with an *another fine mess* expression.

"Well, I certainly hope you're happy," he said.

I began to feel a growing sense of embarrassment. Something told me that lying beneath us was not *The Magnificent Ambersons*. Ron struggled up and, with great exasperation, extended me a hand.

"Well, come on," he said, "unless you're planning to wash your hair."

I let him hoist me. Then Ron began to collect the curtain, bunching it in his arms, before he dropped it on the floor. Left behind it in the tub, the towel was flattened as if the object it sheltered had vanished from the earth.

But it hadn't. No matter what Ron told the others—or promised himself—little shards of a J&B bottle had scattered from its sides, and brown liquor was snaking away, down the drain.

More than embarrassment, I felt regret at having so exposed him.

"So I sneaked away from the party for a pop," Ron said. "So what?"

Unable to meet Ron's eyes, I only mumbled a halfhearted, "Well, let's . . . let's talk about that idea tomorrow, okay?"

Ron waved a furiously dismissive hand. As I shuffled out, I saw him bending at the tub, cupping his hands to catch the bottle's last drops. I knew that he could not afford to buy another.

AT LEAST GUS ZIEGLER HAD HAD THE MOVIE.

That was what I thought as I dragged my aching bones—this time, on the elevator—to my next stakeout. The battle I had endured months before with Gus had at least resulted in a momentary possession of the film. Ron, on the other hand, had just been humiliated, and I had just been a fool.

Now I sneaked to the tenth floor, where Abner Cooley dwelled.

I had no choice in this next target: Taylor Weinrod was, of course, staying in classier digs in town. So I approached 10G, behind which I hoped Abner was letting *Ambersons* sift sensuously through his fingers, like the Midas he imagined himself to be.

My clever scheme: to knock on his door.

There was nothing else I *could* do. And what would happen? Would he fling it open, admit his wrongdoing, and hand me back the film? Who else could Abner be expecting at one-thirty on this morning but me?

I soon had my answer.

Rattling behind me in the hall, I heard the sound of wheels. Coming closer, they rounded the bend. Then I saw a room service waiter.

He was pushing a rolling table upon which sat a stainless-steel cover, preserving the heat of a late-night snack. A bottle of champagne sat chilled in a bucket beside it.

I prayed that the very thing that had caused this crisis would now resolve it: Abner's appetite.

Fidgeting, I watched as the waiter pushed the table past one door, then another, and then another. Finally, he looked up and saw a strange man waving at him from outside Abner's room.

"Hi," I said pleasantly. "Is that for 10G?"

The waiter stopped. Pale and blank-faced, he stifled a yawn before nodding.

"Just can't wait, huh?"

"Well, to be honest," I said, "my wife's asleep. I'd really like to bring the table in myself."

I had betrayed some desperation, and the man eyed me, amused. "You want the uniform, too?"

He made to remove his starched white military jacket, and I smiled. "That won't be necessary."

We both then laughed a little, but he stopped first. "What's in it for me?"

Apparently, I was no master at dissembling, at least not at a quarter of two A.M. with a throbbing shoulder and a banged-up hip. I crushed whatever bills I could retrieve from my wallet into the man's hand. He did not move, so I gave him an extra treat: two half-price coupons for "My Favorite Beer"—Peter O'Toole caricature included—from The Cutting Room.

"Okay," I said, "the food's getting cold. Get lost."

Abner did not answer right away. Standing beside the table, I had a few sweaty seconds before I heard his slow and heavy step and then a phlegm-clearing cry of, "Coming!"

When he whipped the door open, he did not seem to see me. He had eyes just for the table and for the tray upon it.

"Finally!" he said. "I'm famished! I mean, what kind of a dinner is cold cuts . . ."

His final *anyway?* was directed at my face and trailed off into a confused and unhappy gasp. I smiled at Abner, pushed the table past him, and closed the door behind me.

"Jesus Christ!" he said. "Milano!"

He was dressed in purple polka-dot shorts and a PRINT IT! T-shirt, which featured his own face. The picture swelled around his great gut, so that Abner's mouth was at his navel and his eyes upon his breasts. It seemed only appropriate that he had been tattooed, as it were, with himself.

"What the *hell* are *you* doing here?"

I placed a napkin on my forearm. "It's my new gig," I replied. "Now, would Monsieur care to sit?"

I tried to free the champagne from its ice, but I didn't get far. Abner stilled my hand and forced the bottle down.

"Look, Milano," he said, "did someone put you up to this?"

"Nobody knows about this but me," I said reassuringly. "And you can end this whole thing now, if you like."

"End this? What are you, suddenly, my mother?"

I could not believe Abner's moralism, especially when he had been caught redhanded with my film. He made some fuming slow-burn sounds, like an old movie clown. I had a feeling of relief, and then of terrible fatigue. Perhaps, as Agatha Christie might have said, the game was up.

Or not. Abner squeezed and raised the plate cover. Then he lifted the club sandwich sitting there and, as tomatoes fell from it, pushed it right into my face.

"Hey!" I screamed. "What the hell are you—"

"I thought you were a live-and-let-live kind of guy, Roy. Now get out!"

I was pulling bacon and mayonnaise from my face, as what Abner said sank in. "What the hell do you mean? *You're* the one who's gone over the line!"

This remark enraged Abner even more. Yanking up another cover on another tray, he picked up a handful of French fries and started smushing them into my face as if they were hot nails.

I slapped them away, sending several potatoes onto the rug. If Abner was angry enough to destroy his dinner, then this was a new level of indignation for him. As for myself, I had been beaten tonight with instruments of food and hygiene, and I had had enough.

"Look, goddamit," I said, "just own up to what you've done and I'll be on my way!"

"Okay, I admit it. I'm guilty."

The comment should have satisfied, except it did not come from Abner. When I turned in the direction of the third voice in the room, I was stunned to see a familiar face in an unfamiliar pose.

Taylor Weinrod was standing in the bathroom doorway, wearing just a towel.

"So kill us, Roy," he said wearily. "But then get out, okay?"

I looked from one man to the other and, with horror, realized my mistake.

"Jesus. I didn't come here about *this*!" I said very faintly. "I would never . . ."

There was nothing I could say that could have justified my behavior. And I was too proud to admit that *The Magnificent Ambersons* was gone.

"So what," Abner said, "you watched us leave the bar together? Get a life."

I thought about the framed photo of Taylor's family on the table in his LCM office. I also thought that now Abner was *literally* in bed with the powers-that-be. But, backing out, all I said was, "You two, you have my blessing . . . please believe me on that."

"Great," Taylor said drowsily. "Whatever."

As I moved ridiculously toward the door, I saw the special way that Abner was staring at his guest. This was a much better catch than Gus

Ziegler had been last year. His hand drifted toward a fry, but, wanting to look his best, he let it be.

The last thing I saw, as the door closed upon me, was Taylor Weinrod lifting champagne, in a comic toast, to their failed and foolish friend.

THE FIFTEENTH FLOOR WAS MY LAST RESORT.

It was ridiculous, I knew. The Kripps had no motive and were the least likely, at any rate, to be thieves. But I pressed the elevator button anyway.

I traveled up, sore and stained, smelling of fried food. I picked a final crusted piece of potato from my cheek. I tried to forget all I had learned about my trivial colleagues tonight. But, as I had asked myself early on, once you knew a thing, how *could* you forget?

I knocked, bashfully, like a little boy. I knew that I would wake them, but I didn't care. There could be no sleep until I got the film.

To my surprise, the door swung open right away. Claude stood before me, still dressed, with only his tie undone. Behind him, a TV showed Fred Astaire and Ginger Rogers tapping. Their song seemed appropriate: "Pick Yourself Up, Dust Yourself Off, and Start All Over Again."

"Roy!" he said happily. "Come in, my boy, come in!" As I did, he gestured at the screen. "Aren't they marvelous?"

"The best," I said quietly. "The best."

Just as ebullient, Alice came out of the bathroom, in a terry cloth robe, brushing out her hair. "Roy! What a nice surprise!" Then she, too, watched the set. "Aren't they just wonderful?"

"The best."

Unlike the dancing pair, I felt weak in the knees. I stumbled to the bed and sat down. Since I could not bring myself to speak, a concerned Claude broke the silence.

"Roy? Is something wrong?"

"Is there some trouble between you and Jeanine?" Alice asked, concerned.

"No, no," I said, helpless, looking up at them. Their parental aura was strong; so was my need to unburden myself. I could not ask them any incriminating questions. Instead, I felt compelled to explain—and complain about—everything.

"It's just that . . . I'm having some trouble . . . see, something is missing, and I . . ."

Alice sat down beside me and placed a hand on my face. "We all feel that way sometimes."

"Take it from us," Claude said. "We've been at this love thing a long time."

I shook my head. "No, no, it's not that. It's sort of a secret, and I—"

"A secret? Oh . . . I see." Claude glanced at Alice, then both nodded knowingly.

"We know that secrets are hard to keep," Alice said. "We learned that during the incident with little Orson. But sometimes they can bring you closer together."

From this last remark I got a nervous shudder. They were watching me in an owl-like way, and I suddenly felt undressed.

"What do you mean?"

"That it was doubly hard to go through it," Claude said, "having the suspicions we had."

"Luckily," Alice continued, "it's been resolved tonight. And there was a happy ending."

Hearing this, I fell forward, stunned, and put my head in my hands. That the Kripps were aware of my complicity in their child's kidnapping made me dizzy. Yet they seemed, as ever, to be forgiving. Did they know that I had done nothing bad on purpose? I hoped so.

Indeed, their smiles appeared pacific. Only Claude and Alice could make stealing the movie—as I was sure they now had done—into an act of tough love. It was the equivalent of sending me to bed without my supper. And it had worked: I was just about to confess all.

But Claude beat me to the punch. Kneeling beside Alice, he took his wife's hand into his own.

"I never enjoyed a party more," he said, "than I did tonight."

"I know what you mean," she answered. "After we made that call and came in, I could have, well, danced all night."

She looked at Fred and Ginger, then back at Claude, her own Astaire.

"What call?" I asked softly.

"The one to my doctor," Alice explained. "For the results of my test."

"Which was, thank God"—Claude squeezed her hand—"positive."

"We'd been trying to have another baby," she said. "And now we will. At our age!"

Then the Kripps kissed, their secret out.

Now I felt even dizzier, but for another reason. I had guessed so wrong so many times in so few minutes. And I felt just as self-obsessed as the child the Kripps had turned me into. As happy as I was for them, I could not help feeling sorry—for myself.

"I'm sorry," I said. "I mean, I'm glad to hear it. But I'm sorry I . . . barged in."

"Are you kidding?" Alice said. "Being sure means I can turn my attention back to the rest of life. Like your romantic situation, for instance. Now . . ."

I smiled uneasily as the two proceeded to lecture me on the ups and downs of relationships, the back and the forth, the give and the take, how friendship becomes more important than sex, and how men and women are different, but *"vive la différence,"* as Spencer Tracy said in *Adam's Rib*.

"Well, we just hope it helps," Claude said, at last.

"Thank you." I shed a tired tear. "Believe me, it does. And thank you. Thank you!"

When I returned to our room, I found Jeanine asleep. Still in her clothes, she was curled on the bed's outside cover, as if she had tried and failed to stay awake. I lay down and clung to her, like the barnacle I was.

"So?" she asked quietly. "Whodunit?"

"I'll never know," I replied.

The first thing in the morning, I phoned the Fair's organizers. I told them that the posted notice should just say . . .

WE ARE VERY SORRY. TONIGHT'S SPECIAL MIDNIGHT SHOW HAS BEEN CANCELLED.

I GOT OUT OF RHINEBECK THE NEXT DAY.

Before most people were even awake, I had hopped a train back to Manhattan. Reaction to the screening's cancellation was not something I was looking forward to.

Jeanine had wished to accompany me, but I was determined to go alone. It was hard to explain, but I felt too embarrassed, too failed, in front of her. Perhaps once it all died down, and I had returned to my old life, I could face her again, behaving as if I had never heard of *The Magnificent Ambersons.*

But I didn't think so.

"You don't mind staying?" I asked. "Being the lover of a loser?"

"*I* don't care," she said pointedly, "what other people think."

Then she turned away.

———

There was another reason I wanted to get back to town. I had seen on the news that a press conference had been scheduled with Lorelei Reed. So why not rub salt in my wound? I thought.

The lawyer of Alan's accused killer was campaigning to get his client declared unfit for trial. Indeed, the woman's behavior—lashing out at guards, attempting suicide, etc.—didn't suggest she was stable. Still, since she had moments of lucidity, the judge was being obdurate, and the process was slow and painful. Dwayne Ross, the Legal Aid lawyer assigned to her case, now hoped to sway public opinion.

There wasn't much of a public, and very little opinion. Alan Gilbert was a film dork drug user who had been murdered a few months ago, so the event wasn't exactly packed. A handful of Metro reporters milled around the room in the downtown courthouse, where a small makeshift podium had been erected. I flashed an old press pass I had once received for a movie premiere, and sat in the back, undisturbed.

"I'll make a statement, and then take questions. My client is in no condition to speak for herself."

Lorelei had been dressed for the occasion, that is to say, dressed down. She wore a simple, shabby cotton dress, and her hair was only cursorily combed. She sat, staring off, as Ross, a stocky, forthright man in his thirties, stood at a microphone in front of her.

"My client suffers from delusions, brought on by years of crack cocaine use," he said.

"What kind of delusions?" a reporter yelled.

"She imagines that she's being paraded around like a freak," another whispered.

Ross solemnly waited for the cynical chuckling to die down. "Let's just say that she often imagines people are not what they are."

"What does she mistakenly think *you* are?" someone called, and there were comic "suggestions" from my colleagues.

"A good lawyer?" one said.

Without smiling, Dwayne Ross cleared his throat. "This is a woman about to go on trial for her life, my friends. Surely there are funnier things in the world."

There was a bit of doleful mumbling at this, but just a bit.

"Why doesn't he just plead to manslaughter, or something?" one reporter wondered.

"I know," another said. "If she didn't do this, she's done something else."

"Exactly."

I thought of Stu Drayton, out on bail at his art opening, and Webby Slicone, free to rampage before his re-election. I even thought of Ben Williams, who might have been enjoying crack that very instant if it hadn't stopped his overstimulated heart. Then I looked at Lorelei, gazing blankly at the floor—probably medicated that morning—and felt a double dose of guilt.

Maybe if I had chased the murderer as hard as I had the movie, things would have been different. Still, I thought with a sorry laugh, I might have failed as badly at that as I had at keeping *Ambersons*.

"She thinks there are wild dogs in her cell, biting at her," the lawyer was reading from a list of hallucinations. "And that friends of hers have visited. When, in fact, no one has."

He turned over a page of his legal pad. The pathetic quality of Lorelei's life now quieted any derision. But there was no more respect among the press corps; it just meant several people began to leave.

I took the opportunity to move a few rows closer.

"She often sings a song to herself, which has images of disfigurement and self-punishment, cutting and the like. . . . She rarely recognizes the guards she sees daily, or, for that matter, myself."

Ross refused to answer any question directly related to her culpability in the killing. He did say that Lorelei, who was a frequent figure in Alan's vestibule, referred to him as "TV set," in reference to his hosting of *My Movies*. Then there was a long pause.

"Any more questions?" he asked.

No one seemed to have any. Then, just as Ross turned to go, someone finally got the courage to raise his hand.

I caught the next train back to Rhinebeck. It was one of those times when I wished I could drive. The start and stop of someone else at the wheel made me rue every minute we might be late.

If I hurried, I might even make the midnight show.

It was just a crazy possibility, I knew, and one that I wished was wrong. But Lorelei's press conference had made me suspect, with a sense of growing dread, who the guilty party was.

WHEN I OPENED THE DOOR, JEANINE TURNED, SLOWLY. SHE DID NOT EVEN seem surprised.

She was packing her own suitcase, Gus's nylon container still lying on the floor. Brushing a piece of hair back and locking it behind her ear, she only said, "Did you forget something?"

Like most attitudes of bravado, hers masked a lot of fear. Otherwise, why would her hands be shaking as they zipped and locked her bag?

"I wish I could," I answered. "But I can't."

I came toward her, and she pulled the suitcase away, lifting it out of my reach. Then she pressed it against her chest, as if to shield her heart.

"How long have you known?" she asked, and then she sagged, smiling, having heard the cliché. "Isn't that what people always say, at this point in the flim?"

"I just figured it out now, believe it or not," I said. "My detective work is kind of up and down."

The final question in Lorelei Reed's press conference had been mine. Raising a slightly shaking hand, I had been recognized by her lawyer.

"Did she ever say that someone else did it?" I asked.

Dwayne Ross had looked at me a second, surprised, as if I were privy to information. Formerly unspecific about the crime, he decided to reply. After all, I was one of the last people who was left.

"Yes," he said, then paused, anticipating laughter. "She said, the night of the murder, she was passed in the front hall. First by a female *E.T.* And then by Arnold Schwarzenegger."

There was laughter, of course. From everyone but me.

There had been a woman with Alan in Spain. There had been a woman running from Alan's apartment. A junkie might have seen a fleeing Gus Ziegler as the Terminator; that's how Gus would have liked to see himself. And it was possible that Jeanine, the trivial woman, the small eccentric, would appear to her an alien.

After all, I had seen her that way myself once.

Now Jeanine was beautiful, of course, never more so than at this moment, her face all flushed, her fingers nervously patting back that disobedient hair. I would not hurt her by revealing the clue that had brought me back to Rhinebeck. But that remark—a movie reference—combined with her conveniently finding the film gone the night before, had been the goads that got me on the train. She had always been so disdainful of any woman involved with Alan.

"Well," she said. "Better late than never."

I would not say a word to hurt her, nor would I extend a hand. Which is why Jeanine got past me and, carrying the bag, flew out the door.

That didn't mean I couldn't bring her back. Racing through the door myself, I turned and saw her hurtling down the hall, heading for the stairwell.

"Jeanine!"

She disappeared inside it. Coming in a sorry second, I yanked the door open. Staring down, I saw no sign of her. Then, swiveling my head, I realized my mistake: Jeanine was going up.

"Jeanine!"

I climbed, to catch her. Running so fast, Jeanine lost—or kicked off—her shoes, and I turned my head to dodge them as they fell. Then, taking the stairs two at a time, I closed in on her.

We had started on the thirty-third floor, and there were only two more until the roof. Jeanine and *The Magnificent Ambersons* were about to step outside, on the top of the hotel.

IN HER EYES, I COULD SEE THAT JEANINE HAD NOT BEEN THINKING. IF SHE had run down, she might have made it to another floor, and might have gotten away. Instead, she was surrounded by open sky, the town around us, and the gray November day. She turned, seeing this, and knew that she was trapped, and that she had trapped herself. She let the bag fall slowly on the cement.

"Jesus," she said.

She was no pro at villainy; I was no expert at heroics. So I addressed her, as I had so many situations, in the language of the everyday.

"Come on," I said. "Let's try to keep a level head."

"It's a bit late for that," she said with a little laugh. "Isn't it?"

"Not necessarily."

Jeanine laughed again, at my obvious hedging. But I did not back away from earnestness, for it was all I had.

"Just come inside, and we'll discuss this."

Jeanine was walking in a small circle now. Then she stopped.

"Maybe if I'd kept a level head in the first place," she said, "I wouldn't have gotten involved with Alan. I knew he was trouble to begin with. Who didn't? But the pickings are kind of slim for people like us."

"I know," I said, for who would know better?

"I should never have let him talk me into going to Barcelona, and 'lending' him the money for the fare. But the film festival there was kind of fun. And when we saw the name of that pensione, Ambersons—"

"Magníficos—"

"I thought the fun would just continue." She shook her head, her hair now totally rebelling in the breeze.

"You don't have to go on."

The more she revealed, the more I became afraid. People had told me things for all kinds of reasons—guilt, anger, pure indifference—but I didn't know what Jeanine's motive was. I didn't think she was seeking absolution, and that made me frightened.

"When that poor old lady told us about the film," she went on, "I could see that Alan wanted it, and he didn't care about the consequences. One night, after we'd all been drinking, I stayed in the living room, and he walked down from upstairs, all sweaty and panting, and tore a page out of the hotel ledger, the one with our names on it. That's when I knew that something awful had happened."

I wanted her to stop there, at the place where she was innocent. But she went on, helplessly, to the place where she bore responsibility, to the scene before the credits that set the story up. Just like *Of Mice and Men*, I thought.

"On the way back to the States, he was so affectionate. His 'partner in crime,' he called me. He depended on me now, and I liked it, I couldn't help it. People like us need that kind of thing, you know?"

"I do."

"But once we were back in New York, all of it changed. Alan was so cold, he only cared about the movie, and what it would do for him. It just kept getting worse and worse, he didn't seem to see me at all anymore. On the night that he planned to premiere it on his show, I sensed that, once he saw it, it would be over for us. I did our charts, and they confirmed it.

"I know it was crazy, I hardly even liked him. Alan called Gus, to have him shoot the show. I didn't hear him call you. Then, right before he showed *The Magnificent Ambersons*, I"—and here she paused to find the least disturbing word—"I stuck him with the sharpest thing I could find.

"I made it look like a robbery. I ran out, through all the junkies. And I guess Gus showed up after that, found Alan, and stole the film."

She paused then. All I could hear was the wind whipping around the hotel.

"When I agreed to help you find the film, Roy, I never thought you actually would. But you were so much more clever than I gave you credit for. Right after midnight, I was sure that the same thing would happen with you. Except it was different with you. You, I liked."

The past tense of the affectionate term made me even more wary of Jeanine's agenda. Shaken, I stepped forward, to try to change her plans.

"It won't be the way you feared," I said firmly. "I won't let you go. Because I love you, Jeanine. I love you."

It was the first time I had said those words in years. But if Jeanine had heard them before, she didn't want to hear them now. She turned, as if struck, and did not respond. It was too late, she seemed to say, and it had been too late the moment we met.

My case, of course, could just get weaker. Once you've said those words and they haven't saved the day, there's nowhere to go but down. Still, I tried.

"Nothing bad has to happen," I said. "Believe me."

She knew it wasn't true. To cover for Jeanine would be to sentence Lorelei Reed for a crime she didn't commit. I tried to think as that reporter had: If Lorelei didn't do this, she's done something else. But I couldn't do it with conviction. And Jeanine, of course, knew it, because she knew me.

"Something bad has to happen," she said. "Because something bad *has* happened. I just hope it won't be so bad for you."

With that, she picked up her bag again. Then she tossed it, as powerfully as she could, into my arms. Catching it, the force of *Amber-*

sons sent me stumbling back a bit, just long enough for Jeanine to make her move.

Dropping the film, I ran to stop her as she scrambled up the small fence, the only guardrail the hotel had. In an early version of *Meet John Doe*, Gary Cooper jumps from a roof to his death. After negative previews, he is saved.

Today, I was too late. Without looking back, she sprang over the edge. I watched Jeanine fly and then fall, taking with her all the movies she had seen, all the memories she had had, all the love she would never give, to other men, to children, to me.

In one second, she had become a part of the past. And some things from the past never return.

FREE SAMPLES! POSTER SIGNINGS!
GET YOUR PICTURE TAKEN TODAY!

A few days later, I stood in line, like all the rest. I didn't know how many had been paid off or promised something, as I had been at Webby's rally. I just knew that the line of people at Manhattan's Kmart weaved through the main floor and out the door, onto the street.

That bottle in little Orson's hand had just been the beginning; now the U.S. promotional push for Fizz had grown. TV ads, reshot with a California cop, were starting on the airwaves; billboards were stopping traffic on the roads. And Erendira—whose beauty was assumed a most marketable export—was the key to the campaign.

Today, everyone was here to meet the Fizz girl.

From far back in the line, I could see that Erendira had been "improved" for international exposure. Her hair was lush but not too big; she wore a tight black business suit, short but not too sexy. In America, she would be sold as a maternal role model or postfeminist sex symbol, not the basic bombshell that seemed to suffice in Spain.

I got closer to the table. Erendira was autographing a picture of herself posed on a motorcycle and was handing it to a preteen girl. The girl beamed back, then took a free soda sample and went away. Erendira's feet kicked and crossed, with familiar nervousness, above the floor.

Then she looked up and saw me. Her dark eyes shone with sudden warmth. Impatiently, she signed the picture of the man before me—who flashed a camera—and then I was as close to her as I had been in months.

"It's so nice to see you," she said.

"Same here."

"I wanted a picture with *both* of us on the bike," she said softly, "but my boss said no."

I smiled. Then I examined the Fizz bottle, pretending to discuss it, for the benefit of those behind me.

"I have a gift for you," I said.

"You do?" She looked confused.

"Yes. Well, actually, it's not a gift. It was yours to begin with."

With that, I placed Gus's nylon bag, which I had carried all along, beneath the table. Erendira's busy feet came to rest against it. Then she looked up at me, and her whole face flushed.

I no longer wished to keep *The Magnificent Ambersons*. I wanted to give it away, like a coin handed to the homeless, to do some good in the world. And who better to receive it than the woman now appearing at my local Kmart?

Watching me with suspicion, an American P.R. woman beside her moved to speak, but Erendira shushed her.

"Did you catch who . . ." She trailed off, in the public place.

Before responding, I swallowed deeply.

"No," I said. "They got away."

I had told the Rhinebeck police what I knew about Jeanine. They assumed she was a lovesick suicide—the Film Fair brought such lonely people to town. Then I kept the screening cancelled and left before the gossip began.

It was the biggest trivial scandal since Alan Gilbert's death, but no one knew the two were linked. Maybe the New York cops would want to know, but they rarely listened to nerds, hard-boiled or otherwise. For Lorelei Reed, however, I would give it my best shot.

Now Erendira kept staring at me, gratitude making her eyes begin to water. I felt a rush of feeling and moved to take her hand in mine, indifferent to the crowd around us.

In truth, I had been no altruist in offering her the film. Jeanine had been right, there was a risk for a trivial person seeing *The Magnificent Ambersons*: It might take the place of love. But on my way to meet Erendira, I knew it was no longer enough for me to watch the film alone.

"Look," I said, "I want you to know how much I've been—"

Then I saw the ring on her finger.

I swallowed the emotion that had been welling in my throat. I only touched the gold band briefly, and pulled my hand away.

"Well," I said, "congratulations."

She nodded. "Jorge listens to reason," she said, "once he gets something that he wants."

I understood: She was only on loan to America, like a touring work of art. And now, because of me, she would go back with more than just memories.

"You don't know," she said, indicating what lay below her, "what this will do for me."

Would the movie make her feel an equal of her husband? Would it close a family circle and bring her a primal peace? Or would it just provide a publicity hook—Orson Welles's granddaughter, his masterpiece restored—on which to build a big career? From the stillness of her limbs, the crucial calm it brought her, I could tell that, for Erendira, it would do all three.

"Is there anything I can give *you*," she asked, "in return?"

"No," I answered. "It's okay."

I backed away slowly, and watched her disappear behind all those people, so eager for her attention. Held in Erendira's arms now, *The Magnificent Ambersons* disappeared, as well.

I took an autographed picture with me, to remember her by.

EPILOGUE

ONE NIGHT, I SAW ALAN GILBERT AGAIN.

I couldn't sleep, and the Oscar winners for Best Original Song hadn't helped. I started surfing channels, and there he was. At three A.M., in his overstuffed chair, talking a mile a minute, introducing an obscure old film.

From there, channel 297 or something, I switched to an Ed Landers station, one that showed recent movies. I saw Ben Williams in the original *Cause Pain*—or was it the first sequel?—battling a terrorist in his everyman T-shirt.

I next hit the all-news network, also owned by Landers. Here, Webby Slicone was giving an interview, detailing his plans since his landslide re-election a month before. Capital punishment was at the top of his list.

Only I knew why the first two were dead, and the other still—in a political sense—alive. Then I clicked on Landers's old-movie channel, LCM, where Taylor Weinrod worked.

Its new on-air host was Abner Cooley. And only I knew why, as well.

A typesetting job awaited me. I had just completed the latest, long-delayed edition of *Trivial Man*; it would be distributed in the morning. I had made no mention of locating the full version of *The Magnificent Ambersons*, the film find of the century. For detectives, I thought, discretion was part of the deal. So, I had learned, was loneliness.

Then the phone rang.

It was Jody. She wondered who the actor was playing the sheik in the film before me on LCM.

I stared at the man on the screen. Then, to my own shock, I answered, "I don't know."

I really didn't. There was a long pause on the other end. Jody wasn't accustomed to this kind of thing from me, and she wasn't accustomed to not knowing where I was for months on end, either.

Trying not to sound concerned, she said, "What have you been up to, Roy?"

I paused. Then I turned off the TV. And I started to explain.

When I was done, Jody sounded very sympathetic. So I told her that I wanted to solve other mysteries now, not just those to do with trivia. There were other questions to answer, other pieces of the past to find and place together for people. And for myself, as well.

I said it was a new conviction, one that could be easily discouraged. It was fragile, shaky, and needed to be approached with care.

And I didn't laugh when I said:

"Don't even breathe, baby."

ABOUT THE AUTHOR

Laurence Klavan won the Edgar Award for Best Original Paperback for *Mrs. White*, written under a pseudonym. His work for the theater includes the libretto for the Obie Award–winning musical *Bed and Sofa*, for which he received a Drama Desk nomination. He lives in New York City.